Healing Shadows

Joe Gacheru

Chapter 01

"Good night sunshine," Amani's mum's voice, warm and familiar as a freshly baked ugali, drifted through the phone, a fleeting, precious comfort against the sharp, biting chill of the Winnipeg night. It was a lifeline, thin but potent, across thousands of miles. Then, with a soft click, the connection severed, and the line went dead, leaving behind a silence that felt not just vast, but utterly profound and absolute. The digital echo of her mother's words seemed to evaporate into the frigid air, replaced by an overwhelming emptiness. For the first time since she'd moved to this distant, sprawling, and often starkly beautiful city, Amani felt a profound, aching loneliness settle deep in her chest, a physical knot tightening beneath her ribs. The initial surge of excitement, the hopeful anticipation of a new beginning, had completely dissipated, like mist in the sun, replaced by a hollow, gnawing ache. She missed her family—their laughter, their familiar scents, the very rhythm of their lives—with an intensity that stole her breath away, leaving her gasping for air in the silent room.

"O Allah, nourish our hearts... with the bliss of Your closeness... and the coolness of Your forgiveness... and the abundance of Your mercy, please help me," Amani whispered, her voice a ragged, desperate plea, barely audible above her own shuddering breaths. She pressed her face hard into her pillow, the soft down offering a small, futile resistance against the rising tide of despair, muffling the choked sobs that convulsed her body. Hot, relentless tears streamed from her eyes, burning tracks down her temples, and quickly soaked the fabric, leaving a damp patch that mirrored the desolation in her soul. The familiar weight of the pillow, usually a source of comfort, now felt like a heavy burden, a weak barrier against the overwhelming wave of sorrow that threatened to drown her. As she lay there, grappling with the raw, visceral grief of absence, memories, vivid and unbidden, began to flood her mind.

It was as if a dam had broken, and a torrent of the past rushed in, the vibrant, intricate tapestry of her life unfurling before her inner eye with astonishing clarity, each thread a pang of longing.

Her early childhood, steeped in the sun-drenched, vibrant hues of Mombasa, flashed through her consciousness like a cherished film. She remembered the smooth, cool feel of her mother's calloused hand in hers as they walked to the mosque for dawn prayers, the ancient path worn smooth and gleaming by generations of faithful feet. The incessant, gentle murmur of the Indian Ocean's waves served as the ultimate lullaby, a soft, consistent background hum that lulled her to sleep every single night, its rhythmic whisper a constant, comforting presence, a boundless, breathing entity just beyond their doorstep. The invigorating, salty tang of the sea breeze was a constant companion, frequently drifting through the open windows of their small, humble home, carrying with it tantalizing hints of exotic spices – the warm earthiness of cardamom, the pungent depth of cumin, the golden glow of turmeric – wafting from nearby bustling markets and vibrant family kitchens. These were the very scents that permeated her clothes and hair, clinging like an invisible cloak, becoming an indelible part of her being, a fragrant signature of home.

From her bedroom window, a modest square framing a truly grand view, Amani would often gaze out across the cityscape, mesmerized by the elegant minarets that pierced the azure sky. Their slender, graceful spires, adorned with delicate calligraphy and intricate patterns, rose majestically above the terracotta rooftops, shimmering like beacons in the golden light of dawn and dusk, reaching like prayers to the heavens. Five times a day, with a precision that marked the very pulse of the city, the soulful, echoing calls to prayer – the adhan – would reverberate through the narrow, winding streets, a hauntingly beautiful symphony that underscored the community's deep-rooted faith and marked the solemn passage of time. Each call was a gentle reminder, a communal breath taken together, weaving a magic that settled deep into her bones. Her days unfolded in a sensory feast, a vibrant world made lively by the labyrinthine network of narrow alleys, perpetually crowded with spirited merchants hawking their wares – their voices a melodic chant, a bargaining banter, their stalls overflowing with a kaleidoscope of richly coloured fabrics, shimmering beads, and fragrant dried fruits. The joyous shouts of children playing boisterous street games, their laughter echoing off ancient walls like pure, unbridled delight, mingled with the easy chatter of neighbors sharing stories and news outside their small, colorful shops, their voices a comforting hum of interconnected lives, a continuous, comforting symphony. Her family resided in a particularly tight-knit neighborhood, a true village within the city, where every face was familiar, and every door was open, their destinies intertwined. Wizened elders, their faces etched with the wisdom of years and the lines of a hundred unspoken stories, would sit cross-legged on woven mats outside their houses, their voices low and rich with shared wisdom and ancient tales, their presence a grounding anchor in the community's turbulent seas. Children, including a younger, carefree Amani, roamed freely and safely, their laughter echoing as they climbed gnarled, ancient trees whose twisted branches offered leafy sanctuaries, and played spirited games of hide-and-seek amid the kaleidoscope of colorful stalls, their innocent energy a constant, effusive joy that permeated the very air.

Growing up in Mombasa was an immersive experience, akin to being part of a living, breathing painting—a masterpiece rich with a dazzling palette of colors, a symphony of diverse noises, and the deep roots of tradition that stretched back centuries. Every dawn brought forth a fresh tapestry of new sights, distinctive sounds, and captivating smells that continually shaped and deepened Amani's understanding of life itself. Her world, though geographically small, felt infinitely vast and profoundly safe, defined by the warmth of close relationships and the comforting predictability of familiar routines. She knew every one of her neighbors by name, their faces as familiar as her own family's, their lives an intimate symphony she understood innately. Shared meals, often overflowing with laughter and chatter, were a daily ritual that brought everyone together, cementing bonds, an anchor of contentment in their lives. The entire community truly functioned as her extended family, offering an unwavering sense of comfort, stability, and belonging in a city deeply rooted in centuries of history and time-honored tradition. Life flowed peacefully, predictable in its gentle rhythm, and brimming with simple, yet profound, pleasures—like the exhilaration of riding her bicycle along the sun-drenched shoreline, the wind whipping through her hair, the sand cool beneath her bare feet, or the quiet joy of helping her mother prepare the aromatic, traditional Swahili dishes that filled their humble home with delicious, lingering scents, each one a memory in the making.

However, the tranquil harmony of Amani's world shattered abruptly when she was just six years old. Her father, a man possessed of boundless energy, grand dreams that sparkled in his eyes, and an unyielding ambition to expand his burgeoning tourism business, made a monumental decision that would forever alter the trajectory of her young life. He held a fervent belief, an unwavering conviction, that relocating to Nairobi, the bustling capital, could unlock unprecedented opportunities and propel his family to heights they had only ever dared to imagine. The city of Mombasa, with its idyllic sun-kissed beaches, graceful dhows sailing silently across the horizon like ancient ghosts, and charming hotels catering specifically to seaside tourists, had nurtured her childhood in a calm, familiar, and deeply secure way, like a gentle, constant embrace. But Nairobi, a sprawling metropolis renowned for its frenetic, bustling streets and towering, imposing buildings, was a fundamentally different world, a stark contrast in every conceivable way—a concrete canyon compared to Mombasa's whispering palms. Her father, his voice filled with an almost palpable excitement, a cadence of hope and conviction, explained that Nairobi was the undisputed hub of Kenya's rapidly growing tourism industry— strategically positioned close to the world-famous national parks and the exhilarating wildlife safaris that drew countless visitors from every corner of the globe. He spoke passionately of the promise of a brighter future, of greater financial prosperity to support their dreams, and of a wealth of new opportunities for both her siblings and for Amani herself, painting a compelling picture of a future brimming with potential, a glittering mirage she couldn't yet grasp. The transition to Nairobi was nothing short of a profound shock to her young, sensitive senses, a gut-punch that left her reeling. Everything about the new city felt overwhelmingly immense, a dizzying assault on her familiar world, a sensory overload she couldn't process. Nairobi truly sprawled endlessly, an impossibly vast mosaic of cold concrete and unyielding steel that seemed to stretch beyond the very limits of the horizon itself. Towering buildings, immense and impersonal monolithic structures, soared overhead, often blocking out the generous sun and casting long, impersonal shadows over the perpetually busy streets below. The noise was a relentless, deafening cacophony—cars honked incessantly, their horns blaring in an endless symphony of frustration and urgency, vendors shouted their wares in aggressive, urgent tones in the crowded markets, and the distant, monotonous hum of construction filled the air, a constant reminder of the city's relentless, unfeeling growth. In Mombasa, life had moved with a gentle, predictable pace, like the rhythmic ebb and flow of the tides, a slow, deliberate dance. Here, it moved at a breakneck speed, a relentless current, with people rushing in every conceivable direction, their faces set, their movements purposeful, their eyes rarely meeting hers. The open, airy spaces of her beloved coastal hometown, with direct access to the vast expanse of the ocean, were brutally replaced by suffocatingly crowded streets, choked with an endless stream of moving vehicles and a relentless parade of pedestrians. The wide, inviting beaches and the quiet, comforting neighborhoods were gone, replaced instead by frenetic, crowded marketplaces and seemingly endless rows of shops and offices, each one a testament to the city's unceasing, impersonal commerce.

Amani's arrival in Nairobi was a profound jolt, a disorienting rupture from everything familiar. It truly was like stepping, without warning, through an unseen portal into an entirely different world – not just a new city, but a new dimension of existence. This was a world alien in its rhythms, its sounds, its very breath; a place she neither understood nor belonged to, a vast, indifferent landscape where her internal compass, once so reliable by the familiar rhythm of the tides, spun wildly, leaving her utterly adrift.

She couldn't shake the pervasive, suffocating feeling of being utterly small and tragically lost, a tiny, insignificant speck swallowed whole amid the overwhelming chaos and impersonality of millions. The city was a relentless, crushing presence, and she was merely a lost atom in its indifferent throng. Her heart ached with a profound, almost physical longing for the peaceful, rhythmic sounds of the ocean – the whisper of the waves against the sand, the deep, reassuring rumble of the surf – and the gentle, hypnotic bobbing of sailboats near the shore, their masts clinking softly in the breeze. She yearned for the simpler, predictable routines of her old life in Mombasa, the very heartbeat of home: the familiar smells of her mother's cooking, the specific slant of the morning light through her window, the comforting weight of her grandmother's hand.

Nairobi's streets felt cold, hard, and frighteningly impersonal, like an endless, confusing maze of concrete and glass, each towering building a silent, unreadable sentinel. It was a labyrinth inhabited by millions of strangers, each one a mystery, their faces fleeting glimpses in the bustling currents of humanity. A deep, persistent anxiety gnawed at her, a cold dread that settled like a stone in the pit of her stomach. The weight of it was the worry about finding new friends in a place where she knew so little about her surroundings, a city that felt not just alien, but actively unwelcoming, its towering structures and frenetic pace amplifying her isolation. She constantly replayed memories of her old friends – the children she had played with every single day, their lives intertwined with hers. She remembered sharing innocent confidences and whispered secrets under the generous shade of mango trees, their laughter echoing like pure music as they chased kites across the golden sand, their bare feet kicking up dust. Now, those children were ghostly presences, fragile echoes in a world that no longer felt like hers, their vibrant images fading into the vast, lonely expanse of her new reality.

For a long while, the ache of displacement persisted, a constant thrum beneath the surface of her days. But slowly, imperceptibly at first, things started to change for Amani. Her dad's business, fueled by the burgeoning tourism industry after the 2010 devolution, began to flourish, bringing with it a sense of stability and even a touch of prosperity. The city itself, once a hostile entity, slowly began to reveal its hidden warmth. Amani, shy at first, found her footing at her new school, and through the local Madrasa, she hesitantly began to forge connections. Tentative smiles blossomed into shared jokes, quiet conversations grew into boisterous laughter. And true to her loving nature, Amani's mum tirelessly sought out girls of Amani's age within their community, arranging playdates and introductions, a deliberate and successful effort to ensure that Amani was no longer lonely, no longer an isolated island in the bustling city. Things were finally going well; a fragile sense of belonging began to take root. The sharp edges of the city started to blur, replaced by the comforting hum of a life finding its rhythm again. Until that day. That single, devastating day when Amani was not just hurt to the core, but shattered. That day, life changed forever, a seismic shift that cleaved her world in two.

After that fateful, unbearable day, the pain was a raw, gaping wound she couldn't face. Amani instinctively hid herself, seeking refuge not just from the world, but from the relentless torment within. She plunged headfirst into books, losing herself in the intricate plots and vibrant characters of fantasy novels, which became her sanctuary, a shield against the jagged edges of reality. She also found a temporary balm in other activities, the meticulous strokes of a paintbrush, the rhythmic movements of a needle and thread, anything that demanded her complete focus and quieted the tormenting echoes within. These pursuits became her self-prescribed anesthesia, a desperate attempt to numb the searing pain and the crushing weight of her new reality. Hence, when she received the acceptance letter for her student visa to move to Winnipeg, Canada, it wasn't just excitement she felt, but a profound, almost desperate surge of hope. She was ready – more than ready – to forget the pain, to leave it buried beneath the vast distance between continents. She clung to the fervent hope that her new country, this distant, unknown place, would somehow be different, a place where she would finally be safe, where life would not let her get hurt again. Winnipeg wasn't just a city on a map; it was a blank canvas, a fortress she hoped would finally be impenetrable.

Chapter 02

Amani sank into a comfy black leather chair, feeling the weight of the world pressing down on her. The gray floor was calming, mirroring the rainy view outside the waiting room windows. The familiar scents of antiseptic and stale coffee filled the air, bringing back memories of previous visits. She glanced at the clock, noted that it was five minutes past two PM, and realized that she had forty-five minutes to mentally gear up for her appointment with Dr. Alex. The tension in her muscles felt like they were holding back a flood of emotions just waiting to spill out. After four sessions with Dr. Alex, these meetings had become a routine, peeling back layers of her tough past and forcing her to confront it.

Across from her, a man was nervously fiddling with a worn-out notebook, his hands trembling. He avoided her gaze, and the air felt thick with tension. Instead of retreating into her own thoughts like she usually did, Amani decided to reach out this time.

She broke the silence with a gentle yet firm question as the rain continued to patter around them: "Is everything okay?"

He looked up, his eyes filled with uncertainty, and asked if Dr. Alex could help him. "I'm not sure I should be here," he admitted, his hands fidgeting as he spoke quickly.

A wave of empathy washed over Amani, and she offered him a reassuring smile. "He's been a great help to me. Just be honest with him; it really can make a difference."

He let out a nervous laugh and turned his gaze to the window, watching the raindrops slide down like tears. The dreary weather outside contrasted with a flicker of hope inside her as she braced herself to confront her past and embark on the path to healing.

"What brings you here?" Amani asked, hoping to lighten the mood. He replied vaguely about personal issues, his words heavy with unspoken struggles.

"I get that," she admitted, nervously playing with the armrest of her chair. She felt the urge to spill all the heavy truths that were burdening her, but deep down, she knew she had to share them in her own time and in her own way. The soothing sound of rain outside wrapped around her like a warm blanket, lifting her mood with every soft drop. As she thought back to her chats with Dr. Alex, she appreciated the safe space he created for her to speak her mind freely. Yet even with that comfort, memories of her past friendship with Rehema came flooding back when she spotted a photo on the wall. It showed the two of them in a warm embrace, a reminder of their special bond. That image stirred up a storm of mixed feelings—frustration, sadness, and guilt.

 Lost in a tide of memories, Amani found herself caught in a painful whirlpool, reflecting on the day her friendship with Rehema fell apart, leaving her heartbroken. It all started on a sunny afternoon in Plainsview South B, Nairobi, where the air was filled with the sweet aroma of freshly-baked mandazis and the cheerful sounds of kids playing. The Christmas spirit seemed to wrap the neighborhood in warmth and joy, leaving the girls blissfully unaware of the chaos that was about to disrupt their peace. Amani thought about dropping by Rehema's place, feeling a strong longing for her friend's company. She decided against calling first, as it was common in her culture to just show up at a friend's house without any notice.

As Amani strolled through the streets she knew so well, the bright hues of the houses blended together, creating a swirl of memories. Laughter floated from nearby courtyards, and she could smell the delicious scent of mandazis frying somewhere in the distance. The sun hung low, bathing everything in a warm glow, but Amani felt a weight in her heart.

With each step, she thought back to all the moments she had shared with Rehema. They had always been there for each other—sharing secrets, dreams, and even the little struggles of growing up. Amani could vividly remember Rehema's radiant smile and the sound of her laughter ringing in her ears. They had spent endless afternoons under a tree, swapping silly jokes and dreaming about their futures, which seemed limitless and bright.

The humid Nairobi air hung heavy as Amani skipped down the dusty road, her flip-flops slapping a rhythmic beat against the cracked pavement. Each step sent up small puffs of dust that danced in the afternoon sun, momentarily glinting like tiny stars before settling back into the earth. A well-worn Swahili song hummed in her head, a tune she and Rehema had been practicing for their next TikTok video—a melody rich with history and laughter that twined itself around their friendship like a vine climbing towards the sky.

Their TikTok account, "SwahiliSisters," was more than just an online presence; it was a vibrant blossom in Amani's life, unfurling amidst the thorny realities of growing up. It showcased not only their choreography but also snippets of joy caught on camera—moments where carefree spins and infectious laughter seemed to transcend any looming clouds overhead.

Yet beneath this sunny exterior, a storm brewed within Amani. Lately, her conversations with her mum felt like navigating a minefield strewn with sharp words rather than shared stories. At fourteen years old, she stood at an awkward precipice between childhood wonder and adolescent awareness—a precarious age where every choice echoed loudly through the narrow corridors of familial expectations. Her clothes were too childish for her mother's taste; her music too loud for anyone seeking peace; her friends—each one far too everything.

The straightforward decision of selecting a pair of shoes could spark intense discussions that left Amani feeling exhausted and alone, as if she were confined in an echo chamber filled with criticism.

However, this day was different; she was excited to arrive at Rehema's home—the stable ground amid chaotic waters. Rehema possessed an innate understanding without the need for lengthy explanations or gestures filled with exasperation; their aspirations were woven together by melodies both known and unfamiliar. Perhaps working together on another video would alleviate some burden from Amani's heart, providing her with the courage to face whatever awaited her upon returning home.

As she rounded the corner past the tangled bougainvillea cascading over the whitewashed walls, Rehema's vibrant, brightly painted house appeared—an explosion of color contrasting with the subdued backdrop of their neighborhood. The soft strains of "My Journey to Mombasa" floated from within, reminiscent of a welcoming breeze through open windows on a warm day.

"Rehema!" Amani called out, her excitement overflowing despite herself—the sound cracking slightly under the weight of her emotions.

The door swung open to reveal Usiku, Rehema's brother, whose face brightened like the morning sun breaking through the night. "Amani! Welcome!" he greeted her warmly, stepping aside to let her in.

Inside, sunlight poured through sheer curtains that fluttered softly like wings, while colorful fabrics adorned every corner—kanga cloth draped over chairs and intricate beadwork glimmered on shelves filled with trinkets from distant lands or made by local craftspeople. The atmosphere was alive with stories passed down through generations, weaving a rich tapestry of both old and new.

"Where's Rehema?" Amani asked, breathless, as Usiku led her toward the living room, which was filled with plush cushions stacked high. Although Usiku smiled, Amani felt a sense of unease that she couldn't quite identify.

"Rehema will be back soon," he replied, his voice a strange mix of warmth and something unsettling. A chill ran down Amani's spine, but she brushed it off, eager to see Rehema and share their ideas.

"Let's wait inside," Usiku suggested. Amani nodded, expecting him to leave the door slightly open. However, as she entered, Usiku locked it behind her.

"Why are you locking the door?" she asked, trying to keep her composure despite her growing discomfort.

"Just being careful," he said, his smile now more of a grimace. The sunlight seemed to grow harsher, casting stark shadows and dulling the vibrant colors around her. The walls felt as if they were closing in, and Amani sensed an invisible weight tightening around her chest. Feeling increasingly uneasy, she looked around.

"Let me go!" she shouted in a trembling voice, her small frame shaking uncontrollably with fear. Her voice echoed through the dim, shadowy room, desperate and trembling. But Usiku stepped forward, his tall, muscular figure casting a dark shadow that seemed to swallow her whole. His presence was overwhelming, almost oppressive. At just sixteen, he was already strong, his broad shoulders and confident stance making him seem like a fortress. She, only fourteen and slight, was no match for him physically. She pushed at his chest with trembling hands, trying to break free, but he stood firm, unmoving like an unyielding mountain. The struggle stretched on endlessly, each second weighing heavier on her mind. Panic flooded through her veins, clouding her thoughts and numbing her senses. Shadows in the room grew darker, stretching their long, sinister shapes across the walls—an extension of her growing dread. The air felt thick and heavy, making it hard to breathe. It seemed as though the walls themselves were closing in, trapping her in a small world of terror that only grew more suffocating with every passing moment.

In that horrible moment, something inside her shattered forever. Usiku crossed a line that could never be erased, violating her in a way that stole her innocence. A cold, sharp realization swept over her: the carefree days of her childhood were gone. That day marked the end of her safe world, a world where she believed she was protected and loved. The pain of that instant haunted her now, like a hungry ghost that refused to leave her side. The sunlight, once a symbol of warmth and comfort, now seemed distant and faint—like a memory fading into the darkness. What was once bright and full of promise was now overshadowed by the heavy weight of her trauma. The sounds of laughter and joy, the carefree innocence of her childhood, dissolved into a heavy silence that pressed down on her soul. Her world, once vibrant with color and life, now felt dull and muted. The once sweet echoes of her laughter, her carefree voice that filled the air during happier times, had been silenced by the dark truth of betrayal. Everything she held dear seemed shattered.

Days turned into weeks that felt like an endless nightmare. Amani drifted through her life like a ghost, barely aware of her surroundings. Her spirit felt crushed beneath an invisible weight that held her down. The bright colors she remembered from her past faded into dull greys and browns. The joy she once felt from simple things, like playing with friends or singing her favorite songs, had become painful reminders of her broken trust. Every smile from her friends seemed to stab her – a reminder of her lost innocence, her shattered trust. She found it hard to believe anyone anymore. The very act of trusting others became a struggle. Every time someone tried to comfort her or offered kind words, she felt a surge of pain and began to question herself, her worth. She carried an unspoken shame, as if her trauma was a burden only she could bear. Her mind told her that her happiness was just a fragile, fleeting mask, one she had worn before, but that had shattered in an instant. Slowly, her confidence crumbled, replaced by insecurities that froze her in fear.

Her broken trust also pushed her to push away those closest to her. She distanced herself from Rehema, her childhood friend. She wanted to forget those memories, forget Usiku's dark act. She decided she could not keep seeing Rehema or her family, convinced that staying close only meant reliving that terrible moment. She believed that cutting ties with Rehema and her relatives would somehow erase the pain. She felt that if she separated from Rehema's family, she could somehow leave behind the memories of Usiku's violation. To her, this seemed like the only way to find peace, to lessen her sorrow. She convinced herself it was for everyone's good—hers, Rehema's, even her brother's. She thought that ending her friendship with Rehema was a way to shield her from further pain. She told herself that her absence would safeguard Rehema from the heavy burden of her grief. It was her way of creating distance so she would no longer feel the weight of that dark night. She convinced herself that separating from her friend and her family would help her forget, help her move on. But deep down, she knew it wasn't true. Every step away only reminded her of her loss, her pain, her shame. It was like chaining herself tighter, binding her to her suffering. The wounds from that day refused to heal, growing heavier with each attempt to run from her feelings. The more she tried to escape, the more she felt the iron grip of her trauma tighten around her heart, making her believe that she was forever trapped in her grief, chained to the past she couldn't forget.

Deep down, she clung to the hope that this painful wound would eventually heal—that maybe after the chaos, brighter days would come. She dreamed of a time when she could laugh without holding back, when the darkness would fade away, and the shadows that loomed over her life would finally dissipate. Each night, as she lay in bed, she envisioned a future where joy was not a fleeting moment but a constant companion, where the weight of her past would no longer anchor her to despair. The urge for revenge bubbled up inside her, transforming into a fierce quest for justice that ignited a fire within her soul. It was a fire that burned away the remnants of her fear and self-doubt, replacing them with a determination that felt almost palpable.

As time passed, Amani started high school, a new chapter that brought with it both challenges and opportunities. It was here, amidst the bustling hallways and the cacophony of teenage life, that she began to find strength in her suffering. She became a fighter, not just in the physical sense, but in every aspect of her life. Following YouTube tutorials, she immersed herself in the world of martial arts, each lesson a step toward reclaiming her power. The rhythmic sound of her fists striking the heavy bag became a cathartic release, a way to channel her anger and frustration into something constructive. With every punch and kick, she felt more powerful, more in control, envisioning Usiku's defeat as a tangible goal that was within her reach.

As she sat quietly in the waiting room, her hands trembled slightly, but her mind was clear. Her heart pounded, not only from the nerves of seeing Dr. Alex but from a deeper feeling stirring inside her. She had come a long way from that dark night years ago when Usiku took away her innocence. Now, at twenty-one, she felt a strange mix of strength and hope. The pain from her past still lingered, but it had lost its grip on her. It no longer dictated her days or haunted her thoughts as it once had. The ache was no longer something she kept hidden or let control her actions. She had made a firm decision — she was tired of living in fear and silence. She was ready to face her pain head-on.

For years, that memory had held her captive in a small corner of her mind, twisting her sense of trust and safety. But she no longer wanted the fear to define her story. Moving thousands of miles away from where her innocence was shattered marked a turning point for her. She had chosen to leave behind that place and those feelings. Going to university in Canada was part of her effort to start fresh, to rebuild what was broken. Each step she took away from her past gave her a little more strength. She wanted to reclaim her happiness, to find a future she could look forward to without shame or regret weighing her down.

She knew her journey wouldn't be easy. Healing was a slow process, filled with ups and downs. But she believed in her power to heal and grow. She believed she could reclaim her life. This moment in the waiting room symbolized the hope she carried with her. She felt a new resolve taking root inside her. It was time to confront her trauma, to give herself the chance to heal properly. She was ready now, more than ever, to face the memories, to free herself from their hold, and to write a new chapter of her life. With this new outlook, she was preparing to embrace whatever came next, confident she had the strength to move toward healing and happiness.

Her heart raced with increasing intensity as the digital clock's numbers edged ever closer to the precise time of 2:50 PM, each tick sounding like a resounding boom in the silence of the room. With every passing second, the weight of time bore down upon her, elongating the moments into an eternity that seemed to stretch beyond the confines of the present. Nerves coiled tightly within her, intertwining with a growing sense of hope that stubbornly clung to her psyche, refusing to be dislodged. In a bid to manage the rising tumult within, she maintained a facade of stillness, though her hands betrayed her with a subtle tremor that belied the turmoil raging beneath her composed exterior. Each shallow breath she took was a conscious effort to steady herself amidst the whirlwind of emotions swirling within.

Her mind raced through a myriad of potential outcomes, each presenting a different path that could shape her future in significant ways. The uncertainty of what Dr. Alex might convey during their impending therapy session loomed over her like a dark cloud, casting shadows of doubt across her thoughts. Yet, amidst the tumult of her inner turmoil, a glimmer of anticipation flickered, igniting a spark of resilience that bolstered her spirits.

When the door finally creaked open, her entire being tensed in a conflicting dance of relief and apprehension, unsure of what awaited her on the other side. The figure of Dr. Alex emerged into the room, his presence seemingly transformed - exuding a sense of comfort and familiarity that had eluded her in previous sessions. With measured steps, he crossed the threshold, emanating an aura of calm reassurance that enveloped her like a warm embrace. His voice, a soothing lullaby in the starkness of the clinical setting, washed over her, soothing the frayed edges of her nerves. The kind gaze of his eyes met hers, offering a silent pact of understanding and support that resonated deeply within her. In that moment, as his smile unfurled to cradle her in its gentle warmth, she felt a glimmer of hope stir within her, like a fragile flower blooming in the fissures of uncertainty. Dr. Alex's very presence seemed to metamorphose the sterile atmosphere of the room into a sanctuary of trust and compassion - a beacon of solace amidst the tempest of her emotions. And in that simple gesture, in the cadence of his voice, in the depths of his gaze, she found the silent assurance she had been seeking, a lifeline amidst the tumultuous sea of uncertainty that had threatened to engulf her.

"It's great to see you again," Dr. Alex greeted her, his voice calm and steady. "How have you been since we last met?"

Taking a moment to gather her thoughts, she exhaled deeply. "It's been challenging. I've been reflecting on our conversation about moving on from the past."

Dr. Alex nodded, encouraging her to share more. "It's definitely a journey."

"Do you feel ready to take that step?" he asked gently, as if he could sense the whirlwind of feelings within her. Amani inhaled deeply, standing taller as a wave of confidence washed over her. "Yes, I think I am," she affirmed. This gathering was not just another appointment; it symbolized the beginning of Amani's journey toward healing, understanding, and ultimately, freedom. Outside, the rain continued to fall, but inside, the storm within her began to calm, replaced by a growing sense of hope.

She felt a shift inside her, a stirring that had long been dormant, ready to share the weight she had carried for so long. "I was fourteen," she started, her voice trembling, as if the very act of speaking the words could shatter her. "A family friend hurt me... I've kept it bottled up for so long." The admission hung in the air, heavy and raw, as if the room itself held its breath.

Dr. Alex replied with warmth, his eyes softening with empathy. "It takes real bravery to talk about that," he said, his voice steady and reassuring. He understood the courage it took to unearth such painful memories, to expose the wounds that had festered in silence.

"I've never let anyone in," she confessed, tears rolling down her cheeks, each drop a testament to years of unspoken anguish. "I've been so scared and angry. I want to stop feeling this way." The words tumbled out, a floodgate of emotion that she had kept tightly sealed for far too long.

Dr. Alex nodded, his face full of understanding, as if he could see the labyrinth of her pain. "It's totally normal to feel that way after everything you've experienced. Recognizing your pain is a huge step toward healing." His validation wrapped around her like a warm blanket, offering a sense of safety she had longed for.

She inhaled deeply, trying to calm the storm within her. "I didn't tell anyone back then; I thought it was my fault. I've carried that shame for years." The weight of her confession felt both liberating and terrifying, as if she were finally shedding a layer of skin that had suffocated her for too long.

"It's crucial to understand that what happened wasn't your fault," Dr. Alex said gently, his voice a soothing balm. "You were just a child, and you deserved to feel safe. Healing starts when we face those feelings and allow ourselves to mourn." His words resonated within her, echoing the truth she had buried deep down.

"What if I can't do it?" she whispered, her vulnerability clear in her trembling voice, the fear of the unknown creeping back in.

"You can do this. It's a journey," he said gently. "There's no rush; we can take it step by step, at a pace that suits you. Just by opening up to me, you've already shown incredible strength."

She dried her tears and met his gaze, absorbing his words. For the first time in ages, a spark of hope ignited within her. "I want to give it a shot. I want to break free from this pain."

"That's a wonderful goal," Dr. Alex responded. "We'll tackle this together. You're not on this path alone anymore."

The fluorescent lights buzzed suddenly, making her headache worse. Dr. Alex paused for a moment, letting the noise fade before he started talking about regaining power. For a brief second, a glimmer of hope broke through the darkness.

"What's life supposed to be like?" she asked, her voice shaky with uncertainty.

Dr. Alex leaned closer, his expression genuine. "You're not alone. We'll tackle this together."

Hearing "together" was reassuring, sparking a bit of optimism. But the what-ifs still loomed in her mind—what if Usiku found her? What if no one believed her story?

Dr. Alex's steady voice cut through her racing thoughts. "Where is he now?"

"He's gone," Amani replied sharply, her anger bubbling up. In that moment, something shifted within her. She realized she wasn't just a victim—she was a survivor. With Dr. Alex by her side, she felt ready to take on her journey. She would be okay.

Dr. Alex nodded slowly, as if weighing something important. After a few deep breaths, he asked, "What would you do if you saw him again?"

The question pierced through their earlier conversation, reopening wounds that hadn't fully healed. A shiver ran down Amani's spine at the thought of Usiku showing up

Amani paused, her eyes fixed on Dr. Alex, searching for an elusive sign of reassurance. The atmosphere in the room thickened, heavy with the gravity of what she was about to voice. Thoughts swirled like autumn leaves caught in a gust, but this time, they carried *a hint of light*. She had spent countless sessions unraveling the tightly wound threads of her past, and now, for the first time in what felt like eternity, she sensed a sliver of strength piercing through the clouds of despair. Developing a bond with Dr. Alex was like igniting a dormant spark; it suggested there might be a way out of her relentless suffering, a path toward healing, even if it was cloaked in shadows.

Yet, as hope flickered within her, Amani's mind was inexorably drawn back to her home in Kenya, a place where the world had once felt vibrant and full of possibilities. She pictured herself there, storming towards her father with steely determination in her heart and a witty smirk curling on her lips, announcing with sarcastic bravado, "I would kill Usiku." Her thoughts danced dangerously close to that visceral anger, and she clenched her fists, feeling the warmth of fury coursing through her veins. The memory of her father's unwavering support felt like a balm against her turmoil, tempting her to conjure visions of a swift and just retribution. Would the Kenyan authorities have acted in her favor, imprisoning her tormentor? Behind that imagined confrontation laid a tempest of unresolved rage.

Gradually, as she inhaled deeply, attempting to quell the storm brewing within, the reality of her situation began to sink in. She was not in Kenya anymore; Winnipeg bore a different weight, one that forced her to reconsider her approach. It wasn't just a geographical shift; it was a profound transformation within her life and support system. A slow resignation washed over her, yet she grasped onto a thread of agency—she would phone her mother instead of racing to her father. It was less immediate, less powerful, but it was a lifeline, a bridge to something familiar amidst the uncertainty. Although her mother's voice would not fill the space beside her, it could still create a comforting connection, one she desperately sought amid the chaos.

A future plan began to form in her mind, conceived through a blend of frustration and hope. She envisioned the conversation with her mother: one laden with the weight of unspoken pain but also glimmering with the potential for guidance. Together, they could navigate the murky waters of her trauma; her mother's wisdom might illuminate the safest way forward, providing a scaffold upon which Amani could rebuild her sense of self. Even as her shoulders slumped under the burden of the day, the idea of reaching out suffused her with a quiet resolve. Perhaps, through this shared vulnerability, they could elicit a path toward justice and protection that did not threaten her fragile state. As she glanced back at Dr. Alex, she sensed his patient's awareness, quietly waiting, respectful of her unsteady journey through pain to the shores of healing.

Amani looked up, her heart pounding with an unbearable weight, yet an unexpected strength surged within her. "I will talk with mum about the rape incident; I cannot keep it any longer. I want her to help me on what to do. I cannot protect Usiku anymore," she resolved, her voice tremulous yet resolute. In that moment, she uncovered the resilience that lay beneath her sorrow, the shadows of her past illuminated by her courageous choice to confront the sadness that had haunted her for so long. Dr. Alex, seated across from her, watched closely, noting the flicker of determination that danced in her eyes, a spark ready to ignite a path toward healing.

As the gentle rhythm of the rain outside fell against the window, Amani felt its soothing cadence intertwining with her own shaky breaths. The droplets seemed to echo her inner turmoil while also whispering promises of solace and renewal. With each soft patter, she sensed a shift within herself, the fragmented pieces of her spirit beginning to reunite, slowly weaving together what had been scattered by her painful experiences. The once overbearing grief transformed into a mosaic of hope, and though tears brimmed in her eyes, they no longer felt like signs of weakness; they were symbols of her burgeoning strength.

Gathering her thoughts, Amani expressed her gratitude to Dr. Alex, her voice infused with a newfound clarity. "I never imagined I could open up to anyone," she confessed, each word a testament to the walls she had begun to dismantle. Dr. Alex offered her a tissue, his smile warm and inviting, reassuring her that this was indeed a safe space for healing. He spoke softly, his words wrapping around her like a comforting embrace, affirming that support was all around her, waiting patiently as she took her first steps toward reclaiming her narrative. As she dabbed her eyes, Amani felt the rain slowly dissipating her fears, a delicate symphony of droplets softening against the pavement, giving way to a clear sky where hope could flourish anew. The rhythmic pattern of rain transformed into a gentle lullaby, wrapping around her in a comforting embrace, almost like a gentle message from the universe. Each breath she took felt deeper, revitalizing her spirit as if the fresh scent of rain-soaked earth was washing away fragments of doubt that had clouded her mind. The kaleidoscope of colors around her seemed to pop with life; emerald greens and vibrant blooms stood defiantly under the emerging sun, mirroring the rebirth that she yearned for within. As Amani gathered her thoughts, a tidal wave of emotions surfaced. Her tightly-clenched hands were a testament to the shame she carried, gripping her own vulnerability like a lifeline under duress. When she finally spoke, her voice was steady, colored with a newly-found confidence. The words that flowed were raw and honest, each syllable shedding layers of guilt she had long been entangled in, revealing the hidden strength that had been buried too deeply. The realization that her struggles did not define her was like a gentle breeze parting the curtains, inviting brighter days forward.

Dr. Alex leaned back in his chair, his expression a blend of compassion and encouragement as he listened to her share. His thoughtful gaze settled on Amani's white-knuckled grip, a silent acknowledgment of the battles she had faced. "Shame can be a powerful force," he spoke gently, "yet it blinds us to our resilience." As he emphasized that she was not broken but rather a survivor, Amani felt a flicker of warmth blossom within her. Each word he uttered unraveled the tightness in her chest, allowing space for the truth of her bravery. She shifted her focus from the confines of her grasp to the open possibilities ahead, allowing the light of hope to seep through the cracks of her past.

She asked, "What if I can't let go of this feeling?" Dr. Alex responded that the aim wasn't to eliminate it completely but to learn to coexist with it, recognizing that it didn't define her. He likened it to a chapter in a book, not the entirety of her story. Amani paused to absorb this perspective, realizing its significance. Although it had been difficult for her to grasp before, he made it feel attainable. She inquired how she could achieve this, her voice filled with hope despite her past struggles.

Dr. Alex leaned in, his hands resting on the desk as he emphasized the importance of rewriting her narrative. He highlighted the need to acknowledge her pain while also celebrating the growth she had experienced. This process, he noted, required time and patience to truly effect change. Amani met his gaze, a flicker of determination igniting within her. "I want to give it a shot. I'm done letting this dictate my life," she asserted. Dr. Alex nodded, clearly impressed with her mindset. He proposed that they come up with a new mantra for her—something empowering to recite whenever feelings of shame or inadequacy arose. Amani paused, her eyes scanning the room as if searching for the perfect words among the books and the soft glow of the lamp. "What if I say, 'My past does not define me; my strength does'?" she offered thoughtfully. Dr. Alex's smile widened as he commended her for crafting such a powerful mantra. He stressed the importance of focusing on her strengths and encouraged her to repeat it frequently, especially when old negative emotions surfaced. Amani agreed, committing the mantra to her memory. It symbolized her battle against the shadows that had lingered for too long and her desire to reclaim her life. Outside, the rain had nearly stopped, and the streets shimmered under the streetlights, reflecting the newfound calm that was beginning to take root within her. "We should wrap up our session now," Dr. Alex said, glancing at the clock. His voice was both professional and warm, a gentle reminder of the value of time in their therapeutic journey. Amani nodded, a smile spreading across her face as she felt the relief of another fruitful session lift her spirits.

"It was a pretty good day," she said, thinking about all the breakthroughs and insights they had exchanged in the last hour. As Amani gathered her things and headed for the door, she felt lighter than she did when she had walked in. Dr. Alex trailed behind her, his presence a reassuring reminder of the support she had come to depend on throughout her journey.

"Don't forget to book for October!" Dr. Alex called out, giving her a gentle nudge of encouragement. Amani turned back, feeling thankful for his guidance. She had decided to take a break from therapy over the summer due to her school's insurance limits, but she felt good about the progress they had made together. The lessons she learned would help her navigate the upcoming weeks. As she opened the door, a mix of excitement and comfort washed over her, and she was ready to tackle the summer challenges with the skills she had gained in their sessions.

As Amani stepped outside, the wind picked up, sending a chill down her spine. She tightened her scarf and quickened her pace down the sidewalk, focusing on the ground beneath her feet. The city felt heavy around her, with the buildings looking like silent watchers. The only sounds breaking the stillness were the hum of traffic and the distant cry of a siren.

Her mind raced as she replayed the therapy session. Dr. Alex had mentioned it could be anxiety, but Amani wasn't entirely convinced. There was something deeper, something that sent shivers down her spine. She glanced back, but the street was deserted. It was just another calm evening in the city.

As Amani turned onto her street, she saw a shadow dart between the trees. Her heart raced, and she hurried her steps. It could just be a stray cat or a trick of the light, but the feeling lingered. In the three years she had lived in her apartment, she had never felt this way before.

The lights of her building flickered in the distance, a sign of safety she longed to reach. She quickened her pace, breathing heavily. The shadow seemed to grow larger and closer. Suddenly, a figure appeared from the darkness, and Amani felt a hand on her shoulder.

Her heart raced as she turned around, ready to scream, but there was no one there. She spun around, her eyes searching the dark. The figure had disappeared as quickly as it had come. A car passed by, its headlights briefly lighting up the street, but nothing was revealed.

Amani's breath caught in her throat. Was she imagining it? Maybe the therapy session had left her on edge. Yet the fear clung to her, refusing to fade. Taking a deep breath, she began to jog, her eyes fixed on her building's door. Just one hundred meters stood between her and the safety of locking herself away from the outside world.

She surged forward with fresh energy, her feet hitting the pavement hard as if trying to escape the uncertainty trailing her. "Just keep going," she reminded herself, "you'll be home soon." The path she once knew turned into a maze of worry, each heartbeat echoing her vulnerability in the dark.

At last, her apartment building came into view—a symbol of comfort and safety in the night. She stumbled up the steps, fumbling with her keys, her hands shaking as the cold metal pressed into her skin. Just as she opened the door, she glanced back, half-expecting to see that eerie shadow. But the night was quiet, only her heavy breathing and the soft rustle of the wind breaking the silence.

She entered and slammed the door shut, the sound ringing out in the stillness. Leaning against the door, she closed her eyes, feeling the weight of the night pressing down on her. It was just a walk, she told herself again, but that thought did little to lighten the shadows in her mind.

As she sank into the couch, a gentle hum surrounded her, slowly replacing the echoes of doubt with a heavy calm. She couldn't shake the feeling that the night held hidden secrets, lurking just outside her window—waiting and watching. Yet as her eyelids finally grew heavy with sleep, she clung to the hope that the morning light would chase away not just the shadows outside but also the darkness within her.

Amani wrapped the throw blanket tightly around her shoulders, feeling the soft fabric envelop her like a warm shield. Outside, the world felt distant and surreal as moonlight flooded her small apartment in Winnipeg, creating strange shapes on the floor. It was late—too late for anyone sensible to be awake—but sleep eluded her. Shadows moved outside her window, their dance stirring the air in a way that both fascinated and unsettled her.

Almost two years had passed since she had arrived in this new city, so different from her home. The vibrant streets of Winnipeg welcomed her, yet the chilly air mirrored the uncertainty in her heart. Being an international student felt like standing on the edge of an unknown sea, where every wave threatened to pull her under. She shifted her focus to the room, noticing the glow from the lone lamp that lit up her hastily-arranged belongings—books piled high, a small pot of drooping basil, and framed photos of her family, happy moments captured in glass. These memories, like shadows, hovered close, constantly reminding her of the gap she needed to close.

That night, the outside world seemed to seep into her apartment, transforming the quiet into a landscape of shadows and whispers. As Amani sat on her couch, she became convinced she was seeing shapes moving just beyond her line of sight. The faint glow from streetlamps flickered through her window, casting erratic silhouettes that danced across the walls, each flicker making her pulse quicken. The shadows seemed alive, shifting subtly, playing tricks on her mind. Her heartbeat thudded loudly, echoing in her ears, as a wave of fear crept over her. Every creak and rustle sounded magnified in the stillness, almost like the building itself was trying to communicate some unseen threat. She felt her muscles tense, resisting the urge to jump or hide. Her mind raced back to the events earlier that evening, adding weight to her fears. After her therapy session with Dr. Alex, she had taken a walk home through the crisp, cool evening air of West End Winnipeg. The streets were quiet, almost deserted, save for the occasional distant car or the faint hum of the city winding down. Her thoughts had been heavy then, burdened with worries she couldn't quite put into words, making each footstep feel like a small effort against an invisible weight pressing down on her chest.

While she made her way home, her senses seemed sharper. The darkness around her felt alive. Suddenly, a sleek black cat darted across the street in front of her, its striking green eyes glowing eerily in the dark. The animal's sudden burst of speed startled her, and she froze for a moment as the image lingered in her mind. Those eyes, bright and piercing, seemed to hold secrets she couldn't understand. The streetlamp light made them glow like tiny green lanterns in the night. At that exact moment, a single owl hooted softly from a nearby tree. Its call cut through the silence, deep and haunting. The owl's hoot seemed to echo in the stillness, a reminder of the quiet, secret world that hid in the darkness. For someone from her Swahili tradition, these signs carried heavy meaning. A black cat crossing her path was a bad omen, often linked with death or misfortune. The hooting owl was also seen as a warning, a guardian of secrets, often associated with forebodings of bad luck or worse.

Memories flooded her mind—stories from her childhood about superstitions. Her family had often warned her that such signs cannot be ignored. These thoughts made her stomach tighten, and her mind filled with dread. She felt a sudden, overwhelming certainty that something bad was waiting just beyond her sight. She was afraid that she, an outsider in this new city, was somehow singled out for bad luck. The superstitions rooted deep in her culture clawed at her mind, convincing her that danger might be lurking just around the corner, waiting to catch her off guard. The sense of vulnerability grew stronger, especially in the darkness that cloaked her surroundings.

Seeking comfort, she pulled the soft throw blanket tightly around her shoulders, feeling its warm fabric wrap around her like a shield. The texture was soothing, almost like holding onto a piece of home, calming her nerves, if only just a little. Outside her window, the world remained shrouded in darkness, distant and mysterious, as if hiding whatever secrets the night might be holding. Yet beneath her curiosity, a flicker of worry persisted. What if those shadows weren't just tricks of the light or her overactive imagination? What if they signaled real danger in the night? These thoughts made her wonder if she would ever truly belong in this unfamiliar city, so different from her childhood home. She wondered if she'd always be on the outside looking in, longing for a place to call her own. Deep inside, the tension grew. Each new street corner or dark alley seemed to promise adventure, but also held the potential for something more frightening, more threatening.

Then, unexpectedly, a gentle knock broke through her thoughts, pulling her back from her fears. It sounded quiet but insistent, like a whisper, yet it made her jump in her seat. Her heart kicked into overdrive, pounding faster, as if she'd been caught off guard by an unfamiliar force. A shiver ran down her spine as a cold breeze slipped through the cracks of the old building, causing a shudder to ripple through her. Her skin prickled with goosebumps, a sign of her rising unease. She hesitated, feeling a rush of nervous energy, but then summoned her courage. Carefully, she pushed herself up from the couch and approached the door. Her footsteps echoed softly in the quiet room as she moved cautiously, conscious of every sound. The silence felt heavy, like a thick fog settling around her, suffocating and oppressive.

"Who is it?" she called, her voice trembling slightly, trying to sound steadier than she felt inside. The unfamiliarity of the situation made her hesitant, her mind racing with possibilities.

"Hey, it's me, Lydia!" came a bright, familiar voice from the other side. Her neighbor's cheerful sound was a sudden burst of warmth and brightness. Lydia's voice cut through Amani's fears like a ray of sunlight piercing clouds. Lydia was her neighbor—a lively, spirited woman known for her infectious energy, who seemed to thrive on spreading joy. Despite the late hour and the cold night air, she appeared unaffected and full of life. The warmth of her tone brought an immediate wave of relief to Amani.

Lydia stood outside, her vibrant turquoise hair catching the light, cascading over her shoulders. An honest smile stretched across her face, lighting up her features and dispelling some of the darkness clutching her mind. She was a classmate from her orientation, a rare bright spot among the many strangers she'd met since moving here. Lydia was the kind of person who made her feel less alone, even in the silence of unfamiliar surroundings. She looked lively, somehow immune to the cold night outside, her cheeks flushed with excitement. It was as if she carried a warmth within herself that made the cold seem distant.

With a cheerful energy, Lydia lifted two steaming mugs, exuding a warm cocoa aroma that filled the air. "Can I come in? I brought hot chocolate!" she asked with a grin, holding out the mugs as if offering a small piece of comfort. Amani felt a wave of gratitude wash over her. The sight of those mugs, the scent of rich chocolate, and Lydia's cheerful smile made her feel a little safer, a little more connected.

"Of course! I'd love some," she replied, her voice soft but genuine, stepping aside to let Lydia pass. As the door swung open and Lydia crossed into her apartment, Amani sensed that her presence carried more than just warmth—it brought light into the shadows that had been growing in her mind. Lydia's arrival seemed to chase away the lingering fears, replacing them with a fleeting sense of hope and companionship in a city that often felt cold and distant.

As Amani and Lydia settled into the cozy embrace of the couch, a wave of calm enveloped Amani, washing away the tension that had clung to her all evening. It was as if the fog of anxiety was dissipating under the gentle rays of morning sun. The room transformed into a sanctuary—warm and inviting, filled with the comforting aroma of hot chocolate and the distant hum of city life filtering through the window.

They began to share stories, each tale revealing pieces of their lives—hopes, dreams, and fears intertwining like threads in a tapestry of friendship. Amani listened intently as Lydia recounted her childhood adventures, funny memories that brought laughter to their shared space. Each story served as a balm for Amani's troubled heart, turning shadows from her past into mere echoes fading away.

With every sip of her rich hot chocolate, warmth spread through Amani's body, grounding her amid an emotional whirlwind. The drink felt like a source of comfort and courage, encouraging her to open up more about herself.

Lydia leaned forward with sparkling eyes brimming with excitement. "Have you checked out the new developments at Forks Market yet? I heard they've added new trails with character shops along the way!" Her enthusiasm was infectious as she painted vivid pictures of tiny bridges winding through lush greenery and quirky shops filled with handcrafted treasures. The thought ignited a spark within Amani—a flicker of curiosity about exploring this vibrant space she had yet to visit.

"No, I haven't been yet! But I've heard it's stunning," Amani replied eagerly. The idea of wandering through colorful stalls surrounded by friendly faces stirred emotions she hadn't felt in ages.

"We should go tomorrow!" Lydia exclaimed. "There's also a new market by St. Boniface—live music and art displays everywhere! You'll love it!" Her energy filled the room with possibilities that made Amani smile wider than she had in weeks.

As their conversation deepened, so did their connection. Amani found herself sharing worries she had kept hidden—the grief weighing on her heart since moving from Nairobi and the pain stemming from past trauma. She spoke candidly about her therapy session earlier that day with Dr. Alex—the struggle to confront memories that haunted her nights.

In sharing these truths, something shifted within Amani; it was as if Lydia's attentive listening created a bridge between them built on understanding and compassion. When doubts about fitting in surfaced again, Lydia reached out gently placing a reassuring hand on Amani's shoulder. "You're going to be okay," she said softly but firmly. "What happened wasn't your fault—you shouldn't have gone through that."

Amani felt relief wash over her at those words—a simple acknowledgment that offered healing amidst pain. Lydia continued softly, "I'm here for you; you're not alone in this journey." These affirmations touched something deep inside Amani; leaning back against the cushions brought forth an unexpected sense of comfort she hadn't realized she craved.

Gradually, as hours slipped by unnoticed in their small universe filled with dreams and hopes over cooling cups of hot chocolate, outside sounds transformed from threatening noises into soft invitations to embrace life anew.

Time melted away until it became 2 a.m.—a time when most people would be asleep—but not them; they lingered together sharing laughter and vulnerability instead. As Lydia prepared to leave with gentle reluctance evident in her movements, she smiled warmly at Amani one last time before stepping toward the door.

"Don't forget—we're heading out tomorrow! So many adventures await us right here in Winnipeg," she said enthusiastically before leaving behind an echoing promise—a lingering sense of hope embedded deeply within Amani's soul.

In that moment alone after Lydia departed, realization dawned upon Amani: hope wasn't lost—it simply awaited its chance to bloom again like flowers pushing through winter's cold grasp towards bright colors under sunlight.

After Lydia left, Amani found herself standing at the threshold of transformation. The dark corners that had once overwhelmed her began to brighten gradually, as if God had sent Lydia as an angel to guide her. This subtle yet profound shift felt like a warm embrace, with light seeping into spaces previously shadowed by doubt and fear. It promised not just survival but a vibrant joy amid the uncertainty that lay ahead.

The sounds outside her window, which had earlier filled her with trepidation, now felt like an invitation—a gentle call to embrace the world around her. Each note of laughter and every rustle of leaves seemed to beckon her toward new friendships waiting just beyond tomorrow's horizon. With renewed courage swelling within her heart, Amani smiled softly, feeling the weight of despair lifting and being replaced by an exhilarating sense of possibility.

"Thank you, Lydia," she whispered into the quiet night. In those simple words lay a deep gratitude for a friendship that had blossomed unexpectedly—a bond that felt almost celestial in its timing. Lydia had become more than just a friend; she was a guiding light on Amani's tumultuous journey toward healing.

As she prepared for sleep, Amani reflected on how their shared moments illuminated paths previously obscured by fear and uncertainty. Laughter echoed through her mind like a melody of hope, reminding her that joy could coexist with vulnerability.

Tonight was different; it was not merely about closing her eyes but about opening her heart to what lay ahead. As warmth filled those once-dark corners of her mind, she envisioned countless adventures ready for exploration—each one brimming with potential and excitement.

Tomorrow promised more than just another day; it heralded new beginnings steeped in courage and connection. With this thought cradled gently in her heart, Amani surrendered to sleep, ready to embrace whatever awaited her on this beautiful journey toward brighter days ahead.

Chapter 03

May was flying by, school was finished, therapy was on hold until October, and summer in Winnipeg was just around the corner. Amani's new goal was to work at Third Cup and enjoy herself, aiming to save enough money over the summer to help with her tuition.

Every morning, Amani awoke to the lively sounds softly drifting through her apartment window, filling her small space with energy and promise. The streets of Langside Street buzzed with life as shops opened, neighbors greeted each other with cheerful hellos, and the hum of morning traffic gradually grew louder. She could hear the distant chattering of people heading to work, mixing with the clatter of grocery carts and the occasional honk of a car. Sometimes, street musicians played lively tunes, their music echoing off the brick buildings and adding a cheerful rhythm to the neighborhood's constant movement. The smell of fresh bread from a nearby bakery wafted up into her apartment, mingling with the scents of strong coffee brewing at local cafes. Children's laughter echoed from the parks, blending with the chatter of vendors setting up stalls. All of these sounds combined made it clear that Langside Street was an active, close-knit community where life was always in motion. For Amani, waking up to this lively chorus made her feel connected to her surroundings, giving her energy and a sense of belonging that fueled her day ahead. Every morning brought a new chance to witness the neighborhood's everyday magic, reminding her of the simple pleasures that make life in this part of town special. Living on the fourth floor of 415 Langside Street, Amani transformed her small apartment into more than just a haven for sleep; it was a sanctuary where the chaotic rhythm of city life seemed to ebb away. Each time she stepped inside, the air seemed to hum with a gentle warmth, wrapping around her like a protective embrace. The humble quarters, adorned with worn but soft blankets draped across the sofa, exuded a sense of coziness that felt like a warm hug on the coldest days. It was here, surrounded by memories and affection, that she could unwind, shedding the burdens of her day and finding solace in the quietude of her refuge. Photos of loved ones decorated the walls, capturing moments of unfiltered joy—a gallery of smiles that anchored her when the world felt overwhelming. Each snapshot whispered stories of home and hope, infusing her modest apartment with a sense of purpose amid the storm.

Outside her front door, the vibrant neighborhood unfolded into a tapestry woven with struggle and resilience. The streets told tales of lifelong battles against injustices that lingered heavily in the air, enveloping many residents, particularly those Indigenous or newly arrived. As Amani walked past, she often felt the weight of their stories—a profound sadness radiating from neighbors who bore wounds of racism and economic disparity that seemed unyielding. Broken sidewalks echoed the laughter of children playing amidst the gritty realities of life, where fresh produce was a rare luxury, pushing families to make heartbreaking choices. The resilient spirits of her neighbors reminded Amani of her own challenges and the fight she faced to carve out a better life. Yet, against this backdrop of hardship, fleeting gestures of kindness forged connections that became lifelines within this community, each shared moment illuminating a path through the darkness.

In the evenings, after the day's toil at Third Cup, Amani savored her walks through Memorial Park, extending into the lively avenues of Portage and Broadway. The familiar hum of life greeted her; she cherished the sense of belonging that washed over her as she passed by Bean & Leaf. There, the comforting aroma of fresh coffee mingled with the sweetness of pastries, beckoning her inside. Mr. Patel's warm greeting, "Good evening, Amani! The usual?" felt like homecoming after a day spent navigating her new surroundings.

Each visit allowed her to rejuvenate, wrapping her in the harmonious blend of community and comfort, and reinforcing her belief that places of solace could be found, even amid chaos.

Amidst the littered streets of Langside, Amani discovered a vibrant undercurrent of life, pulsing with both struggle and resilience. Though shadows of poverty brushed against the edges of the neighborhood, the heart of the community radiated a warmth that defied the bleak surroundings. Each community meeting held in the local center transformed into a sanctuary where voices converged; ideas soared, and burdens lightened. Amani felt drawn to this kaleidoscope of human experience, each story shared a thread that wove deeper connections among residents. In their meetings, she witnessed the power of unity, realizing that while individual struggles might lay heavy, collective strength seemed nearly unbreakable.

Reflecting on her surroundings brought forth a deeper understanding of hope. It was in these shared experiences—tales of loss, grit, and unwavering spirit—that Amani found her place in Langside's rich tapestry. Inspired by her neighbors, she began committing to small acts of kindness, each interaction a delicate stitch reinforcing the fabric of their community. It was this intricate weaving of lives that lit a spark within her, illuminating dreams she had once deemed unreachable. With each encounter, she unearthed a renewed sense of purpose, grasping the magnitude of what a single connection could instigate—like seeds sown in fertile ground, dreams took root.

Then, on a sun-drenched spring afternoon, Amani's heart swelled as she returned home to the sight of children laughing on the sidewalk. Their joy was infectious, reminiscent of rays breaking through a cloudy sky, a tangible reminder of *life's ebbs and flows*. In the midst of hardship, these moments of pure delight flickered like flames in the darkness, strong enough to illuminate paths ahead. Among the revelers was Leila, a little girl with a boundless imagination, spinning stories as whimsically as she spun in circles.

Amani watched, enchanted by the light that danced in Leila's eyes, a reflection of the hope that persisted in the hearts of all residents of Langside. Here, amidst laughter, she felt the pulse of resilience, emboldening her to embrace the beauty intertwined with struggle—a celebration of life's unwavering spirit.

Leila had a special talent for inviting others into her creative adventures. With her pigtails bouncing, she would lead exciting quests that turned ordinary afternoons into treasure hunts or daring rescues. The other kids loved her, not just for her energy but for her ability to make every game feel magical.

Amani, still feeling the heaviness of the past winter, was drawn to the lively scene on the sidewalk. The children's laughter was contagious, and she found herself smiling despite her worries. It felt like they were casting a spell over the quiet street, brightening the corners of Amani's heart that had felt dark.

"Come play with us!" Leila called out, noticing Amani watching from a distance. Her invitation was bright and warm, much like the sun that bathed the neighborhood in light. Amani hesitated, feeling the unfamiliarity of her new surroundings pressing against her. It had been a while since she had participated in carefree fun, but the sincerity of Leila's offer tugged at her.

With a deep breath, Amani took a step forward. "What are you playing?" she asked.

The parents, who for the longest time were watching Amani as she played with their children, joined the game, too.

"Pirates!" Leila exclaimed, her eyes sparkling with excitement. "We're searching for buried treasure! You can be our captain!"

Amani's heart lifted at the thought. There was something wonderfully freeing about stepping into a world forged by imagination. "Alright, Captain Leila," she chuckled, adopting an exaggerated pirate accent. "Where do we sail first?"

With squeals of delight, the children rallied around Amani, who felt their eagerness wash over her like a soothing wave. They crafted makeshift eye patches from strips of cloth and drew treasures in the dirt with sticks. From that moment on, she became a part of their world, sharing laughter and camaraderie with children who had no idea of the battles she was fighting internally.

As the sun began to dip below the horizon, painting the sky with hues of orange and pink, Amani realized how much joy a simple afternoon had brought her. In the heart of her new neighborhood, amidst whimsical tales and raucous laughter, she had found connections that reminded her of the resilience present in life's simple pleasures.

"Can we do this again tomorrow?" Leila asked, her face beaming with hope.

Amani looked at the eager faces surrounding her, each one lit up with the thrill of the adventure they had just shared. The thought of returning to this vibrant world, where laughter drowned out her worries, filled her with a warmth she hadn't felt in ages.

"Absolutely!" she replied, her voice brimming with enthusiasm. "But only if we promise to find the most legendary treasure of all!" The children gasped, their eyes wide with wonder.

"What kind of treasure is that?" one of the littler girls asked, her pigtails swinging as she bounced on the balls of her feet in excitement.

Amani placed a hand on her chin, feigning deep contemplation. "The treasure of friendship!" she finally declared, her smile infectious. The kids erupted in giggles, and she felt a wave of joy wash over her—this was the kind of magic she had missed.

Leila clapped her hands, rallying everyone's attention. "Then it's settled! Tomorrow, we will become treasure hunters! We'll need maps and clues, and we can even make a flag!"

As dusk settled around them, the children began to disperse, their laughter echoing in the crisp evening air. Amani lingered, feeling a deep sense of gratitude for this unexpected turn in her day. The parents, who had smiles plastered on their faces, approached her.

"You fit right in with them," one mother said, her warm gaze filling Amani with a sense of belonging. "They're lucky to have you as their captain."

Amani felt a flush of warmth in her cheeks. "Thank you. I think I'm the lucky one. I haven't felt this lighthearted in a long time."

Amani and Leila's parents were starting to become friends. They invited Amani over for dinner after spending the afternoon at Rock and Horse Park. Amani couldn't say no to the invitation because it meant she could hang out a bit longer with her new friend Leila.

"We're from Lebanon," Ahmad, Leila's dad, reminded Amani. "I hope you remember that."

"Yes, I remember," Amani replied.

"We have a special Lebanese dish for you," Ahmad said with a smile as he headed to the kitchen to help his wife, Fatima.

"I love trying food from different countries," Amani said, while Leila and her brother moved closer, excited to show her their photo albums.

"Check this out," Ali, Leila's younger brother, said as he pointed to a picture in the album. "That's me at Assiniboine Park Zoo!"

Amani leaned in closer to get a better look at the pictures. The joy on Ali's face was infectious as he pointed out different animals in each photo.

"Wow, you look so happy! Did you see all the animals there?" Amani asked, genuinely intrigued.

"Yeah! I saw lions, elephants, and even a penguin!" Ali exclaimed, his eyes sparkling with excitement. Leila chimed in, "We went there last summer. It was so much fun! You should come with us next time."

"I would love that," Amani replied, feeling a warmth in her heart at the thought of spending more time with her new friends. Just then, Ahmad and Fatima emerged from the kitchen, carrying a beautifully arranged platter filled with something unfamiliar yet enticing.

"Here it is," Fatima said, setting the platter on the table. "This is called tabbouleh. It's a salad made from parsley, tomatoes, mint, onion, and bulgur. And we also have some kebabs for you to try."

Amani's mouth watered at the sight. "It looks amazing! I can't wait to taste it," she said eagerly.

As they sat down to eat, Amani couldn't help but feel grateful for this unexpected and wonderful day. The aroma of the food, the laughter from Leila and Ali, and the warm atmosphere of their home made her feel like she was part of their family.

"What's your favorite Lebanese food?" Amani asked, curious to know more about their culture.

Leila thought for a moment before responding, "Definitely the kibbeh! It's like a meat pie, but with spices and bulgur. You'll have to try it with us next time!"

After dinner, Ahmad and Fatima invited Amani to tell them about her journey from Kenya to Winnipeg. "We're just really curious," Ahmad said with a smile, while Fatima, Leila, and Ali sat quietly, eager to hear. Amani grinned as she began to explain how she had relocated to Winnipeg a year earlier to pursue a Bachelor of Science in Psychiatric Nursing at the Brandon University, Winnipeg Campus.

Amani took a deep breath, her eyes reflecting memories from her journey. "You know, it wasn't an easy decision to leave Kenya," she began, her voice calm yet filled with emotion. "I grew up in Nairobi, surrounded by my family and friends, and the thought of leaving my home was daunting. But I always dreamed of pursuing higher education in nursing—specifically psychiatric nursing—because I wanted to make a difference in people's lives."

Fatima leaned in closer, intrigued. "What was the process like for you to move to Canada?"

Amani chuckled softly, recalling the numerous steps she had to take. "First, I had to research universities that offered my program. After narrowing them down, I applied to Brandon University. The application process was intense, with essays and references, but I was determined. Once I received my acceptance letter, it felt like a dream come true!"

"That sounds exciting!" Ahmad interjected. "But how did you prepare for such a big move?"

Amani nodded, her expression turning more serious. "Preparing for the move was overwhelming. I had to get my visa and arrange travel, which involved a lot of bureaucracy. I also had to say goodbye to my family, which was heartbreaking. They were supportive, of course, but it was tough to leave my life behind."

Leila piped up, "What was your first impression of Winnipeg when you arrived?"

Amani's eyes lit up. "Wow, it was a shock! The weather was completely different—so cold compared to Nairobi. I remember stepping off the plane and feeling that rush of icy air hitting my face. I thought to myself, 'What have I gotten into?' But the people here are so welcoming. The community made me feel at home, which helped ease the transition."

Ali listened intently, clearly fascinated. "How was your experience at university? Was it difficult to adapt to a new education system?"

Amani smiled, recalling the challenges she faced. "Initially, the coursework was intense. The focus here is different—you really have to engage in discussions and think critically. But I found support through my professors and classmates. I joined a study group, which became my little family away from home. We helped each other navigate our courses and shared experiences about living in a new country."

Fatima looked thoughtful. "What's been your favorite part of living in Winnipeg so far?"

Amani thought for a moment. "I'd say the sense of community. There are so many multicultural events, and I've learned about different cultures through food and celebrations. I even joined a local group that offers support to newcomers, which has been invaluable."

Ahmad's smile grew warm as he looked at Amani. "It's clear you've changed a lot since moving here," he said. His voice carried genuine admiration. "Do you have any plans for what comes next?"

Amani nodded confidently, her eyes bright with focus. "Absolutely," she replied, a firm tone in her voice. "Once I finish my degree, I want to get involved in mental health work. I want to support people who often feel overlooked or ignored, those who are struggling silently. My biggest goal is to build bridges between different cultures when it comes to mental health care. I believe everyone deserves services that respect their background, beliefs, and ways of understanding the world. Too often, mental health treatments are one-size-fits-all or don't consider cultural differences, which can make it harder for people to seek help and truly get the support they need."

Amani's face lit up with passion as she spoke about her dreams, her words reflecting a deep sense of purpose. The others listened intently, sensing her conviction and the importance behind her words.

Then, Amani turned to Fatima and asked, "Can you tell me about your journey from Lebanon to Winnipeg? I'd love to hear how you and Ahmad made that move." Her curiosity and respect showed in her gentle tone, eager to understand a story that seemed full of meaning and sacrifice.

Leila, sitting nearby, grinned and nodded eagerly. "I want to hear it too," she said softly, her eyes searching Fatima's face for details. She looked at her parents, who exchanged knowing glances, and then at Ahmad, waiting patiently for the story.

Ali, their younger brother, chimed in quickly, "I want to hear it as well. It's like a chapter from our family's story, and I think we all need to hear it." His voice was full of genuine interest and pride.

Fatima smiled warmly at her children and glanced at Ahmad. Her eyes briefly flicked to her parents, the quiet strength of her memories shining through her expression. As she settled into her chair, she took a deep breath, and a tender, thoughtful look crossed her face.

"You know," she began softly, "it's been quite an adventure for us. Ahmad and I grew up way back in Beirut, in the heart of Lebanon. Life there was full of energy—bright markets, lively streets, and a constant hum of life. But it also had its tough sides. Political unrest, economic struggles, and uncertainty shadowed many of our days. We faced challenges, yet we found comfort in our family and community.

"We were lucky enough to have relatives in Winnipeg who could help us when we decided to make a change. Before Leila was born, Ahmad's brother helped us navigate the complicated process of moving. We applied for permanent residence status, and eventually, we received good news—our new home in Winnipeg. It wasn't easy to leave behind Beirut, a city filled with both chaos and beauty, but we believed a better future was waiting for us here."

Fatima paused, her eyes softening with the memory. "It took a lot of courage to leave everything behind—the familiar streets, friends, and the life we knew. It was a mix of fear and hope, blending into a single strong feeling that we wanted a better life for our children." Her voice grew a little thicker with emotion. "We wanted Leila and Ali to grow up safe, free from the worries that come with instability. We dreamed of a place where they could follow their dreams without being held back by circumstances beyond their control."

She looked at her children with love, a quiet pride shining through. "That's what drove us to start fresh in Winnipeg, to build a future where they could thrive. It wasn't just about escaping chaos, but about giving them the chance to grow into the best versions of themselves in a safer, more stable environment."

Fatima's words carried a mixture of hope and determination, but also a deep understanding of sacrifice. The room grew still, each person absorbing her story, feeling the strength behind her choices. Their shared history brought everyone closer, weaving a tapestry of resilience and hope. Each family's journey was a testament to their enduring spirit.

As Fatima finished, the warmth in their circle deepened. Her story, filled with struggles and sacrifices, resonated strongly with everyone present. It reminded them all of why they came to this new land and what they hoped to achieve here. The political instability in Lebanon cast a long shadow over her family's future, especially for her children. Her voice wavered just slightly as she said, "We knew we wanted better for Leila and Ali—more than anything, a life where they could grow without fear and have the freedom to chase their dreams." Her words hung in the air, full of quiet resolve and unwavering love, a testament to her unwavering faith in a brighter future.

Ahmad interjected with a mix of excitement and nostalgia, *"The day we arrived in Winnipeg felt like stepping into a new world."* His words painted a vivid picture of their arrival, where eager hearts battled the fears of the unknown. The thrill of a fresh start was quickly entwined with anxiety—the biting cold, the quest to find their footing in an unfamiliar land, and the challenge of embracing a new culture. He remembered those first few weeks as a tumultuous blend of joy and uncertainty, a delicate dance between hope and trepidation.

Fatima's eyes lit up as she recounted her first day at school, where she was upgrading her computer skills. *"Everyone was so different, but they were friendly,"* she reminisced, reflecting on how she had felt adrift at first, yet gradually found her place among her classmates. The initial anxiety faded like shadows at dawn, replaced by the warm glow of connection and friendship. She recalled the smiles that welcomed her, making it easier to transform the sense of isolation into a feeling of belonging in this new chapter of her life.

As she continued, Fatima observed how time had a remarkable way of reshaping their experiences. *"Once we settled, we found a community that embraced us,"* she said with awe. The cultural festivals, vibrant and colorful, served as a bridge to her past, evoking cherished memories from home while allowing her to share her heritage with others. The realization struck them that life in Winnipeg had its own unique beauty—a beauty forged in the merging of cultures and collective histories. Amani nodded, her heart full, feeling the bond among them solidify into something profound. *"It's incredible how, despite our different backgrounds, we all share similar struggles and triumphs. That's what connects us,"* she affirmed, her words echoing the essence of their gathering. Ahmad leaned back, contemplative. "It's so true, Amani. Our journeys may differ, but ultimately, they're about finding a place where we belong—where we can help one another and uplift our communities."

Fatima let out a contented sigh, a soft exhalation that seemed to carry the weight of gentle understanding and quiet joy. Her eyes, luminous with warmth and deep satisfaction, reflected the soft glow of the room. She paused for a serene moment, letting the wave of profound connection wash over her—a tangible bond with her cherished family, and now, a new, equally profound kinship with Amani, whose presence radiated calm wisdom. Then, her voice, a gentle murmur yet remarkably clear, filled the comfortable silence. "And in sharing our stories," Fatima began, her gaze sweeping from Ahmad to Amani and back again, "we unconsciously, yet powerfully, build bridges—bridges that span the distances between different cultures, between families whose paths might otherwise never truly cross, and even, most profoundly, within ourselves, connecting our past experiences to our present understanding. When we bravely open up about our individual journeys, our triumphs, and our vulnerabilities, it creates a unique window for others. It helps them to genuinely see the world through our eyes, to walk a mile in our shoes, if only through imagination. It's through these narratives that we truly learn about each other's unique traditions, the silent struggles that shape us, and the overflowing joys that uplift our spirits. For instance, sharing the vibrant details of how Ramadan is celebrated at home, with its communal meals and spiritual reflections, or recounting the boisterous laughter and shared histories of a family reunion, can offer friends an authentic, intimate glimpse into the very fabric of our lives. These precious exchanges, these honest unveilings, are like gentle hammers chipping away at the thick walls of misunderstanding, allowing light to flood in and helping us to build lasting bonds of trust and mutual respect. They serve as potent reminders that beneath the surface of apparent differences, we all possess a shared humanity, more fundamental commonalities than divisions, and that this deep understanding, once fostered, creates an undeniable sense of unity. Listening intently to each other's stories also naturally cultivates empathy, that vital ability to share and understand the feelings of another—a skill so utterly essential in a world that often feels fractured and profoundly divided. When we choose to share honestly, with open hearts and minds, we inherently promote respect and profound kindness. That, truly, is the deepest gift of true community—the creation of a nurturing, inclusive space where every single individual feels profoundly valued, truly seen, and deeply heard. It's far more than just talking, more than just exchanging pleasantries; it's about weaving a tapestry of shared experiences that creates an undeniable sense of belonging, a feeling so strong it can inspire and uplift not just the speaker and the listener, but everyone involved, radiating outwards."

Ahmad responded with a bright, eager nod, his entire being alight with enthusiasm. His excitement was palpable, almost a living thing, contagious in its purity. He leaned forward, his eyes sparkling. "I think the absolute best part is that we get to teach others about our cultures, too!" he exclaimed, a wide, genuine smile spreading across his face, lighting up his features. "I absolutely love sharing my favorite Lebanese foods with my friends at school. Like when I bring in homemade hummus and crispy falafel, watching their faces when they try it, or when I tell them excitedly about the special ways we celebrate Eid, with all the family gatherings and delicious sweets. It's such an amazing chance to proudly show them what makes us who we are, what makes us proud of where we come from and our heritage. Sometimes, their eyes literally light up with wonder and curiosity when they taste something new and exciting, and it's genuinely so much fun to watch them learn and ask thoughtful questions about our traditions. Sharing these vibrant parts of my culture doesn't just feel good; it makes me feel incredibly proud and deeply connected, not just to my friends, but to my roots. It reminds me, powerfully, that food, stories, and traditions are not just customs; they are incredibly powerful tools, beautiful languages that help others truly understand and appreciate us for who we are. When we take the time to patiently teach and explain, we are actively helping to build and bridge gaps that might otherwise remain stubbornly closed, perpetuating misunderstanding. It's not just about showing off our culture; it's about authentically sharing who we are, our very essence, so others can see and celebrate the inherent beauty in both our differences and our surprising similarities."

Amani nodded in thoughtful agreement, her face glowing with a gentle, inner sense of pride, a quiet radiance. "And sharing your experiences and values, your deepest beliefs, makes you undeniably stronger," she added, her voice a warm, soothing balm, rich with deep sincerity. "When we courageously talk about what truly matters to us, what shapes our moral compass, we inherently build confidence in our convictions and cultivate an inner resilience that helps us weather life's storms. It's like carefully planting precious seeds of understanding and compassion that, with time and nurturing, grow into even greater empathy and shared humanity. We learn, with each shared story, how to support each other more effectively, more genuinely, especially when someone is navigating a particularly tough day, feeling overwhelmed or lost. For instance, my family has always instilled in me the profound importance of listening carefully, truly hearing, and being patiently present, no matter what challenges arise or emotions are expressed. In doing so, we consciously create a robust, unbreakable circle of trust, a safe haven where everyone feels unequivocally safe, deeply valued, and genuinely cared for. It's a truly beautiful, reciprocal cycle—learning profound lessons from each other's unique stories and instinctively offering unwavering support in return, a constant give and take of wisdom and comfort. This profoundly transformative process helps us all to clearly see the immense strength within ourselves, strength we might not have known we possessed, and to recognize and celebrate the incredible power within each other, making us far more united and understanding in everything we do, in every interaction. These deeply forged bonds don't just enrich our individual lives; they make our entire community richer, profoundly more caring, and ultimately, far more capable of facing any challenge or adversity together, as one unbreakable unit."

Fatima's curiosity, ignited by their profound words, visibly grew, and she leaned in slightly, a subtle shift in her posture, her eyes shining with an almost childlike eagerness, brimming with unasked questions. "What words of encouragement or inspiration would you share specifically with my family?" she asked softly, her voice barely above a whisper, yet filled with an undeniable eagerness to absorb Amani's thoughts, to glean wisdom for her own beloved kin. Her poignant question hung in the air for a moment, a weighty silence settling over them as everyone, in their own way, thought deeply and introspectively about it, pondering what singular sentiment or guiding principle could truly bring the most profound unity and enduring strength to their family bonds.

Amani took a slow, deliberate breath, as if gathering her thoughts, then shared her insight with a gentle, reassuring smile. "I'd tell your family to practice empathy towards all, without exception, and I know, Fatima, that you already do it so beautifully, because you have shown it to me in countless ways," she said thoughtfully, her gaze steady and kind. "We all, every single one of us, carry our own intricate, often invisible stories—histories of joy, pain, loss, and triumph—and knowing, truly knowing, that someone else genuinely understands our feelings, validates our experiences, and shares our burdens, can make an immeasurable difference in navigating life. In my work as a nurse, especially within the delicate and often challenging field of mental health, I witness every single day how radical compassion, how genuine understanding, fundamentally changes everything. Approaching others, whether patients or family members, with an open heart and an inherent kindness helps them to feel unequivocally safe, seen, and utterly supported, allowing them to lower their guards and begin to heal. When we truly listen— not just hear words, but truly listen with our soul—and genuinely try to see the world through someone else's eyes, even if their perspective differs vastly from our own, it can miraculously heal old wounds, bridge emotional chasms, and build a profound, unbreakable trust. Empathy, in its purest form, helps us to gracefully navigate and ultimately move past disagreements, past those stubborn misunderstandings that can fester and divide. It serves as a gentle yet potent reminder that everyone, at some point, struggles, everyone carries burdens, and everyone, more than anything else, needs kindness and understanding. That, I believe, is the fundamental key to making any family stronger, closer, and more deeply caring every single day."

Fatima listened intently, absorbing every word, her face filled with an almost reverent admiration for Amani's profound and wise words. "That's powerful," she said softly, the words a hushed testament to their impact. "For us, for our family, the word that resonates most deeply, the quality we strive for, would be resilience—that unwavering ability to rise again, to stand tall after facing challenges that threaten to overwhelm us, and to face each new day, no matter how daunting, with an unbreakable spirit of hope. No matter what hardships fate throws our way, no matter how formidable the obstacles, we strive to keep going, to persist, learning invaluable lessons from each setback, transforming pain into wisdom. Life, as we all know, often relentlessly throws unforeseen obstacles in our path—whether it's crushing financial struggles that test our very foundation, debilitating health issues that drain our strength, or complex family problems that fray our communal bonds—and sometimes, in the thick of it, it feels utterly overwhelming, like a crushing weight. But resilience, for us, means precisely this: not giving up, not surrendering, even when every fiber of our being screams for rest or defeat, even when the path ahead seems impossibly difficult. It's about finding that deep, inexplicable strength from within, that innate human capacity to keep moving forward, persistently, no matter how tough things genuinely get, no matter how many times we stumble. We cling to the unwavering trust that better days will come, that the darkness will recede, and we hold onto hope—that invisible yet potent anchor—that we can, and will, overcome any challenge placed before us. Resilience is what empowers us to rebuild our lives, piece by painstaking piece, after life's most devastating storms have passed; it allows us to face each new dawn with courage in our hearts and boundless optimism in our spirits. More than that, it profoundly shapes our future, for it teaches us, through every trial, that difficulties and suffering do not define us or our worth—it is our unwavering response to them that does. This inherent strength, this quiet determination, passed down from generation to generation like a sacred torch, keeps our collective spirits alive, keeps our dreams burning brightly, and helps us to continually build a hopeful, brighter future, not just for ourselves, but for all who follow."

Ahmad added, "And always stay connected to your roots. They form the foundation of who you are, no matter where you are in the world."

Amani felt incredibly grateful for the opportunity to welcome Leila, an eleven-year-old girl, into her life. In return, Leila had introduced her to her wonderful family, creating a beautiful bond between them.

Amani realized that it was getting late and decided to head home. Ahmad and his family kindly offered to give her a ride to her Langside apartment, which was just a short five-block distance away.

As they made their way to the car, Amani felt a warmth in her heart, grateful for the connections she had formed with Ahmad's family. The night air was crisp, but the shared warmth of their conversation wrapped around her like a cozy blanket.

Once they settled into the car, Fatima turned to Amani with a bright smile. "Thank you for joining us tonight. It's not often that we get to share our stories like this. It helps us remember where we come from, and it creates new bonds."

Amani beamed in response. "Thank you for including me. Your stories are inspiring and remind me of the importance of community. It's amazing how much we can learn from each other."

As they drove through the quiet Winnipeg streets, the city lay illuminated under a blanket of stars. Amani gazed out the window, taking in the sight of snow-dusted rooftops and quiet, tree-lined avenues.

Leila, seated in the backseat beside her younger brother Ali, whispered excitedly, "Amani, do you think we could have a potluck with our friends at school? We could all bring food from our cultures!"

"Oh, that would be fantastic!" Amani encouraged, turning slightly in her seat to face the two siblings. "It's a great way to celebrate diversity and share our traditions. I would love to bring some of my favorite dishes."

Ahmad chuckled lightly. "I can already picture it—the culinary festival right in your school's cafeteria, a true representation of our beautiful melting pot of cultures."

Fatima nodded, her eyes sparkling with enthusiasm. "We can all contribute recipes, too! Food has a unique way of bringing people together. It's a connection that goes beyond words."

As they reached Amani's apartment, she turned to them, her eyes twinkling with gratitude. "You guys are wonderful. I truly feel lucky to have met you all. Let's make that potluck happen!"

"Definitely," Leila said, bouncing in her seat with excitement. "And maybe we can even teach our friends how to cook some of the dishes!"

Amani laughed. "That sounds like a plan. I'm in! But you have to promise—no pressure on the cooking; it's all about having fun together."

Ahmad parked the car and they all climbed out, Amani feeling a little reluctant to say goodbye. Fatima enveloped her in a warm hug, her voice soft as she said, "Remember, Amani, you're always part of our family now. We look forward to more gatherings and making more memories together."

With that, Amani waved goodbye and headed up the stairs to her apartment, a smile stretching across her face. The bonds of community and shared stories had enriched her life in ways she could never have anticipated. She glanced back at the car, hoping to hold onto this moment forever. Inside her heart, she knew this was just the beginning of many beautiful friendships that would grow and flourish.

Once Amani arrived at her apartment, she rushed out to the balcony to admire the stunning moon hanging in the night sky. It glowed brightly, almost as if it were beaming down at her, radiating a soft light that reflected her inner joy. After securing the balcony door, she found it hard to let go of the sweet memories of the day. Thoughts of treasure maps and laughter-filled dinners with her new friends—who seemed like family—swirled in her head. She cherished the moments spent with Ahmad, Fatima, and their kids, Leila and Ali; they brought so much happiness into her life.

Feeling that warmth, she felt compelled to call her mom back in Kenya to share all about her wonderful evening with the family.

Amani picked up her phone, her heart fluttering with excitement as she searched for her mom's contact. The anticipation of sharing her joy brought a smile to her face. She dialed the number and listened to the ringing, imagining her mother's voice on the other end.

When her mom finally answered, Amani couldn't help but let out a soft laugh. "Mama! You won't believe the wonderful day I just had!" she exclaimed, her voice bubbling with enthusiasm.

Her mother chuckled warmly. "Tell me everything, Amani! I want to hear all about it."

Amani settled into her balcony chair, the moonlight casting a gentle glow around her. "I spent the day exploring with Ahmad and Fatima. We found this amazing spot by the river where the kids could run wild. Leila and Ali are such bundles of energy! We even made treasure maps and had a picnic on the grass."

As she spoke, memories rushed back to her—the sound of laughter echoing in the air, the delicious aroma of the food they had shared, and the way the sunset had painted the sky in hues of orange and pink. Her mother listened intently, occasionally interjecting with questions or laughter, urging Amani to share more vibrant details.

"And Mama," Amani continued, her voice softening, "it felt like I was part of something beautiful, like I really belonged. They've welcomed me so warmly into their home. I never expected to make such great friends so far from home."

Her mother's voice was full of pride. "I always knew you were meant to connect with others, my dear. That's your gift. Just remember, family isn't always about blood; it's about the bonds you create."

Amani nodded, even though her mother couldn't see her. Those words resonated within her. "You're right, Mama. It's like I've found a little piece of family here."

They continued to chat, sharing stories and laughter under the watchful eye of the moon, bridging the physical distance with heartfelt connection. As Amani hung up, she felt that familiar warmth spread through her again, filling her with gratitude for both her new friends and her enduring family ties. Tonight, with the moon shining brightly above, she felt a sense of peace and belonging that she had longed for amidst the changes of her new life.

Chapter 04

As Amani hopped into her car, the heat of the sun seeped through the driver's window, and she rolled it down to let in the fresh air filled with hints of blooming flowers. The roads would soon be lined with vibrant greens and the occasional burst of wildflowers as summer took hold. She turned up the music, a playlist curated for the perfect beach vibe, each song resounding with happiness and nostalgia.

The drive to Grand Beach was one she knew well—a stretch of highway that twisted through scenic landscapes. Amani relished this part of the journey; it was a time to breathe, to disconnect from the mundane daily grind, and to connect with her friends and nature. On the way there she picked up Christina, Samantha, and Maya—her favorite best friends.

As they piled into the car, laughter filled the air, each friend bringing their unique energy to the mix. Christina slotted into the back seat, immediately reaching for the aux cord, eager to introduce a few new songs to their playlist. "You guys have to hear this one; it's all over TikTok!" she exclaimed, her excitement infectious.

Samantha adjusted her sunglasses and leaned forward, chiming in, "Only if we can play that beach anthem I sent you earlier. It's got the perfect summer vibe!" Maya, who was flipping through her beach bag in search of snacks, nodded in agreement. "And don't forget my epic playlist from last year. Those songs always bring back good memories!"

With the music flowing and the windows down, they sped down the highway, the wind dancing through their hair. Amani felt an overwhelming sense of joy as they passed picturesque sunflower fields and glistening lakes, each landmark tugging at her heartstrings with nostalgia. The world outside sparkled under the sun, promising a day filled with laughter and unforgettable moments.

As they neared the beach, the scent of saltwater mingled with the floral fragrances from earlier. It was a scent that spoke of freedom and adventure, and it pulled them closer to their destination. "I can't wait to dip my toes in the ocean!" Maya exclaimed, her eyes shining brightly with anticipation.

"Just remember to reapply sunscreen this time," Samantha teased, recalling last year's beach day where Maya had turned the color of a lobster.

Amani chuckled, her heart swelling at the camaraderie they shared. "Don't worry, I've got you covered," she assured them, her voice filled with warmth. This was what summer was all about—shared stories, playful banter, and diving into the moments that mattered most.

As they pulled into the beach parking lot, the sun hung high in the sky, creating a perfect backdrop for their day. They stepped out, the sound of waves crashing nearby quickly enveloping them, and the sight of the sprawling beach stretched out like a canvas filled with sunbathers and laughter. Amani's heart swelled with happiness as she joined them, the salty breeze tousling her hair and the shimmering expanse of Lake Winnipeg sparkling under the radiant sun. The air was alive with the sounds of children laughing and splashing in the water, while the scent of sunscreen enveloped them, creating an atmosphere of pure bliss.

"Let's get started!" Maya exclaimed, her excitement contagious as she glanced at the volleyball net just a few feet away. The group wasted no time diving into the game, their laughter echoing across the beach as they jumped and dove for the ball. Amani felt a rush of adrenaline as she leaped to send the ball soaring, her friends cheering her on. Each serve and spike reignited her spirit, reminding her of carefree summers spent with friends, where worries faded into the background.

After their exhausting but exhilarating game, they decided to explore the nearby boardwalk shops, their spirits high. Amani's eyes widened with delight when she spotted a quaint little boutique, its window displaying an array of stunning jewelry. One necklace, in particular, seemed to call out to her—a delicate silver pendant shaped like a wave, glistening in the sunlight.

"Go on, Amani! You have to try it on!" Lila urged, nudging her toward the entrance. With a little persuasion, Amani stepped inside, her heart racing with the thrill of a potential treasure. Emerging from the boutique, she beamed with joy, the necklace nestled in her hands like a precious gem—an unexpected delight that would forever remind her of this summer day.

As the sun began to set, painting the sky in hues of orange and pink, the friends settled down for a delicious beachside dinner. They spread out their picnic blankets and shared sandwiches, fruit, and refreshing drinks, the simple meal seasoned with laughter and stories from their childhood. Time seemed to slip away, and the world felt perfect in those moments.

After dinner, they gathered around a bonfire, the flames crackling and dancing in the twilight. Amani watched as Maya expertly roasted marshmallows, the golden brown sweetness melting into gooey perfection, ready to be sandwiched between chocolate and graham crackers. It was an evening filled with storytelling, each tale weaving a tapestry of shared experiences that bonded them even closer.

But as the stars twinkled overhead, a sense of adventure began to stir within Amani. She felt restless, yearning for something more than a serene evening by the lake. "What if we go for a night swim?" she proposed, her eyes sparkling with mischief.

"Are you crazy?" Christina laughed, but her tone held intrigue. "It's dark out there!"

"Come on! It'll be fun! We can't let the day end just like this!" Amani urged, her heart racing with the thrill of spontaneity.

After a moment of hesitation, Lila and Maya exchanged excited glances, igniting the spark of adventure within them. "Alright, let's do it!" Maya cheered, and soon they were all in agreement.

With a mix of excitement and nervousness, the group made their way to the edge of the water, the cool breeze brushing against their skin. The moonlight shimmered on the surface of the lake, creating a magical pathway that seemed to invite them in. They stood at the water's edge, laughter bubbling up like the waves lapping at their feet.

"Okay, on the count of three!" Amani declared, her heart pounding with exhilaration. "One... two... three!"

They plunged into the water, the coolness enveloping them like a refreshing embrace. Amani surfaced, gasping in delight as she glanced at her friends, their laughter echoing in the night. They splashed and played, the stars twinkling above like a canopy of dreams, the world around them fading away as they lost themselves in the moment.

But as they swam farther from shore, Amani felt a twinge of unease. What if they swam too far? The thought lingered in her mind, but the thrill of adventure pushed it aside. They laughed and splashed, creating ripples in the water that shimmered like silver under the moonlight.

Suddenly, Christina let out a yelp. "What was that?" she exclaimed, her eyes wide with surprise as something brushed against her leg.

"Probably just a fish!" Maya laughed, but her voice trembled slightly.

Amani felt a shiver run down her spine. "Let's swim back," she suggested, her instincts kicking in. The earlier thrill of adventure began to shift into a sense of caution.

As they turned to head back, the waves seemed to grow choppier, and Amani felt a sudden rush of panic. "Swim faster!" she urged, her heart racing. The shore felt farther away than it had moments ago.

Just as they began to panic, Amani spotted a flicker of light in the distance—an old wooden dock jutting into the water. "Over there! We can rest!" she shouted, pointing toward it.

With renewed energy, they swam toward the dock, the light guiding them through the darkness. As they reached it, Amani grabbed hold of the wooden posts, her heart pounding. They pulled themselves up onto the dock, gasping for breath and laughing nervously at the thrill of it all.

As they lay on the wooden planks, the stars above twinkling like diamonds, Amani felt a rush of gratitude. "That was insane!" she laughed, her voice filled with exhilaration.

Maya grinned, her eyes sparkling. "Best adventure ever! I can't believe we did that!"

Samantha joined in, "It was a little scary, but we made it! And we'll always have this story to tell!"

As they lay there under the vast sky, Amani felt a sense of euphoria wash over her. The fear that had crept in moments ago faded away, replaced by the warmth of friendship and the thrill of adventure. They shared stories and laughter, the bond between them solidifying in the glow of the moonlight.

When they finally swam back to the shore, the sun was just beginning to peek over the horizon, painting the sky in shades of gold and pink. Exhausted but happy, they settled down on their beach towels, the warmth of the sun enveloping them like a comforting blanket.

As Amani lay there, listening to the gentle lapping of the waves, she reflected on the incredible day they had shared. The warmth of the sun, the sound of her friends' laughter, and the thrill of adventure had etched a memory in her heart that she would carry with her forever.

"Come on, guys, it's getting dark," Samantha called out, her voice echoing through the park. The sun had begun to dip below the horizon, casting long shadows across the picnic blanket and the remnants of their afternoon snack. Maya and Amani looked up from their book and phone, respectively, squinting at the sudden shift in light.

"Yeah, you're right," Maya said, folding her novel with a sigh. "But the fireworks are supposed to start soon."

"I don't think we're gonna make it," Amani chimed in, glancing at her watch. "I've got to be up at five to open the shop."

Samantha nodded, the seriousness of the situation etched on her face. "We can catch them another time. It's not worth you being late for work."

The four friends began to gather their things, the laughter and chatter of the day giving way to the quiet rustling of plastic bags and the clink of bottles being recycled. The park, which had been a whirlwind of activity just moments before, now felt eerily still, as if the world was holding its breath in anticipation of the night to come. As they packed up their picnic basket, a cool breeze whispered through the leaves above, carrying with it the faint scent of rain. The air was electric with unspoken tension, hinting at a storm that was slowly building on the outskirts of the city. Christina shivered, wrapping her sweater tighter around her shoulders.

"You okay?" Samantha asked, noticing Amani's discomfort. Amani nodded, forcing a smile. "Just a little chilly," she lied, hoping to keep the mood light.

But as they made their way to the car, the first drops of rain began to fall, the sound of their footsteps now accompanied by a gentle patter against the pavement. The sky grew darker with every step, the street lights flickering to life like a string of pearls in the growing night.

The car was parked on a side street, and as they approached, the distant boom of thunder rolled towards them, a harbinger of the storm's impending arrival. Amani felt a twinge of excitement mixed with a hint of fear, a thrill that was all too familiar to her.

"Guys, hurry up," Amani urged, already halfway to the car. "We don't wanna get caught in this."

With a final look at the now-desolate park, Christina, Maya, and Samantha quickened their pace, the wind tugging at their hair and clothes. The storm was almost upon them, and Amani couldn't help but feel a strange sense of foreboding, a feeling that this night was going to be far from ordinary.

The rain picked up speed, turning from a gentle patter to a steady downpour. Amani fumbled with the keys, droplets of water clinging to her lashes and obscuring her vision. "Come on, come on," she murmured under her breath as she finally managed to unlock the car. The three friends dove inside, the warmth of the interior a stark contrast to the chilly air outside.

"Whew, that was close!" Maya exclaimed, wiping her wet hair out of her face. Amani couldn't help but agree, her heart pounding in her chest. The storm had rolled in much faster than any of them had anticipated.

Christina leaned into the front seat, her eyes wide. "Amani, are you sure you're okay to drive?"

Amani nodded firmly. "I've driven in worse in Nairobi." She laughed and then turned the ignition, the wipers swiping back and forth in a steady rhythm, the only sound in the otherwise quiet car. The headlights cut through the rain, casting two yellow beams into the darkening night. As they pulled out of the parking spot, the storm's intensity grew. The wind howled around the car, pushing against the windows and making it difficult to see.

Maya leaned forward, her nose almost touching the windshield. "Maybe we should find a place to wait it out," she suggested nervously. The rain was coming down so hard now that the wipers struggled to keep up.

But Amani had made up her mind. She had to be home. "It's okay, I got this," she said, her knuckles white on the steering wheel. The car splashed through puddles that had quickly turned into small lakes, the headlights reflecting off the shiny black asphalt.

The road grew slick, and the visibility dropped to almost nothing as the storm unfurled its full power. The windshield wipers swept back and forth in a hypnotic dance, but even they couldn't keep up with the onslaught of rain. Amani's heart raced as she navigated the familiar streets, the world outside a blur of light and shadow.

"You're doing great," Samantha offered, her voice a gentle reassurance from the backseat. But the storm was growing more fierce, the wind tugging at the car as if trying to steer it off-course. Thunder rumbled, a bass line to the symphony of rain that surrounded them.

The rain poured relentlessly as Amani gripped the steering wheel, her heart racing with each pounding drop that met the windshield. She was navigating the winding roads, her focus sharp despite the late hour. Beside her, Christina sat tensely, her knuckles white as she clutched the door handle, eyes darting nervously between the storm-soaked landscape outside and her friend's determined face.

Suddenly, a figure emerged through the sheets of rain, waving frantically. Amani's heart skipped. "Oh my God, look!" she exclaimed, pointing. The figure was a young man drenched and desperate, his outstretched arm pleading for help.

"Are you crazy?" Christina exclaimed, her voice barely piercing the storm's roar. "We can't stop in this weather!"

"I can't just leave him there," Amani insisted, urgency swelling in her heart. "He needs help!"

With a mix of trepidation and resolve, she turned the wheel and pulled over to the side of the highway. Rain drummed heavily on the metal roof, the sound an ominous reminder of the tempest surrounding them.

Amani rolled down the window, bracing herself for the icy blast of wind. "Hey! Do you need a ride?" she shouted over the storm.

The soaked young man staggered forward, his voice strained. "Yes! My car broke down a few miles back. I need to get to a gas station!" He was shivering, and Amani could see the desperation in his eyes.

Christina's doubts were palpable as she shifted nervously in her seat. "What if he's dangerous? We shouldn't—"

But Amani, fueled by compassion and the man's obvious distress, turned to him and said, "Get in." This was not how she had envisioned her evening, but leaving him stranded felt even worse. The man clambered into the backseat, water pooling on the upholstery, the smell of rain and dampness filling the car.

As they pulled back onto the road, Amani's focus was solely on the task at hand. "Do you know where the nearest gas station is?" she shouted, struggling for clarity amidst the cacophony of raindrops.

"Yes! Just follow Highway 59 towards Winnipeg!" he responded, his voice trembling from cold and fear. Desperation emanated from him, adding to the weight in the car.

As they drove, the familiar landscape morphed into shadows and silhouettes, the harsh rain transforming the world into a distorted version of itself. The illuminated signs of fast-food chains and roadside motels flickered in and out of view, like ghostly apparitions taunting them.

"Are we close?" Amani asked, her heart thumping against her ribs as the darkness thickened, wrapping around them like a sinister shroud.

"Just a few more miles," the young man stammered, his voice barely rising above the roar of the storm.

Then, as they approached the gas station, flickering lights bleeding into the darkness, an unsettling feeling coursed through Amani. The pumps loomed ominously, their screens displaying distorted numbers that danced like moths to a flame. Something felt wrong, but she pushed it aside, focusing on getting the man to safety.

She slowed the car, and when they stopped, he practically leaped out, turning to them with wide eyes. "Thank you! Thank you so much!" he said, relief washing over his features.

Amani barely nodded, feeling a knot of anxiety tightening in her stomach. As soon as he shut the door, she pressed her foot down on the accelerator, eager to leave the unsettling atmosphere behind.

"What was that noise?" Christina's voice pierced through the silence, filled with newfound anxiety. The sound—a low rumble followed by a high pitch, like metal scraping against metal—sent a shiver down Amani's spine.

Maya, in the passenger seat, turned to Amani, her face pale. "I'm just grateful we're safe," she said, trying to inject positivity into the moment.

But the tension in the car thickened like the storm outside. Amani remained silent, drowning in her own tumult of regret. She had acted on impulse; had she put them in danger by trusting a stranger? "I shouldn't have done that," Amani finally said, her voice shaking, tears prickling her eyes. "I made a mistake letting him in..."

"Hey," Maya said gently, reaching over to offer comfort. "You did what you thought was right. You helped someone in need."

"But what if—" Amani started, but Christina interrupted.

"We don't know who he was, Amani. You could have put us in danger," she said, her caution giving way to frustration.

The delicate balance of their friendship seemed to teeter on the edge of that truth, and Amani felt the weight of their shared fear hang heavy in the air.

"I...I'm sorry," Amani whispered, her tears finally spilling over. "I just couldn't leave him alone. I thought it was the right thing to do."

Maya squeezed her hand. "Intentions matter. It wasn't your fault the storm was scary. It wasn't your fault that man was in trouble. What matters is that we stuck together."

As the wipers fought against the falling rain and the road smoothed out ahead, Amani felt the storm's furious melody begin to soften, but the echoes of the night would linger—a haunting reminder of their vulnerability and the fine line that separated kindness from recklessness.

Amani gripped the wheel tighter, taking a deep breath as she finally found a moment of clarity. Maybe compassion could lead them into the unknown, but as Maya had said, it could also light the way home—something she desperately needed to believe in right now.

Ahead, the clouds gradually parted, revealing a patch of star-speckled sky as if the universe itself sought to reassure her. In that fleeting moment of clarity, Amani made a promise to herself: to pursue kindness, even when it felt daunting. They had ventured into the storm together. And while the night had tested their resolve, it also illuminated their bond—stronger than any storm, brighter than lost fears.

Suddenly, a car swerved sharply in front of her, the headlights blaring briefly before disappearing into the darkness behind them. Amani felt her heart race as instinct kicked in; she slowed down, hands steady on the wheel, reminding herself that their safety was paramount. The world was untrustworthy, a sentiment she could feel echoing with intensity through the rainy night.

The rain kept pounding steadily against the windshield in a relentless, muffled thud. Each drop hit with its own rhythm, like a drumbeat that echoed the storm brewing outside. It made a constant, dull symphony that seemed to match the tension inside the car. Amani's eyes stayed fixed on the wet, twisting road ahead, her gaze sharp despite the gray gloom that shrouded everything around her. She focused hard, her hands gripping the steering wheel with determination. Her mind was racing, but she forced herself to stay calm, pushing aside her rising anxiety. The heavy rain blurred her view, making every turn more challenging. As the sheets of gray clouds rolled over the landscape, visibility shrank minute by minute. The outside world was fading into a mist of doubt and uncertainty, yet she kept her attention locked on the road, fighting the instinct to panic. She knew she had to stay collected if they were to make it through the storm.

In the back seat, Christina and Samantha had gone quiet. The earlier burst of tears had drained the energy from their bodies. Their faces, pale and strained, bore the weight of today's emotional toll. Shadows of worry marked their features—further evidence of how deeply the day had shaken them. As they leaned back in their seats, they seemed lost inside their own thoughts. Their eyes flickered slightly as they processed what had happened, but words were scarce. They looked through the windshield, yet they saw only the rain and gray sky. Amani, sitting at the front, could sense the heaviness that hung around them like a thick fog. It was as if the car had become a small world of its own, where silence was deafening and emotions collided in the tight space.

The atmosphere inside grew more tense with each passing mile. A thick silence settled over the car, broken only by the faint swish of the windshield wipers sweeping water off the glass. The wipers moved quickly, like a metronome keeping pace with the pounding rain, but they couldn't erase the mood inside. Every so often, Amani caught glimpses of Christina and Samantha, noticing how their hands trembled slightly or how they pressed their lips tight in an effort to hold back tears. She felt a deep sense of responsibility settle upon her shoulders—not just for the physical safety of everyone in the car, but for the emotional safety too. Behind her, she could feel their unspoken pain, like a fragile web of feelings that needed care and understanding.

She understood her role now stretched beyond just driving. She was the one anchoring them in this storm—both the weather and the emotional storm inside the car. She kept her focus on the road, knowing they couldn't afford any mistakes right now. Still, her mind wouldn't stop racing. She wished she had words that could soothe their fears, ease the ache she could feel in their quiet despair. But instead, she relied on her steady presence, the simple act of staying silent and alert to give them a sense of security. It was all she could do, for now. She hoped her silence and calmness might offer some comfort, as they faced the unknown—uncertain about what lay ahead, but oddly comforted in knowing they weren't alone. In that small space, amid the relentless rain and unspoken worries, she silently promised to steel herself for whatever came next, to keep them safe, and to hold their fragile hopes, however small, until the storm passed.

As the headlights from the rogue vehicle faded into the darkness, Amani allowed herself a moment to reflect on what had brought them here: the tumultuous evening that started with laughter, prepping for a weekend getaway, and ended in this anxious drive home through a storm that seemed almost sentient in its ferocity.

"Do you think we should pull over?" Christina's voice shook slightly, a fragile sound that faintly broke the heavy silence that had fallen over the car like a thick, suffocating blanket, pressing down on them, stealing the air. Her words seemed to hang in the air, caught precariously between her raw nerves and the growing fury of the storm outside, each syllable a question mark punctuated by a rumble of distant thunder.

Amani, her own heart thrumming with an uneasy rhythm, looked into the rearview mirror. Her eyes met Christina's trembling face, which was starkly illuminated by the soft, flickering glow of the dashboard lights, casting a ghostly pallor upon her features. Christina's skin was unnaturally pale, almost translucent in the dim light, and her wide, shimmering eyes, usually so bright and full of life, now betrayed a mounting tide of fear and gnawing doubt. A wave of profound empathy washed over Amani, a painful tightening in her throat that made it difficult to swallow. She saw her friend's hands, not just trembling, but clutching the seatbelt strap with a white-knuckled grip, as if it were the only thing grounding her to reality. It was clear Christina was scared, a raw, primal fear that resonated deep within Amani herself. An urgent desire to reassure her, to tell her everything would be fine, surged through Amani, even if she wasn't entirely sure herself.

"We can make it," Amani said softly, her voice struggling to find its usual strength, a hint of hesitation barely perceptible beneath a forced resolve. "Just a little longer." The words fell from her lips, an incantation whispered more to convince herself than Christina. The mere thought of pulling over right now sent a chill through her, colder than the rain. Stopping meant risking the storm's full, unbridled fury, becoming a static target for swirling winds and plummeting visibility. It could also mean encountering other drivers who might not be as cautious or as friendly in this treacherous weather, their desperation potentially adding another layer of danger.

The rain, thick and relentless, hammered against the windshield, a deafening drumbeat on the roof. Thick strips of water cascaded down the glass, making visibility difficult, distorting the world outside into a smear of grey and black, punctuated by blinding flashes. Lightning ripped across the sky like giant, jagged scars, momentarily illuminating angry, bruised clouds before plunging the world back into a deeper, more profound darkness. Every instinct in her body, honed by years of navigating unpredictable roads, screamed at her to keep going, to press on, no matter how shaky her hands trembled on the steering wheel, no matter the growing ache in her shoulders. She gripped the cold, hard plastic, willing her fingers to stay steady.

She hesitated, trying to siphon every ounce of courage from some forgotten wellspring deep within her. Then, a different story, a vibrant memory from last summer, surfaced, a lifeline to keep her grounded amidst the chaos. "Hey," she started, her voice a deliberate effort to sound calm and warm, to inject a much-needed lightness into the heavy air. "Do you remember that time when we got caught in that freak storm while camping? The one where Maya kept laughing, even as the rain soaked through our clothes and turned our campsite into a muddy swamp?" A faint, genuine smile touched Amani's lips as the memory blossomed. "That night was pure chaos, absolutely ridiculous, but also, without a doubt, one of the funniest moments we've ever had." She paused, allowing the warmth of the recollection to spread. "Maya just kept cracking jokes, her voice bubbling with mirth, about how we looked like drowned rats, shivering and miserable. She was so incredibly lively, even with the rain pounding down on the flimsy tent and us fumbling around in the dark under the stormy sky, trying to secure everything. When everything else felt overwhelming, her sheer, infectious laughter made it bearable, even genuinely funny."

Sitting in the back, just as the moment of nostalgia reached its peak, Samantha couldn't help but scoff softly, a sound that was both affectionate and slightly sarcastic, breaking the spell. "Yeah," she said with a hint of dry humor that softened the edge of her words, "and then we spent the next morning trying to dry out our things, only to discover our sleeping bags were absolutely soaked through, clinging to us like damp second skins." Her tone, however, carried a mix of wry amusement and warmth, as if she, too, was still reminiscing about the chaotic absurdity of it all—yet appreciating how it had all miraculously transformed into a cherished story they'd tell for years to come. Amani's smile grew, a gentle reminder that even the roughest, most uncomfortable moments could, with time and the right company, truly turn into good memories.

"Exactly!" Amani affirmed, her voice now filled with quiet confidence, bolstered by the shared past. "We made it work. That night, even with the mud, the mess, and the relentless rain, became one of our favorite stories to recount. Maya kept joking about how she was going to be the 'queen of the rain,' demanding a crown of twigs and leaves, and before long, we couldn't stop laughing, even with mud squishing between our toes and wet clothes clinging uncomfortably to us. The storm outside was fierce, thrashing the trees and rattling the tent, but inside that tiny, fragile tent, huddled together, we found a way to make it fun, to find joy in the absurdity. It was chaos, yes, but also the kind of night that forged a deeper bond between us, that brought us closer together." She risked a quick glance at Christina in the mirror. Christina's lips were still pressed in a soft line, but her rigid features seemed a little softer, a little more at ease, a hint of the tension seeping out of her shoulders.

"Yeah," Christina whispered, her voice trembling noticeably less than before, the soft remnants of her earlier fear slowly giving way to a fragile and tentative hope. Her wide eyes flickered with something like a faint spark of reassurance, a tiny flame in the dim light. She took a deep, shuddering breath, her shoulders relaxing a tiny bit more, as if she had just managed to shed a heavy cloak of dread. A tense silence stretched for a moment, filled only with the relentless sound of rain pounding on the car roof, a continuous roar, and the mournful whine of the wind howling in the distance, a haunting symphony of the storm. Then, from the backseat, Samantha broke the silence again, her voice cutting through the atmospheric din. "You're right, Amani," she said, her tone more sure, more grounded now. "We can do this. We've handled worse, remember? We're okay, right?" She asked softly, her words carrying a gentle, steady confidence that made Amani hold her breath in sheer relief. It was the affirmation she hadn't realized she desperately needed.

Amani inhaled deeply, as if to draw in some of the newfound calm that Samantha's words had brought. Inside, she felt a complex mixture of lingering worry and stubborn resolve, but also a strange, comforting sense of shared strength. The air outside had thickened further, heavy with moisture and the sharp, clean scent of rain and ozone, but as the car moved steadily forward, a different aroma began to drift in—a clean, earthy smell, like wet soil and damp leaves, that grew stronger with each passing mile. Just ahead, piercing through the dense rain curtain, a faint, almost ethereal glow emerged. Tiny halos of soft, diffused light spread gently across the dark, sodden landscape, a luminous promise of warmth and safety after the storm's unyielding chaos. She spotted the welcoming, shimmering outline of the city—lights flickering like a constellation of tiny stars fallen to Earth, each one a beacon of hope, confirming that the worst, the truly terrifying part, was finally behind them.

"Winnipeg here we come!" Amani exclaimed, feeling a surge of pure, unadulterated excitement bubble up once again, washing away the last vestiges of her own fear. Her voice lifted above the fading roar of the storm, vibrant and filled with triumphant hope. "We're almost there, just a little more!" Relief visibly flooded Christina's pale face as she let out a long, shaky breath, a soft sigh that seemed to release all the tension she had been holding. Her shoulders slumped fully in relaxation, and a faint, genuine smile, beautiful in its simplicity, finally appeared on her lips. "Thank goodness," she breathed softly, her voice rich with longing for comfort. "I really needed a warm drink. A huge one."

Amani's mind raced ahead, already conjuring images of that cozy diner they often talked about, their designated haven. The place where the hot chocolate was always thick and rich, a decadent dream, topped with impossibly high mountains of whipped cream that looked like fluffy clouds. The place that offered a warm, inviting escape after long, arduous days or wild, unpredictable nights like this one. She pictured them sitting at the worn wooden counter, wrapped in the comforting warmth of thick, borrowed blankets, the air fragrant with the inviting smell of fresh coffee and sweet desserts, a symphony of comfort. It was a place where laughter flowed as easily as the coffee, where friendships were built and strengthened over simple, sweet moments. That thought, so vivid and comforting, made her smile even wider, fueling her with a renewed and potent sense of hope. Her heart raced with anticipation for that warm, peaceful moment, and she knew, deep down in her very core, that they'd get there soon. They would survive this storm, not just physically, but emotionally, and end the night with comforting drinks and stories to last a lifetime.

With a deep breath, she pressed the accelerator gently, feeling the response of the car beneath her fingers. The engine responded softly, a quiet purr that seemed to hug them as they moved forward. Outside, the rain beat down hard, heavy drops pounding the windshield, but as they pressed on, it appeared to soften just a little. It was as if the storm was giving a small nod of approval, acknowledging their resolve to keep going despite the chaos outside. The wind howled around the car, swirling tears of rain that blurred the world outside into streaks of gray and silver, yet inside, a quiet determination grew stronger. They knew they were nearing the safety of home, where familiar faces, warmth, and peace awaited them after the long, testing night. The storm, with all its fury, had brought out a new strength in them. It reminded them of their resilience—how they'd stayed hopeful even when the skies opened up with such violence. Their love for each other deepened through these trials, bonding them more firmly. They thought of their friend waiting at home, her bright spirit shining out even through the storm, ready to welcome them with open arms. Her vibrant energy was brighter than any lightning that split the sky. She was the anchor that kept their hearts steady, the beacon guiding them through the storm's dark clouds.

"Just a little longer," Amani whispered again. Her voice was soft, yet steady, carrying a weight of confidence that arranged itself between her words and their hearts. They clung to that promise, feeling the truth buried in her voice. Every mile they crossed felt like a small victory over the chaos outside, as if each turn brought them closer to the safe haven waiting beyond the rainy curtain. Their journey through the storm was more than just driving—it was a test of their strength, their faith, and their connection. They pulled their fears inside, replacing them with hope, trusting that warmth and safety were just around the bend. The darkness outside was thick, but they found comfort in the certainty of what awaited them. They knew that once they crossed that threshold, everything would settle—the storm, the worries, the exhaustion. The storm had tested them, but it hadn't broken their spirits. Instead, it had woven a stronger bond between them, one stitched with shared struggles and their unwavering love.

Beside her, Christina looked out at the rain-slick landscape rushing past the windows. Every streak of rain seemed like a challenge, but her heart was filled with a sense of purpose that kept her grounded. She felt the pulse of hope beating loudly inside her chest. Suddenly, without thinking, she decided to do something spontaneous to lift their spirits. She cleared her throat and softly began singing. Her voice floated gently, almost shy at first, then gaining strength. "I'm chasing fireflies, in a world that feels so wide," she sang, her voice blending with the sound of rain and wind. The words seemed to echo memories from her childhood, moments of wonder and longing. Her singing made the cramped car feel warmer, more alive—like a cocoon wrapped in shared hope. Her laughter burst out suddenly, loud and bright, breaking the heavy silence with a spark of joy. The song they shared wasn't just words; it became a source of comfort, a reminder of simpler times, of dreams that still flickered like tiny sparks inside each of them. It was a hymn to resilience and to the power of hope, even in moments like these.

The familiar lyrics resonated between them, filling the small space of the car. The words wrapped around them like a soft blanket, soothing and energizing at once. They spoke of inside journeys, of finding strength amid chaos. Christina's voice wove through their minds, lifting spirits that felt heavy from the night's ordeal. "Through the storms and heartaches," she sang, her voice rising and falling gently. The words echoed feelings of perseverance, of learning to spread wings despite winds that pushed back. She sang of dancing with memories, about embracing pain and hope alike, holding on to the belief that brighter days would come. As her song faded into the rain, Amani responded, adding her voice unexpectedly strong and clear. Her singing guitarist style filled the tiny space with a raw power that no one had anticipated. It was as if the struggles they'd faced turned into a song of triumph, a melody flowing with their collective strength. The rain tapped against the windows like slow applause, each droplet a note dancing in harmony with their voices. Their words and song became a silent prayer, lifting them above the darkness and reminding them that, no matter how fierce the storm, they would arrive safely. That night, music became their refuge, transforming their fear into hope and turning the chaos outside into a chorus of resilience inside.

"What are you girls doing?" Samantha laughed, her voice rising cheerfully despite the storm outside. "I want in!" She threw her arms up in a playful gesture, and with that, Amani could no longer contain the smile breaking across her face.

"Go ahead, Sami!" she encouraged, her spirits noticeably lifted as the car became their makeshift stage, the downpour providing a fitting backdrop for their impromptu concert.

As they sang, their voices rising and falling, memories danced in Amani's mind: the countless summer festivals they'd braved together, the nights spent talking until the sun painted the sky in hues of dawn, and the recent harrowing days that had tested their limits. Each note they sang stripped away the fears and uncertainties, leaving only the pureness of their connectedness.

Amani adjusted her speed, and as she did, she felt the storm begin to relent, the rain lightening as if the heavens themselves were joining in the celebration of their journey.

With each chorus of their favorite road-trip anthem, the song that had become their soundtrack, they felt the warmth of coming closer to something familiar and safe. It was a melody that carried the echoes of countless summer nights spent joking around, inside jokes that only they understood. Every time they hummed that tune, they were reminded of shared adventures, late-night talks about dreams and fears, and the simple joy of being together. As the familiar notes filled the car's cozy interior, they sensed that they were pulling closer to the true meaning of home—not just a place on a map, but a feeling rooted deep in moments of comfort, connection, and belonging. It was a sense of relief that washed over them, a quiet peace that settled in their chests, knowing they had each other. Home was personified by the smile of Elena waiting for them at the end of the road, someone whose presence made everything brighter and easier. She didn't just greet them when they arrived; her warmth radiated like a comforting light after a long, burdensome journey. Her steady eyes and gentle laugh were the anchors in their lives, always there to steady them when the road ahead seemed uncertain.

Elena, their reliable group study partner, was more than just a friend. She was the one who had shared their late-night study marathons, fueling their brains with coffee as they crammed for exams. She was the one who cheered them on during moments of frustration, offering encouragement when they felt overwhelmed. Whether it was dissecting complex math problems, reviewing chapters for history class, or practicing presentations, Elena had been there, helping them push through the hardest parts. She had stood beside them in moments of anxiety, her calm resolve offering a sense of stability in a chaotic world. Her unwavering positivity was contagious, lifting spirits when spirits were low. The group's plans for a beach day, meant to be a carefree break from all the stress and deadlines, had lost some of that spark when Elena called. Her voice sounded genuinely sorry, apologizing for missing the fun they'd all looked forward to. She explained how busy her mornings were, how she couldn't find anyone to cover her shift at her group home. This wasn't just any work; it was a place where she poured her heart into caring for others, a role that showcased her deep empathy and sense of responsibility. Her feet were planted firmly in her commitments, and her kindness shone through her words.

Elena had promised to still meet them after the beach, waiting like a beacon of hope at her apartment. She told them she'd make hot chocolate—the rich, warm drink that always seemed to taste better when shared with friends—and prepare her famous loaded nachos, with the crispy, savory toppings they all loved. Her plans to be part of the day, even if only in small gestures, made them feel less disappointed. They hoped her shift would end early so she could join them, knowing her warmth and good humor would add to their fun. Outside, the storm raged on, relentless and loud, drumming against the car windows as if trying to drown out their thoughts. The heavy rain was a reminder of the long, tough stretch they'd endured—bad weather, stressful exams, disagreements, and personal setbacks all blending into one exhausting phase. But despite the storm's chaos, they couldn't stop thinking about her. Her face, her voice, the way she laughed—a sound more beautiful than any song—could pierce through the noise and bring light back into their minds. They imagined her sitting at her kitchen table, her eyes bright, her voice bubbling with excitement as she planned to see them later.

They could almost hear her laughter, pure and melodious, cutting through the rain's roaring din. That sound wasn't just noise; it was like sunlight breaking through heavy clouds, warming their hearts even on the coldest days. It was a bright burst of happiness, a pure, bubbly joy that stood in stark contrast to the stress and exhaustion they carried. Her contagious spirit brightened their spirits in ways words couldn't express. Her warmth, her kindness, her instinct to always help others—that was what everyone needed right now. It was like a shot of relief for their weary souls, a reminder that even on the darkest days, a little kindness and laughter could make everything seem lighter, easier to face. Her presence, even from afar, was a soothing balm that made their worries fade, if only for a moment. They clung to that image of her—her laughter ringing clear, her smile unwavering—as a symbol of hope and comfort amidst the storm both outside and within themselves.

As they drove along the winding, tree-lined road, the pervasive chill of the stormy night began to subtly recede. The oppressive blanket of darkness, which had cloaked the landscape for hours, softened its formidable grip, yielding to a deep indigo hue. Above them, the heavy, brooding charcoal clouds that had hung like a threat now seemed to dissipate, thinning at their edges as if a celestial hand gently pulled them apart. This gradual clearing unveiled vast, serene swaths of sky, allowing the first brave pinpricks of light to pierce through. Tiny stars, like diamond dust scattered across velvet, appeared shy and almost hesitant, trembling softly as if unsure whether to fully emerge after the tempest's wild, untamed chaos. The asphalt ribbon of the road, slicked by recent rain, stretched endlessly ahead, an ancient guide curving gently through the hushed countryside. It flowed like a current, patiently guiding them not just over miles, but toward a specific haven: a small, unassuming house tucked away on a distant hillside. Even from afar, the house exuded an aura of safety and intrinsic warmth, a stark contrast to the lingering dampness outside. It wasn't large or grand; rather, its very essence was coziness, its windows glowing with a soft, inviting light, and its welcoming porch seemed almost to beckon them, promising an embrace of comfort and an abundance of love that permeated every single corner.

A palpable, almost magical quietude had settled within the car, a serene bubble that insulated them from the lingering turbulence outside. It was a peculiar alchemy, transforming the roaring tempest into a distant, muted echo. Within this sanctuary, they had seamlessly found their shared rhythm – a comfortable synchronicity of breath and unspoken understanding that deepened their connection far beyond mere words. While the wind howled its final laments and errant rain lashed against the windows, inside the vehicle, a profound peace reigned. Their voices, clear and strong, resonated with an honest vulnerability, carrying not just their hopes, but also the whispered fears of the uncertain night. They sang together, a spontaneous, joyful chorus that started as a hum and blossomed into full-throated harmony, each note a deliberate act of defiance against the storm. It was an eclectic mix of beloved classics and spontaneous, nonsensical melodies, their voices rising and falling, intertwining seamlessly. Every shared note felt like a gentle push forward, an invisible force fueling their collective confidence and solidifying the unbreakable bond between them as they pressed on through the slick, reflective dark streets of Winnipeg, streetlights blurring into elongated streaks of gold and red. This wasn't merely a song; it was a living, breathing testament to their enduring friendship, a vibrant reminder that, together, they possessed the strength to face any challenge that lay ahead.

Suddenly, Amani's gaze, which had been fixed on the hypnotic swirl of the windshield wipers, sharpened. Her eyes caught a faint, almost imperceptible flicker in the inky blackness ahead—a nascent glow in the vast distance that, with each passing second and every meter they covered, blossomed into a more distinct and unwavering beacon. It was unmistakable: the welcoming, steady illumination from Elena's apartment building, now a tangible landmark in the heart of Transcona, finally visible along the familiar stretch of Kildare Avenue. The sight, now just four precious blocks away, acted like a powerful magnet, a comforting pull that seemed to physically draw them further along the road, promising not just the end of their long journey, but the imminent solace of rest, the familiarity of home, and an all-encompassing warmth that seeped into their weary bones.

"Just a little longer," Amani murmured, her voice a soothing balm, steady and imbued with a quiet confidence that radiated through the shared space. A gentle, knowing smile touched her lips as she glanced around at her friends, her words carrying the profound pride and deep satisfaction that came from navigating this entire unpredictable journey together, side by side, through the storm and into the dawn.

Chapter 05

The aroma of freshly brewed coffee mingled with the sweet, yeasty scent of rising dough as Caroline and Amani settled into their morning duty at Third Cup. Amani, the quiet artisan of the two, was already deep in her domain behind the counter, coaxing flour and butter into golden perfection. Caroline, with her bright smile and easy laugh, took her usual post at the front, ready to greet the day's first customers. The café was a symphony of soft clinks from ceramic cups, the gentle hiss of the espresso machine, and the low hum of early morning chatter – a comforting tableau that marked the start of another bustling day.

The place had a unique, lived-in charm, a cozy haven of mismatched antique furniture and walls adorned with local art, bathed in the warm glow of hanging Edison bulbs. Sunlight, still sleepy, slanted through the tall front windows, illuminating dust motes dancing in the air. Amani, amidst the familiar rhythm of kneading and shaping, found her thoughts drifting. In a past life, she had often sought solace in the quiet, isolated moments of her personal space, away from the clamor of the world. But at Third Cup, a transformation had subtly occurred; here, she rediscovered the profound joy of shared experiences, of being a vital thread in a vibrant tapestry. The solitude of her former days now felt less like peace and more like a gentle ache for connection.

Just as the last batch of blueberry muffins, plump and glistening golden-brown, filled the air with an intoxicatingly delightful aroma – a rich, fruity sweetness that promised comfort – the bell above the door chimed, announcing the arrival of Mr. Jenkins. He was a regular, a man whose presence was as reliable as the sunrise, his kind eyes twinkling perpetually beneath his impressively bushy, silver eyebrows. He strode directly to the counter, taking a deep, theatrical breath as if inhaling pure bliss. "Ah, the aroma of success!" he exclaimed, his voice a jovial rumble that always brought a smile to tired faces. "Your pastries, Amani, they're not just good, they're legendary! They could win awards! If there were a contest for the best blueberry muffin in the world, we'd already be champions, crowned and celebrated!"

Caroline, ever quick-witted, exchanged a playful, knowing glance with Amani, a silent agreement to indulge their favorite regular. "You know, Mr. Jenkins," she chimed in, her voice light and teasing, "if we ever did win that top prize, we'd have to celebrate with free muffins for life for our most loyal customers!"

Mr. Jenkins's laugh boomed, a hearty sound that echoed pleasantly through the café. "That's a deal I'd gladly accept! But only if Amani is the one baking them," he joked, his eyes crinkling at the corners, which in turn made a faint blush creep up Amani's neck. A small, self-conscious smile touched her lips.

"Oh, come on, Mr. Jenkins, I'm not ready for that level of fame!" she chuckled, shaking her head in a gesture of genuine, if slightly exaggerated, modesty. Yet, deep down, a warmth spread through her chest. She enjoyed the praise more than she let on, but the sheer weight of such high expectations also brought with it a familiar, subtle pressure. Turning away from the counter, she sought refuge in the familiar motions, her hands moving automatically through the preparations for the next set of orders – slicing bagels, grinding coffee beans, wiping down surfaces – while her mind drifted, pulling her further and further away from the bustling present.

As she meticulously arranged the golden-brown pastries on the cooling racks, each one a testament to her skill, vivid memories of her childhood came rushing back with an almost physical force. She could almost hear her grandmother's joyful laughter, a clear, bell-like sound, blending seamlessly with the comforting clink of ceramic cups and saucers in that cozy, sun-dappled little bakery. It was a place where flour dust motes danced in the air, where the scent of cinnamon and rising bread was a perpetual embrace, and where every customer, no matter how briefly they stayed, felt like an extension of their own warm, chaotic family. Though those days seemed distant, separated by years and miles, moments like this, immersed in the familiar comfort of baking, helped her feel viscerally connected to those treasured memories, a lifeline to a past she cherished.

Caroline, ever perceptive, noticed the subtle shift in Amani's demeanor. She quietly joined her behind the counter, gently sliding a freshly-baked muffin onto the display, its warmth still radiating softly. "You're different today, Amani," she observed, her voice soft, laced with a genuine concern. "A little quieter than usual. What's on your mind?"

The gentle question caught Amani off-guard, pulling her abruptly from her reverie. She hadn't fully realized how lost in thought she had become, how deeply she had been submerged in the past. "Just... thinking about home, I suppose," she admitted, her voice a little softer than usual. "Sometimes I forget how much I miss it. How much I miss them."

"There's a saying I love," Caroline said, her voice dropping to a comforting murmur as she leaned casually against the counter, her gaze warm and understanding. "Home isn't just a place, Amani. It's the people you share it with. The comfort they bring, the memories you make."

Amani's heart swelled, a quiet ache turning into a profound sense of recognition. The truth in those simple words resonated strongly with her, vibrating through her very being. As if on cue, her eyes landed on a young mother at a nearby table, valiantly trying to juggle her squirming toddler's enthusiastic antics while simultaneously attempting to scroll through her phone. The mother, catching Amani's eye, offered a small, knowing smile, a shared understanding – a universal language of life's daily juggling act – passing between them over the gentle clamor of the café. It was a fleeting moment, but it spoke volumes.

"Look at that," Amani said, a new lightness entering her voice as she tilted her head toward the scene, a genuine, unburdened smile gracing her lips. "She's doing her best to write the next chapter of her own little adventure. Just like us! Everyone here is, aren't they?" "Exactly," Caroline replied, her smile widening in affirmation. "We're all spinning our own stories here, moment by moment, connection by connection. And you, Amani, are a big, beautiful part of ours."

With a renewed surge of determination, a spark of resolve kindling in her eyes, Amani set down the pastry she was holding. She took a deep breath, the comforting scents of the bakery filling her lungs, and turned fully to face the other patrons. Her voice, usually reserved, now held a spirited, almost theatrical enthusiasm that cut through the café's gentle hum. "Hey, everyone! Gather 'round! We have a new special today! A truly buttery blueberry muffin that even Mr. Jenkins, our esteemed connoisseur of confections, thinks is award-winning!"

The café, which had been a low murmur of conversation, erupted in a delightful flurry of playful banter and curious exclamations. Heads lifted from laptops, newspapers were lowered, and conversations paused as people turned, smiles spreading across their faces. Amani's voice, no longer hesitant, held a vibrant spark of excitement, a genuine joy that banished the lingering darkness of nostalgia in that very instant, replacing it with the exhilarating promise of connection and shared laughter.

"And, if you're lucky," she added, leaning forward conspiratorially, a mischievous glint in her eyes, "I might even throw in some chocolate drizzle!" Her feigned secrecy made the entire group erupt in good-natured laughter, a warm wave of camaraderie washing over her.

"Count me in!" shouted a sharp-dressed businesswoman who had been intensely sketching ideas on a napkin, her eyes lighting up with a hint of mischief, abandoning her work for the promise of a sweet treat.

Mr. Jenkins clapped his hands together with a booming, joyful thud. "That's the spirit, Amani! I'll take two, with extra drizzle, if you please! You've convinced me!"

Amani found herself utterly swept up in the lively exchange, her words weaving her deeper and deeper into the vibrant fabric of the café community. Laughter bounced back and forth, a joyful symphony that filled every corner, every nook and cranny of Third Cup, creating a melody of camaraderie that felt more like a true home than any building ever could. She was no longer just the baker; she was the heart of the morning, a connector, a laughter-maker.

Caroline leaned close, her voice barely above a whisper, her eyes shining with affection and pride. "See?" she murmured, a gentle smile gracing her lips. "You don't just bake pastries, Amani. You bake joy. You're home."

And in that moment, as Amani served the first round of blueberry muffins drizzled with chocolate, she realized she had found her place. The Third Cup wasn't just a café; it was a canvas, and together, they were painting a beautiful story—one laugh, one muffin at a time.

Amani filled her cup with a latte, gently mixing the frothy milk and a sprinkle of cinnamon that danced in the air. The comforting scent wrapped around her, a warm embrace against the crisp autumn breeze that rattled the café's windows. This was a cherished ritual, one that gave her the courage to face a world that had felt so daunting just a year ago.

Memories of the tough two years rushed back to her like a series of bright snapshots—each one was a reminder of the challenges she had endured. After leaving her beloved Kenya, Amani found herself wading through the stormy seas of grief and uncertainty. Like many international students, she mourned the harsh Winnipeg winters, learning to bundle herself in layer after layer of clothing. The warmth of the sun felt like a distant memory as she shivered. When the snow fell, it felt as if she might drown on solid ground, struggling to breathe in the icy air. She missed her mother's cooking and longed for her father's protective presence. Starting anew in Winnipeg was no easy feat. It was during this trying period that she stumbled upon a café; its delightful pink façade caught her eye one rainy afternoon as she sought comfort in a warm drink and a momentary escape from her struggles. Not long after, she applied for a waitress position and was welcomed aboard.

Initially, the café felt unfamiliar, a lively space where laughter bounced off the walls and soft conversations filled the air. The first few weeks were filled with her uncertainty. Could this be the place where she would reconnect, not only with herself but also with the vibrant community around her? Each day, she watched the patrons with a mix of curiosity and caution. Friends gathered at tables, sharing secrets and creating memories over steaming mugs. Young parents, laughter spilling from their lips, chased after toddlers who darted around, their joyful shrieks cutting through the café's buzz. Artists tucked away in corners filled their sketchbooks with scenes of life unfolding before them.

As the months went by, her initial hesitance transformed into a sense of belonging. Amani found a rhythm in the café that echoed the heartbeat of the city outside. No longer just an observer, she became woven into the fabric of this haven. Through shared smiles with regulars and conversations about life's little pleasures, she began to rediscover who she was. The café became more than just a place; it was a home.

The gentle murmur of conversation created a warm, inviting backdrop, a symphony of hushed tones and contented sighs that mingled seamlessly with the rich, intoxicating aroma of freshly-brewed coffee. It was a scent that spoke of comfort and possibility, layered subtly with hints of warm pastries and dark chocolate. Soft, amber light spilled generously from industrial-chic pendant lamps, casting long, dancing shadows and creating intimate cocoons of warmth where patrons, weary from their day, settled in for their evening respite. Some were hunched over glowing laptops, others lost in the pages of well-worn books, while many simply indulged in the quiet luxury of shared silence or the comfortable rhythm of low-pitched chatter.

Behind the polished oak counter, Caroline moved with a practiced grace that was almost meditative. She wiped her hands on her linen apron, the familiar, rhythmic movements of her craft grounding her, making her feel utterly at home in this bustling haven she had created. Every tamp of the espresso machine, every perfect pour of steamed milk, was executed with an effortless precision that belied the focused attention she gave each cup; her presence was as comforting and reliable as the rich, dark java she brewed. Beside her, a vibrant counterpoint, Amani darted around, her signature streaks of shocking pink hair a blur as she fulfilled drink orders with the lively spring in her step that seemed to defy the late hour. For them, the bustling café was more than just a place of work; it was their canvas, and their artistry—from the delicate foam art to the precise measurement of syrups—flowed freely as they crafted each unique drink.

"Two espressos and a cappuccino coming right up!" Caroline called across the counter to Amani, her voice clear and resonant, even as she adjusted the grind on a batch of Sumatra beans. She watched from the corner of her eye as Amani, with nimble fingers, tossed fresh mint sprigs into a tall, frosted glass, the crisp green contrasting beautifully with the clear ice. A soft, satisfying crunch echoed as she expertly muddled the fragrant leaves with simple syrup and a splash of sparkling soda water, preparing a refreshing mojito that promised a burst of cool sweetness.

Just as Amani was about to lift the beautifully garnished drink—a delicate lime wheel perched on the rim, a tiny straw nested beside it—to a waiting customer, whose eyes were already fixed on the vibrant concoction, a familiar voice cut through the café's gentle hum. Mr. Jenkins, a beloved regular who occupied the same worn armchair in the quietest corner every evening, waved his hand enthusiastically. His thin, wire-rimmed glasses had slid down to the very tip of his nose, and his lips stretched into a broad, infectious smile, the genuine warmth of it brightening his otherwise perpetually stern features, carving cheerful crinkles around his eyes. "Hey there, girls! Over here!" he called, his voice a little raspy with age but carrying a distinct joviality over the gentle clinking of cups and the soft ripple of laughter.

Caroline exchanged an amused glance with Amani, a playful smirk tugging at the corner of her lips. "Looks like the mayor of Third Cup needs us," she joked, a term of endearment they'd long bestowed upon him due to his steadfast presence and his habit of holding court from his corner. With a shared unspoken understanding, Caroline made her way around the counter, untying her apron as she went, with Amani trailing just a step behind, already anticipating a delightful interlude.

As they approached his table, adorned only with a well-thumbed paperback and his usual unsweetened black coffee, Mr. Jenkins gestured for them to sit. It was a rare invitation, a departure from his usual routine of quiet contemplation and a polite nod before departure. He was a retired school principal, a man whose stern public facade belied a wonderfully quirky sense of humor and an unmatched penchant for storytelling. Whenever he visited, he would unfailingly regale them with vivid, often hilarious, tales of mischief from his days in the classroom – stories that always, without fail, ended in hearty, genuine laughter, reminding them that even the most formidable figures held a treasure trove of delightful human experiences.

With a flourish, Mr. Jenkins gestured to the table, where a small stack of colorful envelopes sat neatly arranged. Each one bore a different whimsical sticker on it.

"What's all this?" Amani asked, her curiosity piqued.

"Ah, my dear ladies, these are for you," he said, patting the envelopes as if they were precious treasures. "Today is your lucky day!"

Caroline raised an eyebrow, glancing at Amani, who was equally puzzled. "Lucky day? What's the occasion?"

"Today I decided to write a little something for my favorite baristas!" he exclaimed, his eyes twinkling. "Inside those envelopes are invitations to my annual poetry night! I host it every year to celebrate the beauty of our community, and I want both of you to come and share your talents!"

Amani's face lit up. "Mr. Jenkins, I didn't know you had such a flair for poetry!"

Mr. Jenkins chuckled. "Oh, dear, I merely appreciate it! This year, I'm trying something new and inviting people to share their own. I thought about you two and your artistry. You give so much joy to the world with your craft here—imagine sharing that creativity on a stage!"

Caroline felt her heart flutter. She and Amani had often joked about showcasing their mixology skills as an art form, but they had never envisioned stepping into the spotlight in such a way. "You really think we're good enough?" she asked.

"Of course! Everyone has a story to tell, and there's poetry in every cup of coffee you pour and every cocktail you mix!" His enthusiasm was infectious, and Amani nodded eagerly, her excitement bubbling over.

"What if we combined poetry and drinks?" Amani proposed. "We could create signature cocktails inspired by different poems! That could be our act!"

Caroline clapped her hands together, a spark igniting in her eyes. "Yes! We could turn it into a whole experience—each drink crafted with passion and a piece of poetry to go with it!"

"Now you're talking!" Mr. Jenkins chuckled heartily, his laughter mingling with the café's ambience. He pulled out his phone, and as he started to type, his fingers danced over the screen. "Look at you two! The world needs more of this creativity and joy. I'll get you the details for the event; I can't wait to see what you come up with!"

As they headed back to the counter, the café around them pulsed with life, yet it felt as if they were in their own little world, buzzing with the excitement of a new adventure. Amani and Caroline exchanged glances, their smiles broadening as they began to brainstorm ideas for their performance.

Just then, the door chimed softly as a pair of newcomers entered— a young couple, their faces aglow with the thrill of discovery. They moved closer to the counter with hesitance, eyes darting between the chalkboard menu and Amani, whose warmth radiated like the aroma of her brews.

Amani greeted them with a bright smile. "Welcome to Third Cup! It's so lovely to see new faces. What can I get for you?"

The young woman, her hair framing her face in soft waves, leaned slightly forward, her excitement bubbling to the surface. "What do you recommend?" she asked, her voice filled with the hope of a new adventure.

Amani's eyes twinkled. "Our caramel macchiato is a favorite for first-timers, but the dark chocolate mocha—" she paused dramatically, leaning in as if sharing a well-guarded secret "—is pure magic. It's like a warm hug on a cold day!"

The couple erupted into giggles at her enthusiastic pitch, their initial shyness melting away. "Okay, we'll take one of each!" the young man declared, his voice playful as he draped an affectionate arm around his partner's shoulders.

The rich, bittersweet aroma of melting chocolate already filled the air, a comforting prelude to the warmth Amani was about to serve. With practiced grace, she lifted a heavy ceramic pitcher, its contents a deep, glossy brown, and carefully poured the velvety liquid into two waiting mugs. A delicate swirl of steamed milk followed, blossoming into a perfect, frothy cap on each, before a final flourish of finely grated dark chocolate dusted the surface like powdery snow.

As the last sprinkle settled, Amani glanced up, a soft smile playing on her lips. Across the counter, the couple, who had initially entered with a faint air of newness and perhaps a touch of apprehension, seemed to visibly relax. The soft glow of the café lights caught the subtle shift in their shoulders, the way their gazes, initially scanning the unfamiliar space, now softened, surrendering to the quiet ease of her presence and the promise of warmth the hot chocolate offered.

"What brings two bright faces like yours to my little corner of the world?" Amani asked, her voice soft but clear, her curiosity a genuine warmth rather than an intrusion. She knew, from years of watching strangers come and go, that every visitor carried a unique narrative, a whispered reason that led them to her door.

The young woman, with a vibrant red scarf loosely tied around her neck, offered a playful, almost conspiratorial roll of her eyes. "Well," she began, a hint of cheerful weariness in her tone, "we've just moved to the city. Everything feels new, a little overwhelming, but mostly exciting! We're on a quest, you see, a mission to uncover the very best local spots. And we figured, what better place to begin our grand adventure than with the quintessential local experience – coffee?"

The young man, whose dark, expressive eyes mirrored his partner's enthusiasm, nodded vigorously, a lock of hair falling over his forehead. "Exactly!" he chimed in, leaning slightly forward. "It's kind of our thing, you know? Hunting down hidden gems, trying out the places where the locals truly go. It's how we get to know a new place, really feel its pulse."

"Ah, that's absolutely wonderful!" Amani exclaimed, her smile broadening. She carefully placed the two steaming mugs on the polished wooden counter, the frothy topping now adorned with an intricate swirl of golden caramel that glistened enticingly under the warm café lights. "You're not just in for an adventure," she continued, a note of genuine excitement in her voice, "you're about to fall in love. This city... it's not just buildings and streets. It has a soul of its own, a rhythm you'll soon find yourselves dancing to. Oh, and you simply must find your way to Pine Ridge for sunset. The colors that paint the sky there, spreading across the whole valley... it's truly breathtaking, something you carry with you long after the sun dips below the horizon."

With eager hands, the couple lifted their mugs. The young woman took a tentative sip, her eyes closing briefly as the warmth spread through her. When she opened them, they were no longer just sparkling; they were alight with pure, unadulterated delight. "Oh my goodness," she breathed, a soft sigh escaping her lips. "This is... this is absolutely incredible!" She leaned closer to the young man, a look of shared wonder passing between them. He took a longer, more contemplative sip, a slow smile spreading across his face as if savoring every nuanced flavor. Their shared smiles, bright and genuine, didn't just illuminate their faces; they seemed to cast a warm, golden glow across Amani's entire café, a silent testament to the simple joy found in a perfect cup. Watching them, listening to their quiet murmurs of appreciation, Amani felt a deep, profound sense of happiness bloom within her, a familiar warmth that settled firmly in her chest. This was why she did what she did – to offer a haven, a moment of connection, and a taste of something truly special.

Prompted by the magic of the moment, the couple began sharing their own stories—not just about what brought them to Third Cup, but about their lives, dreams, and love for exploration. They spoke of their previous home, a quiet town, and how the decision to move had felt both thrilling and terrifying. "We wanted to feel alive, to embrace the chaos and the beauty of a city," the young man confessed, a hint of vulnerability in his tone.

"And we plan to soak it all in!" the young woman added, her determination sparkling in her eyes. "We want to meet people, try every corner café, and attend all the street festivals!"

Amani nodded, her heart swelling with camaraderie. "You're going to love it here. Just like coffee, life is best savored one sip at a time.

And trust me, the best memories are made when you least expect them."

As the couple reveled in their first taste of Third Cup's offerings, Amani wiped her hands on her apron, absorbing their infectious energy. The soft chime of the door echoed once more, carrying with it a gentle breeze and the sound of laughter that floated like music through the café.

Amani turned to see a group of students enter, cheeks flushed from the brisk air outside. They clustered together, navigating the space shyly until Amani welcomed them with the same warmth she had given the couple.

"Welcome! What can I get for you?" she asked, ready to embrace this new wave of guests.

The students rallied around the counter, peering at the chalkboard menu as if it were a treasure map leading to delicious excitement. One of them, a tall young woman with vibrant tattoos trailing down her arms, stepped forward. "What's your top seller? I need something to keep me awake for my study marathon!"

"Ah, you've come to the right place!" Amani replied with a smile. "Our nitro cold brew is a favorite among students. It's refreshing, and the caffeine packs a punch!"

"Okay, I think that's a winner!" the young woman exclaimed, her eyes lighting up.

As she placed the order, the couple finished their drinks and nudged each other playfully. The young man, still grinning, leaned towards Amani. "Do you always get this kind of crowd? It's so lively in here!"

Amani laughed, her heart swelling with gratitude. "Every day has its charm. It's like a little slice of life all rolled up in coffee. Each person brings their own story, their own energy."

As the sun dipped lower in the sky, casting a golden hue through the window, the café felt electrified with connection. The couple found themselves drawn into the laughter of the students, sharing stories of their own past and making new friends. They appeared like characters in a vibrant painting, swirling together in the rich atmosphere of Third Cup.

"Who knew we'd find such a welcoming crew on our first day in the city?" the young woman said, her eyes darting from one smiling face to another, her heart echoing the chorus of camaraderie surrounding them.

"It's the magic of coffee," Amani chimed in from behind the counter, carefully drizzling white chocolate into a cup. "It fuels connection, helps break down barriers."

The clock chimed seven pm, and Amani felt the weight of her day's work melt away with each resonant note. As customers drifted out into the twilight, their laughter and light conversations fading into the cool evening air, she found herself in a familiar rhythm, collecting her things to head home. The café was a refuge for so many—an intersection of stories that blended seamlessly but never lost their uniqueness. Every shift, each latte served, had woven Amani deeper into the fabric of this welcoming city of Winnipeg, her adopted home.

Stepping outside, she smiled as the crisp autumn breeze caressed her cheeks, a gentle reminder that summer's warmth was yielding to the change of seasons. The sun, a glowing orb of amber, cast long shadows that danced along Langside Avenue. Amani slipped her coat closer around her, savoring the moment, her heart alight with the remnants of the day.

Her thoughts, like the ceaseless ocean tides she once knew, spiraled back to the sun-drenched days of her early childhood in Mombasa. It was a time before the family's momentous move to the bustling, landlocked energy of Nairobi, a time when her world was a seamless canvas of vibrant blues and yellows. She remembered the crystalline waters of the Indian Ocean, mirroring the endless cerulean sky, and the golden, powdery sand kissed by a sun that always seemed to smile. Her days had blended into a symphony of natural sounds: the rhythmic hush and roar of waves breaking on the shore, the distant calls of fishing dhows, the playful shrieks of children chasing retreating water, and the rustle of palm fronds in the warm, salt-laced air. There was an unburdened freedom in those early years, a careless innocence that the harsh realities of adulthood had since eroded.

Yet, along with these cherished, almost luminous memories, came a flood, at times a torrent, of family expectations. The unspoken pact, woven into the very fabric of Kenyan family life, was that after graduation, she would not only support herself but also contribute significantly to the well-being of her parents and younger siblings. This responsibility, an invisible yet crushing burden, weighed heavily on her spirit. Families in Kenya, with a deep-seated belief in the transformative power of education, often invest every shilling, every hard-earned savings, even taking on significant debt, to send their children to university. Their hope, their fervent prayer, was that these children would secure professional degrees – medicine, law, engineering, or, in her case, nursing – to earn enough money not just to sustain themselves but to uplift the entire family from the cycle of poverty. It was this profound, almost sacred duty that had propelled her across continents, the reason she came to the vast, unfamiliar expanse of Winnipeg. She had diligently chosen to pursue a degree in Psychiatric Nursing, a pragmatic and calculated decision, not a childhood dream. She knew jobs were almost guaranteed anywhere in Canada, a beacon of hope in her quest for financial stability. By becoming a Psychiatric Nurse, she would earn enough to support herself in a new country, and, crucially, to send money back home to Kenya, fulfilling the unspoken promise she carried in her heart.

She then remembered the exact day she left—the bittersweet farewell that tore at her heart even as it promised liberation. It was a poignant goodbye to a world that, despite its beauty and familial warmth, had ironically confined her spirit within the rigid, often suffocating, boundaries of her family's aspirations. Boarding that plane to Canada felt like more than just a journey; it was a profound metamorphosis. It was like breaking free from a chrysalis, shedding the old, tight skin of prescribed destiny and societal obligation. As the aircraft soared, leaving the familiar red earth and vibrant greens of Kenya behind, she felt herself morphing, not into a creature of defined purpose, but into something gloriously wild and uncontainable, ready to unfurl wings she hadn't known she possessed, soaring towards an unwritten future.

In Winnipeg, Amani discovered her wings. The city welcomed her with open arms, an eclectic mix of cultures and stories that inspired her to delve into her own. The café had become her sanctuary, a place where her laughter mingled with tales of strangers. Her colleagues, quirky and genuine, were like family, each sharing their own narratives and passions, allowing her to shed the expectations of her past. Yet shadows from her former life occasionally whispered in the corridors of her mind.

As she unlocked the door to her cozy apartment, a wave of warmth enveloped her, almost like a hug. The familiar creak of the door greeted her like an old friend, and her heart surged with joy as she took in her sanctuary. Her walls were adorned with photographs chronicling her journey—a stunning collage of adventures, laughter, and moments that echoed her current mantra: she was finally becoming herself.

That evening, she settled by her window, a steaming cup of chamomile tea warming her hands as she prepared to pour her thoughts into her journal. The pages had become her confidante, a therapeutic release for the spectrum of her emotions—the light, shadow, and everything in between. Sipping slowly, she felt the delicate flavor of the chamomile wrap around her like a blanket, inviting her to dig deeper.

As she flipped through pages filled with sketches of dreams and the trials of her heart, something stirred within her—a sense of empowerment. She understood that acceptance wasn't a destination, but rather a dance, a graceful intertwining of her past and present. It was time to reclaim her narrative.

A flicker of inspiration ignited in her heart as she opened her journal once more. The blank pages were eager for her insights, thirsty for every word she had yet to write. A flurry of thoughts spilled forth, each line a tapestry of her identity—an intricate blend of cultures, expectations, and dreams. She poured her soul into the ink, releasing the expectations that had once imprisoned her and allowing them to transform into a celebration of her individuality.

As the sky deepened into an indigo canvas, and the stars began to twinkle like little guardian lights, Amani felt a swell of pride coursing through her veins. The journey was just beginning—this was the first chapter of her own story, told in the language of liberation and self-discovery.

The clock struck ten pm, yet in that moment, time felt suspended in her new reality. Laughter and whispers from the past intertwined with the quiet anticipation of the future. The sweet scent of chamomile enveloped her, wrapping her in a cocoon of comfort. In her heart, she knew it was time to call her mother. Although Nairobi was eight hours ahead, the evening's embrace urged her to connect with the roots of her family.

Amani's fingers lingered on the sleek, cool metal of her phone, a quiet hum settling in her chest. Around her, the soft glow of fairy lights woven through a bookshelf cast warm shadows, and the scent of freshly brewed tea mingled with the subtle aroma of a burning candle – a scent she now associated with 'home.' She reveled in this sanctuary she had meticulously crafted in Winnipeg, a space that mirrored the burgeoning sense of belonging blossoming within her spirit. The deep, contented sigh that escaped her lips was a testament to the journey, acknowledging the quiet battles fought and the small, hard-won victories. Her mother's homely voice, a sound as comforting as a well-worn blanket, warm and familiar even across continents, awaited her on the other end. Amani chuckled softly, a bright, hopeful sound, anticipation blossoming like a rare flower in her chest. It was time to share not just the mundane details of her day, but the unfolding chapters of her new life—a vibrant mosaic of struggle and triumph, of loneliness overcome and new connections forged.

With a gentle, almost reverent tap, the line connected, and from the moment her mother's voice, clear and resonant despite the distance, filled the air with a bright, "Amani, my sunshine! How's my Winnipeg warrior doing today?" the thousands of miles between them dissolved. It was as if her mother was right there, sitting on the plush sofa beside her, her presence a tangible comfort. As Amani spoke, recounting anecdotes and sharing her latest revelations, the background laughter and voices of friends still chatting in her cozy apartment transformed into a symphony of connection that spanned oceans. The subtle clinking of teacups, the muffled hum of comfortable conversation from her friends in the kitchen, blended seamlessly with the echoes of a life lived far away. She could almost feel the golden heat of Nairobi's sun through the phone, sense the vibrant energy of its streets, illuminating their long-distance bond in a way only profound love could. Her mother's stories, rich with the colours and everyday rhythms of home, began to weave a tapestry of nostalgia that danced through Amani's heart, a comforting balm wrapping around the lingering shadows of her past; the whispers of familiarity and home gently smoothed over the edges of homesickness and the solitary moments of her adaptation. "Amani, remember the time we got lost in Karura Forest?" her mother chuckled, the richness of her laughter echoing not just in the walls of her apartment, but deep within the chambers of Amani's heart, mingling with memories that flickered like fireworks—the damp earth smell, the rustle of unseen creatures, the sheer boundless thrill of childhood adventure. "You were so convinced we'd become intrepid forest explorers, adventurers in search of hidden treasures, armed with nothing but your boundless imagination and a stick for a sword!"

"I do! I thought we'd find a secret cave or maybe a treasure chest full of gold, just like in your old storybooks!" Amani laughed, the sound bright and unburdened, a pure echo of that childhood joy resurfacing.

"Or maybe some native creatures that'd want to befriend you and join your grand quest," her mother added, teasingly, the affection evident in every syllable. The pure, unadulterated joy in her voice reminded Amani how profoundly she missed these spontaneous, comforting moments—how vital they were for grounding her spirit and affirming her identity.

As her mother regaled the details of Nairobi's latest developments—the new art galleries, the bustling markets, the ever-changing skyline—Amani found deep solace in this blend of old and new. The world felt vast, stretching endlessly beyond her Winnipeg window, yet in those moments, with her mother's stories painting vibrant pictures of home, she was linked to her deepest roots, intertwined with the very essence of who she was. She envisioned the bustling, vibrant streets of South B, the cacophony of matatu horns, the fragrant steam rising from street food vendors, and the lively, intimate café culture she had grown up with. She contrasted it with her new life in Winnipeg—the crisp, clean air, the gentle hush of snow-covered streets in winter, the quiet charm of its neighbourhoods—an embrace of the unfamiliar that was slowly, patiently softening the edges of her heart, allowing new joys and experiences to settle in.

Soon they shifted the conversation toward Amani's life in Canada. It was her turn to describe the eclectic blend of cultures she'd encountered, the snippets of broken conversations with strangers over steaming cups of coffee, and the laughter of her colleagues at the café—a place where every cup of chai carried its own story.

"Mum, the people I work with... they're incredible," Amani said, her enthusiasm bubbling over. "They're just like us—full of stories and dreams. It's like walking into a new world every day!"

"And you've found your wings, haven't you? You're soaring above your past, exploring all that life has to offer," her mother encouraged, her voice a soothing balm that eased Amani's anxieties.

"Yes, I am," Amani replied, her heart swelling with pride. "It feels like every moment here is helping me become the person I'm meant to be."

After more laughter and reminiscing, the conversation drifted gently down paths of shared dreams. "What are your plans now, my sunshine?" her mother asked, her interest piqued.

"I've been thinking of writing more—more than just my journal. Maybe I can compile my experiences, the stories of the people I've met, and weave them into something larger." A flicker of inspiration ignited in her chest at the thought.

"That would be wonderful! You have a gift for storytelling, my dear. Just remember to keep your heart in every word you write." Amani could hear the pride in her mother's voice, and it encouraged her to reach beyond her comfort zone.

"Thank you, Mum. I promise I will," Amani said, her thoughts already cascading into new ideas. Perhaps her words would resonate with others who found themselves at the crossroads of two worlds, who were learning to synthesize the past with the present.

As their call lingered, the night crept deeper, wrapping Amani in a blanket of serenity. The stars twinkled brightly outside her window, each one a reminder of where she had come from and the myriad of possibilities still ahead. Embraced by the warm sentiment of her mother's love, Amani felt empowered, as if the very act of sharing her journey was an act of reclamation.

"Goodnight, my sunshine," her mother's voice resonated, a gentle anchor that steadied her for the journey ahead.

"Goodnight, Mum. I love you," Amani whispered, the warmth of her mother's love wrapping around her like a cocoon, deepening her sense of home.

With the call ended, Amani turned back to her journal, inspired by their exchange and driven by the need to document her truth. As she wrote, she felt the words flow freely, unencumbered by the past, infused with the brilliance of her present. In that moment, under the watchful gaze of the stars, Amani realized that she was not just writing a story—she was creating her life, one page at a time. The dance of acceptance continued, and with every word inked and every leading thought embraced, she soared higher, breaking the invisible chains that had once held her back. She was becoming not only herself but a beacon of light for others navigating their own shadows. And Winnipeg, with its diverse stories and cultures, had gifted her wings.

Chapter 06

Amani and Leo were working together at Third Cup that Thursday afternoon. Amani enjoyed having Leo as a partner since he always brought a fun vibe to their shifts. "Hey, Amani," Leo called out, his voice cheerful as he frothed the milk for a cappuccino. "Did you hear about the open mic night happening here next week? We should totally perform!"

Amani chuckled, wiping the counter. "Perform? I can barely sing in the shower without scaring my neighbors! But I'm in for cheering you on. What do you have planned?"

Leo grinned, his eyes sparkling with excitement. "I've been working on a new song. Just need a little backup! Come on, it'll be fun!"

"Alright, I'll think about it," Amani finally replied with a playful smirk. "But only if you promise not to make me sing any high notes!"

"Deal!" Leo responded, laughing as he handed a customer their drink. The afternoon wore on, but the camaraderie and joy they shared kept their spirits high, making the rain-soaked day feel brighter than ever.

As the bell above the door jingled again, heralding yet another arrival, Amani straightened up and turned with a bright smile. It was Mia, a college student who often studied at the café while sipping various blends. Today, her eyes sparkled with newfound excitement.

"Hey, Amani!" Mia called out, adjusting her oversized glasses. "Can I get a matcha latte today? I need a little pick-me-up for my cramming session."

"Coming right up!" Amani replied, her fingers dancing over the matcha powder as she prepared Mia's order. The sound of the whisk against the bowl was oddly soothing, almost like a rhythmic chant amidst the café's steady hum.

While she prepared, Leo swept over to Mia's table, where a stack of books flanked her laptop. "Studying hard for your finals, huh?" he asked, his tone light but curious.

"More like cramming because I procrastinated!" Mia laughed, brushing a strand of hair behind her ear. "But I'm surviving thanks to your fabulous coffee!"

Amani chimed in as she placed the vibrant green drink before Mia. "And here's hoping this matcha will turn your cramming into a study party!" She winked, pleased to see Mia's face light up with delight.

Just as Mia dug into her study supplies, the café filled with a group of friends bursting through the door, smiles gleaming and laughter cascading like confetti. They were familiar faces—friends from the neighborhood who often gathered for weekly catch-ups at Third Cup.

"Hey, squad! What are we feeling today?" Amani greeted them, welcoming the surge of energy they brought along with them.

"Surprise us!" one of the friends, Jake, called back playfully, a mischievous glint in his eyes.

"Alright!" Amani replied, her creative instincts kicking in. "Let's do a flight of mini lattes! Each with a twist!" She quickly whipped up a pumpkin spice, a lavender honey, a chai, and a rich dark chocolate mocha, arranging them on a wooden serving board as Leo assisted by finding festive cups.

The friends oohed and aahed over the colorful lineup, snapping pictures with their phones. "You two are the dream team!" one remarked, diving in eagerly to taste the treats. As laughter and chatter filled the space, Amani felt a sense of fulfillment wash over her—she loved sharing these moments.

As the rain pattered softly against the windows, creating a gentle backdrop, Amani noticed a few other patrons drifting away with the afternoon sun hidden behind thick clouds. The café atmosphere tightened to something more intimate, perfect for the poetry reading on the horizon.

"Are you ready for tonight's performance?" Leo asked, swinging back towards Amani with a playful grin.

"Oh, I'm all set! Just need to finalize my piece," Amani replied enthusiastically, thoughts racing with the imagery she wished to convey.

"Are you going to pull a dramatic reading like last time?" he was teasing her with a glimmer in his eye.

"Only if you promise to do interpretative dance again," Amani shot back, giggling as she tossed a napkin at him.

Just as they exchanged playful banter, the door opened once more, and in stepped Mr. Johnson, a retired teacher known for his love of philosophy. He ambled in, a sturdy umbrella in one hand and a twinkle of wisdom in his eye.

"Aha! The café masterpiece is in full bloom!" he exclaimed, shaking off droplets of rain. "What's brewing this fine afternoon?"

"Just spreading joy one latte at a time!" Amani replied, serving him his favorite Earl Grey with a side of lemon wedge.

As Mr. Johnson settled into his armchair, the familiar creak of the seat echoed through the café, a sound that had become synonymous with the warmth of community. Amani smiled to herself as she watched him. He was more than just a regular; he was a treasure trove of stories and wisdom, always ready to share his insights wrapped in the delightful cloak of playful banter.

"Have you written anything about our charming little café?" Amani asked, leaning over the counter, eager for a glimpse of his poetic world. The air around them was filled with the scent of roasted coffee beans mingling with the sweet notes of baked goods, a perfect backdrop for creativity.

Mr. Johnson chuckled, his eyes sparkling behind round spectacles that perched precariously on the edge of his nose. "Ah, my dear Amani, I might just devote an entire ode to your espresso. It brews not just coffee but also camaraderie!"

The café hummed with a light buzz as other regulars nodded in agreement, their own cups in hand, savoring moments both flavorful and fleeting. Amani felt a rush of gratitude. Here they sat, bound by the aroma of caffeine and the warmth of familiar faces, sharing snippets of life over sips of their beloved beverages.

As Mr. Johnson pulled the poems from the newspaper, Amani's curiosity piqued. Each poem was handwritten with a delicate flourish, capturing thoughts on nature, human connection, and the whims of life itself. He read aloud, his voice soft yet resonant, weaving words that danced in the air like the soft notes of a piano.

"In the quiet of rain, life reveals its grace; each droplet a story, each splash a trace."

The usual symphony of clinking mugs, soft chatter, and the rhythmic hiss of the espresso machine gradually faded into an attentive hush. The café, usually a vibrant hum of activity, became entirely absorbed in the rich, resonant cadence of Mr. Johnson's storytelling. He sat, a warm, inviting presence, his voice weaving intricate narratives that seemed to draw the very air out of the room. Amani, behind the gleaming counter, paused in her tasks, observing the transformation. The familiar faces – the hurried businesswoman, the perpetually sketching art student, the elderly couple who always shared a scone – all morphed into still, wide-eyed, captivated listeners. In the quiet, shared space, a unique kind of magic unfolded, uniting them in the unfolding drama of Mr. Johnson's words. It was a rare, collective experience that transcended their individual worlds, subtly drawing them closer together in an unspoken bond.

Finally, with a gentle sigh that seemed to release the last vestiges of his tale, Mr. Johnson concluded his story. A soft, collective breath rippled through the café, followed by a smattering of appreciative murmurs and quiet claps. Amani, her own mind still buzzing with the echoes of his narrative, felt an irresistible urge to understand the wellspring of his talent. "Mr. Johnson," she asked, her voice a soft counterpoint to the returning ambient sounds, "what fuels your creativity the most? Is it the wide, unpredictable outside world, or the countless tales you hear from others, perhaps even right here in this very café?"

He took a deliberate moment, his gaze drifting over the faces of his listeners, his fingers lightly drumming a soft rhythm on the ceramic of his well-loved mug. A thoughtful, almost knowing grin began to bloom across his kind face. "Ah, Amani," he began, his eyes twinkling, "life, my dear, is like a rich tapestry. Each thread, no matter how humble or grand, is vibrant with feeling - filled with the warmth of laughter and the poignant ache of sorrow, the exuberance of joy and the quiet sting of heartache. It's in every fleeting chat I have, every new face I encounter, every familiar smile that greets me here, day after day. Just look around you, Amani - there's a veritable feast of stories waiting, always, for us to simply pay attention and listen!" His sweeping gesture encompassed the entire café, inviting Amani to see the silent narratives unfolding all around her.

Inspired by his words, a new perspective blooming in her mind, Amani then returned to the comforting familiarity of the counter. With a cheerful, professional call that cut through the reawakened buzz, she prepared to take the next order. "Robust dark roast for Mr. Thompson!" she announced, her voice clear and bright. Her gaze fell on the elderly gentleman by the window, his spectacles perched on his nose, deeply absorbed in the rustle and crinkle of his morning newspaper, utterly oblivious to the café's transient hush and reawakening. Behind her, Leo, with his usual quiet efficiency, moved with practiced ease. He quickly measured out the dark, aromatic grounds, poured the steaming water precisely into the French press, and let it steep, the rich coffee scent already beginning to unfurl in the air. A moment later, he pressed the plunger down with a satisfying hiss, pouring the potent brew into a steaming ceramic cup and handing it to Amani. She, with the practiced grace of a seasoned barista, executed a swift, almost artistic flick of her wrist, sending a perfect spiral of cream tracing white against the dark surface. When she delivered the piping hot coffee to Mr. Thompson, he lowered his newspaper, his eyes crinkling at the corners as he beamed at her, clearly pleased with the drink made just to his precise taste. "It's all in a day's work, Mr. T," she teased gently, playfully ruffling the corner of his newspaper with a light touch. "Enjoy your time here!" She lingered for a moment, absorbing the quiet satisfaction of the exchange, before turning back to the endless, beautiful tapestry of her café and its patrons.

During the bustling morning rush, the café, affectionately known as Third Cup, buzzed with a vibrant, almost chaotic symphony of sounds—the hiss of the espresso machine, the clatter of ceramic on saucers, and the low hum of countless conversations. The air was thick with the comforting aroma of roasted coffee beans and freshly baked pastries, as patrons discussed everything from the latest captivating new book releases to the juiciest tidbits of local gossip. Sunlight, slanting through the large front windows, illuminated motes of dust dancing in the air and cast a warm glow on the polished wooden tables.

In one cozy corner, two university students, their textbooks splayed open but largely ignored, were locked in an animated debate, their voices rising and falling as they passionately argued the merits of a newly opened, trendy café nearby versus the tried-and-true comfort of Third Cup. Across the room, a young mother, her brow furrowed with a mixture of amusement and exasperation, wrestled with her two energetic little ones, who, with sticky fingers and eyes wide with mischievous intent, made repeated, determined lunges for her cooling blueberry muffin. Their giggles and her gentle reprimands added another layer to the café's lively soundscape.

Amidst this lively chaos, Amani, her hands still damp from washing a stack of mugs, paused, drying them absently on her apron. Her gaze swept across the room, catching Leo's eye over the rim of an empty coffee pot he was wiping down. She nodded subtly towards a couple seated near the window, her expression intrigued by the subtly unsettling scene unfolding between them.

The couple, a young man and woman, were indeed engrossed in conversation, their heads bent close, but there was a palpable, almost suffocating tension radiating from their small table. Despite the intimacy of their whispered words, they pointedly avoided making eye contact, their shoulders stiff, their hands clasped tightly in their laps or gesticulating in small, agitated movements. Leo, his brow furrowed slightly as he observed them, finally straightened up. "Looks like a storm brewing over there," Leo mused, his voice low, just for Amani. He speculated, his gaze still on the couple, "Could be a breakup in the making, or maybe just a really serious discussion about, oh, I don't know, whose turn it is to clean the cat litter." He offered a small, wry smile. Amani let out a deep sigh, the sound barely audible above the café's hum, a ripple of genuine sadness crossing her face.

"Oh, I hope not," she murmured, her voice tinged with a wistful regret. "I really wish things didn't turn out that way for them. They're usually so endearing, always laughing together." She paused, then added, "Just last week, they were practically bubbling over, showing me photos of the itinerary for their upcoming vacation - all the arrangements were done for Costa Rica."

Leo merely raised his shoulders in a nonchalant shrug, a faint, almost cynical smirk playing on his lips. "Well," he quipped, "maybe Costa Rica wasn't the best choice, then. Being confined to a small hotel room, even in paradise, can sometimes reveal that people truly cannot tolerate each other." Just as Amani was about to retort, the conversation was abruptly cut short.

Out of nowhere, the whimsical bell hanging above the ornate entrance — a collection of repurposed silver spoons that chimed with a surprisingly clear, joyful note — rang with an enthusiastic jingle, disturbing their quiet moment. All heads turned as Elise, a familiar and much-loved regular whose vibrant personality was as much a part of Third Cup's fabric as the aroma of coffee, burst through the door, a whirlwind of breathless energy. "You won't believe what just went down!" she exclaimed, her voice bubbling with excitement, her cheeks flushed a bright, triumphant red, her eyes sparkling.

Amani, her curiosity immediately piqued, hurried over. "Elise, what's happening? You look like you've just won the lottery!"

Still beaming, Elise took a deep, dramatic breath, as if to contain her overflowing joy. "I," she announced, her voice rising in a celebratory crescendo, "have landed the main role in the upcoming play at the local theater! We're performing a rendition of Pride and Prejudice!"

Amani gasped in delight, her face mirroring Elise's elation, and pulled her into a warm, congratulatory hug. Leo, grinning broadly, also joined in, playfully picking Elise up and spinning her around briefly, her joyous squeal echoing through the café.

Setting her down gently, Leo chuckled. "Elise, that's incredible news! You'll make a fantastic Elizabeth Bennet. Spirited, witty, a little bit sassy – perfect casting! When's the show?"

Elise, still vibrating with excitement, clapped her hands together. "Next month! I need everyone there, you hear? Both of you bringing the loudest applause in the entire house!"

"Sounds good!" Amani exclaimed, already reaching for the small, dog-eared notepad attached to the cash register. With a flourish, she swiftly recorded the date, her pen scratching decisively.

Throughout the rest of the day, as the sun moved across the sky and cast an ever-shifting golden light on the café, the anecdotes kept pouring out. Customers came and went, each leaving behind fragments of their lives – a funny story about a pet, a proud declaration of a child's achievement, a quiet confession about a difficult week. Amani and Leo, working in comfortable synchronicity, exchanged meaningful looks, their eyes meeting over steaming mugs or across the bustling counter, as they joined in the laughter and touching moments, silent witnesses to the small, intimate glimpses of life circulating through Third Cup, much like the rich, fragrant coffee they so expertly offered.

Right before shutting down for the day, as the last stragglers departed and the golden light faded into the soft glow of interior lamps, the café began to calm down. The frenetic energy of the morning dissipated, replaced by a soothing quiet that allowed Amani and Leo to tidy up after the remarkably busy day. The clatter of dishes became more deliberate, the wiping of counters a rhythmic hum.

"You know," Leo mentioned, leaning against the now-clean counter, a thoughtful expression on his face, "I've been thinking, with all the stories we hear in here... I believe it would be a really good idea to organize a special event for our regular customers. Something like hosting an open mic night where they could share their own personal stories, their poems, anything."

A spark ignited in Amani's eyes when she heard the suggestion, chasing away any lingering fatigue. Her face lit up with a sudden, brilliant smile. "Leo, that sounds like a fantastic idea!" she exclaimed, her voice brimming with a fresh wave of enthusiasm. "We could highlight talents within the neighborhood, give everyone a platform, and provide a truly unique space for our community to come together!"

While engaging in this lively discussion, the café, now quiet and still save for their voices, seemed to transform into a hub of immense potential, almost humming with the energy of future possibilities, similar to the warm, comforting contentment found in the bottom of the cup of joy they offered each day. Amani and Leo came to the profound realization that Third Cup was, and always had been, more than just a place for coffee. It was a cherished space for forging genuine connections, for the quiet exchange of stories that bound people together, and for fostering a deep sense of belonging through warm conversations and shared, often unexpected, experiences.

In the lively, now quiet, café, they started making initial arrangements for an evening dedicated to celebrating the diverse and interconnected lives that thrived within the establishment's walls, realizing, with a sense of wonder, that they had just scratched the surface of what Third Cup truly meant to its beloved patrons.

As the final customer, a rumpled man with a perpetually surprised expression, pushed open the door and stepped out into the cool evening air, the small bell above the door, which had announced a hundred arrivals and departures throughout the day, offered its last, soft chime, a gentle sigh of farewell. Amani and Leo were left in the sudden, palpable quiet that always descended once the last patron was gone. It was their favourite part of the day, a transition from public bustling to private possibility.

The scent of roasted coffee beans, a ghost of the day's activity, still hung faintly in the air, mingling with the fresh lemon tang of cleaning spray. Amani moved with a practiced grace, her cloth a silent whisper across the polished tabletops, erasing the rings left by countless mugs. Leo, meanwhile, stacked chairs with rhythmic clunks, the sound echoing slightly in the suddenly vast space. Yet, the silence wasn't truly empty. It was punctuated by their easy conversation, a comfortable rhythm of shared thoughts and observations that had less to do with the day winding down than with the dreams winding up.

Amani paused, leaning on a freshly wiped table, her eyes unfocused, gazing past the smudges of the day to something only she could see. A slow smile bloomed on her face, transforming her tired features into something alight with anticipation.

"I can just see it now," she murmured, her voice softer than usual, a whisper against the quiet hum of the refrigerators. "We could have a little stage, right there," she waved a hand towards the prime corner spot between the espresso machine's gleaming chrome and the large bay window that overlooked the quiet street. "Not a big, fancy thing, just a raised platform. And we'd string so many twinkly lights – fairy lights, proper ones – from the ceiling, draping them down like luminous vines. It would create this incredible, intimate glow, warm and inviting."

Leo, who had just finished stacking the last chair, leaned against the counter, a faint smudge of flour on his cheek from the morning's bake. He watched her, a familiar affection in his eyes. "And what would go on this 'incredible, intimate glow' stage of yours, Amani?" he asked, a hint of amusement in his tone, but also genuine curiosity.

Amani's eyes snapped back to him, sparkling. "Everything!" she exclaimed, sweeping her arm wide. "Open mic nights, local acoustic sets, poetry readings, maybe even a spoken word night. Imagine - this space, alive with music and stories, not just the clatter of cups and the hiss of the steamer."

Leo pushed off the counter, walking over to stand beside her, looking at the empty corner with a new perspective. "A regular hub, then," he mused, a thoughtful frown creasing his brow. "It would certainly draw a different crowd. And we'd need, what, better acoustics? Maybe some soundproofing for the late nights?" His practical side was already kicking in, but the initial warmth of her dream had clearly taken root.

"A garage band? Perfect! They can help drum up excitement." Amani laughed, her enthusiasm infectious. "And we'll have a sign-up sheet for anyone who wants to perform. I bet the regulars have some hidden talents!"

Leo nodded, his eyes brightening. "Like Mr. Thompson—he still plays the harmonica, doesn't he? He could open the night with a little blues."

"Absolutely! And Elise could do a dramatic reading from Pride and Prejudice!" They both burst into laughter, picturing the scene. The café wasn't just a job to them; it was a patchwork of lives, loves, and laughter.

As they continued cleaning, the sun dipped lower, casting long shadows across the wooden floor. The warmth of the day began to fade into a cool evening breeze. In a corner, the two college students from earlier were still lingering, discussing their findings from the new café down the road, completely unaware of the time.

"Hey, look at them," Amani said quietly, nudging Leo with her elbow. "They're so engrossed that they don't even realize they're the last ones here."

"That's the magic of this place," Leo replied, glancing over. "It's like they're in their own little world. Everyone comes together, even if they don't know it."

With a gentle smile, Amani looked at the artwork adorning the café's walls—local artists' pieces that told stories of the neighborhood. "What if we also included poetry nights? Or local art showcases? We could really bring the community together."

Leo raised an eyebrow, clearly intrigued. "You're onto something big, Amani. This could turn into quite the showplace for creativity."

The ideas began to flow like the coffee they poured during their busiest shifts, new energy brimming with each suggestion they shared. They pulled out a notebook and started scribbling ideas: poetry slam nights, local art displays, themed trivia nights possibly linked to local history.

Amani smiled so brightly her dimples showed, a genuine, radiating warmth that seemed to fill the quiet café. She leaned slightly against the cool countertop, her eyes sparkling as she vividly imagined the space transformed: every table occupied, not just by customers, but by burgeoning friendships and shared passions. The aroma of lingering coffee would mingle with the buzz of excited chatter and the warm, golden glow of lamplight reflecting off polished wood, a haven where ideas could truly spark. "Can you imagine the stories we could hear?" she mused aloud, her voice a soft murmur in the hushed room, picturing tales of triumph and heartache, whispered confessions and boisterous anecdotes. "Maybe Jenna and Mark will come back and share their latest relationship adventures—you know how wild their dating life is! And wouldn't it be hilarious if they finished with some impromptu karaoke?"

"Or," Leo added, a low rumble of a chuckle starting deep in his chest and bubbling up, "we could ask customers to share their funniest, most absurd customer service stories. Imagine the sheer chaos and hilarity! I bet we'd get everything from rogue squirrels in drive-thrus to confused grandmas trying to pay with chickens." He shook his head, still amused by the thought. "That would certainly keep things interesting, wouldn't it?"

As they brainstormed, the last lingering echoes of laughter from the final customers of the day slowly faded into the background, replaced by the rhythmic, comforting tick-tock of the antique wall clock near the counter. The vibrant energy of the workday had dwindled, leaving behind a serene, near-silent stillness that settled over the café like a soft blanket. They both instinctively glanced at the clock, then at each other, realizing it was well past closing time, the "Open" sign long since flipped to "Closed," but neither felt the slightest urge to leave just yet. The café, usually a bustling hub of activity, had transformed, under the cloak of night and their shared vision, into their own private sanctuary, a blank canvas where their dreams were beginning to vividly unfold.

Finally, with the last napkins folded, the espresso machine gleaming, and tabletops wiped down to a high shine, the quiet hum of the mini-fridge was the only remaining sound. Leo grabbed the sturdy broom, its bristles swishing rhythmically against the polished concrete floor as he began to sweep stray crumbs and dust toward the door. Across the room, Amani meticulously restacked the vibrant, artfully arranged jars of various pastries that hadn't sold, gently nudging a blueberry scone here, a lemon square there, ensuring they looked inviting for the morning rush.

"Alright, Amani," Leo said, his voice lowering, shedding its playful tone for something more serious and focused, the rhythmic swoosh of the broom pausing. "We should really nail down a date to launch this open mic night. We can start promoting it immediately on social media—get some fun graphics going—and put up eye-catching flyers around town. But first, we have to get our regulars excited!"

"Yes!" Amani replied instantly, her heart giving a joyful leap, a rush of pure adrenaline flooding through her. The thought of bringing their shared vision to life, of sharing this exciting new chapter with their loyal patrons, made her pulse quicken. "Let's announce it during the morning rush! When the café is buzzing and everyone's already hyped on coffee. We'll create an electric buzz!"

The two friends exchanged determined glances, the spark of inspiration lighting up their faces.

As they locked up the café, Amani took a moment to breathe in the familiar warm aroma that always set the tone at Third Cup. "I can't wait to see how this evolves. It feels like we're about to open a whole new chapter for our community."

"Absolutely," Leo said, slinging his arm around her shoulders as they walked out. "Here's to the stories yet to be told—and the connections yet to be made." Amani tried to avoid the hug, but Leo was so excited about the energy they had together, he could not help but express it.

With that shared sentiment, they walked into the chilly evening, energized by the warmth they had built within the walls of Third Cup, ready to stir the community's heart with stories, laughter, and, most importantly, connection. Little did they know, they were about to embark on a journey that would strengthen their bonds, introduce new talent to the world, and create a tapestry of shared experiences that would truly make Third Cup the heart of their community.

Chapter 07

Amani's day began with the soft glow of morning sunlight streaming through the sheer curtains of her small apartment, casting a golden hue on the simple furnishings. It was a moment she usually cherished, basking in the peace and solitude that the early hours brought. But this morning was different—the tranquility was shattered by the violent ringing of her phone against the wooden bedside table.

The distinctive, slightly tinny melody of her mother's ringtone, a sound usually associated with comforting normalcy, suddenly shredded the afternoon's quiet stillness like an urgent alarm. Amani's heart, which moments before had been beating a calm, steady rhythm, now bucked and leaped, skipping a frantic beat as she answered. A cold dread, familiar yet always unwelcome, began to seep into her veins, coiling tightly in her chest.

Her mother's voice, usually so steady and comforting, now splintered with a raw, breathless urgency, each word felt like a shard of cracked porcelain, dropping into an unfathomable abyss of fear. "The house... it caught fire, in the kitchen," she hurriedly explained, the explanation tumbling out in a desperate, rushing cascade, panic evident in every high-pitched inflection, every gasping pause. Amani could almost see her mother, hunched over the phone, her brow deeply furrowed, fine lines etched by worry, her hands probably wringing together until her knuckles were white, caught in that agonizing limbo between the crushing weight of disaster and the fragile relief that everyone was safe. Yet, that sense of safety was like a wafer-thin layer of ice over a treacherous, bottomless chasm—the true chilling nature of the call, the extent of the damage, had only just begun to sink into Amani's reeling mind.

As her mother continued, speaking of extensive repairs and the urgent, immediate need for a substantial sum of money, a devastating wave didn't just crash over Amani; it was a tsunami, dragging her back through time, pulling her treasured memories along with it through the current of cold reality. Images of her childhood home, that cherished sanctuary, filled her mind's eye, each vibrant scene now tinged with a profound, aching melancholy. She recalled the warm, golden glow of family dinners casting long shadows across the walls, the rich, savory aroma of her mother's Sunday pot roast or freshly baked apple pie wafting through the air, and the uninhibited peals of laughter that used to echo from the living room—now imagined as ghostly whispers among the soot-stained, skeletal remnants of a life once vibrant. The thought of the holiday decorations that had adorned every nook and cranny, the twinkling fairy lights that transformed the living room into a winter wonderland, the scent of pine and cinnamon that filled the air, now reduced to grotesque, melted lumps and fine ash, sent a profound shiver down her spine. The vibrant reds and greens of Christmases past were now mere shadows under blackened, gaping ceilings, the joyful spirit extinguished.

"I'll do what I can, Mom. It'll be okay. I promise," Amani heard the words leave her mouth, steady and firm, as though her voice itself was constructing a fragile bridge over the chasm of despair, trying to connect her mother's panic with a desperate, self-willed hope. Yet, within her, a different reality swirled – uncertainty, thick and choking like acrid smoke in a once-happy home, threatened to engulf her resolve. The daunting prospect of helping prompted her to dig deeper into her already sparse resources, her mind racing through a frantic inventory of practical solutions – extra shifts, selling prized possessions, reaching out for any lifeline – all amid the overwhelming emotional turmoil that tightened her chest. She could hear the deep-seated tremor in her mother's voice, a tremor that resonated with the strength of their shared history – a history forged not just in laughter and joy, but in countless quiet acts of resilience, in weathering storms together. Amani clung to that fragile thread of hope, willing it to hold, to become a lifeline, as she prepared to rise to the immense occasion, to steel herself for the odd, disorienting blend of cold pragmatism and searing heartache that lay inevitably ahead.

The click of the phone as she hung up echoed in the oppressive silence of her tiny Canadian apartment. Amani remained seated on the edge of her bed, the worn duvet a thin barrier against the encroaching chill. The weight of the situation, a crushing burden she hadn't anticipated, settled heavily onto her shoulders, pressing down until her very bones ached. She felt utterly torn, not just by circumstance, but by an internal schism. On one side, the profound, unwavering responsibilities that bound her to her family in Kenya – her aging parents, her younger siblings, the dire need for their family home, the very nexus of their lives, to be rebuilt. On the other, the fierce, hard-won independence she had cultivated in Canada, a dream she had chased across continents, a fledgling life she was desperately trying to nurture. This conflict didn't just tug; it rent at the very core of her being, pulling her violently in two opposing directions, each demanding her absolute allegiance.

As the hours bled into late afternoon, marked only by the shifting grey light outside her single window, Amani found herself pacing the cool laminate floor of her sparse apartment. Her anxiety, a knot of icy dread, coiled tightly in her stomach, tightening with every circuit she made from the kitchenette to the living area. The most daunting task loomed: reaching out for help. Her mind spun with a tumultuous battle: pride, once a sturdy shield, now felt like a heavy cloak of shame. How could she, the independent, resourceful Amani who had flown across the world to build a new life, admit such a profound vulnerability? Mingling with this internal conflict was the paralyzing fear of judgment, the phantom whisper of rejection. Could she truly bring herself to ask for financial assistance from her friends, many of whom were striving themselves, carrying their own unseen burdens and responsibilities? The very thought felt like confessing a colossal failure.

With a deep, shuddering breath that seemed to gather all the fragmented pieces of her courage, Amani finally stilled her pacing. Her fingers trembled ever so slightly as she opened the WhatsApp application on her phone. She created a new group, adding first her closest friends from back home in Kenya, then those she had recently forged connections with in Canada. It was a leap of faith, a moment of profound vulnerability. She typed, then deleted, then retyped, her heart pouring into a few carefully chosen lines. She explained the devastating situation with raw honesty, describing the fire, the damage, the urgent need for their home to be more than just ashes and broken walls. And then, the hardest part: she humbly, almost shyly, asked for any support they could offer, financial or otherwise, emphasizing that even the smallest gesture would be a beacon of hope.

The response was not just surprising; it was a tidal wave of unwavering solidarity that washed over her, dissolving the icy knot in her chest. Messages began to ping in, one after another, then calls, then a cascade of support that brought tears to her eyes. Her friends rallied around her with an astonishing speed and unity. They didn't just offer comfort and compassion; they immediately brainstormed practical help. Mariam, ever the organizer, took charge with decisive efficiency, proposing and swiftly setting up a virtual fundraiser, complete with a payment portal and a clear goal. Others chipped in without hesitation, their generosity a testament to their unwavering belief in her, their kindness overwhelming Amani with a profound sense of gratitude that left her speechless.

The following weeks unfolded in a whirlwind of collaborative efforts that transcended time zones and borders. Amani's friends, a vibrant network of compassion, mobilized their own communities, spreading the word about her family's desperate situation with incredible zeal. Flyers, beautifully designed by a friend with a knack for graphics, adorned local cafés and community boards, silent appeals for help. Social media campaigns gained incredible traction, with posts shared thousands of times, each share a ripple expanding across the digital ocean, carrying Amani's story to new ears and hearts. The outpouring of generosity was staggering, each donation a tangible expression of care. With every notification of a contribution, a part of the heavy shadows of shame and self-doubt that had clouded her heart lifted, replaced by a radiant warmth.

With each donation, Amani felt an invisible thread strengthening, connecting her to this sprawling, global community of support. It was a sense of connection and belonging that transcended borders and distances, making her feel less isolated in her struggle. Her family's home began its slow but steady healing process. The burnt, desolate shell of the kitchen, once a symbol of their loss, slowly transformed. New timbers rose, walls were plastered, fresh paint gleamed, and the scent of new wood replaced the acrid smell of smoke. It became more than just a kitchen; it was a symbol of resilience and renewal, aptly dubbed the "Phoenix Kitchen" by her friends, rising from the ashes of adversity, vibrant and hopeful. Amani's gratitude knew no bounds. She worked tirelessly, her days filled with communicating updates – sending photos, short videos, and heartfelt messages – to her friends, celebrating every small step, every nail hammered, every tile laid, toward rebuilding her family's sanctuary.

Amidst the initial chaos and lingering uncertainty, Amani found herself embracing this unexpected journey of community, vulnerability, and profound personal growth. Her days, once heavy with worry, were now filled with a vibrant blend of relief and surprising joy as she witnessed the astonishing transformation taking place in her family's home. It was a living testament to the unparalleled power of unity, the quiet strength found in shared vulnerability, and the unwavering support of a community that had become her extended family. She had not only rebuilt a home but had discovered a new, deeper meaning of connection and belonging.

One crisp late summer afternoon, as Amani prepared for a video call with her parents, a familiar ritual began. Her gaze drifted instinctively towards a small, artfully arranged shelf that served as her personal altar to home. Adorned with a collection of curated mementos – a faded photograph of her family laughing on a sun-drenched beach, a small, intricately woven basket her grandmother had crafted, and a smooth, cool river stone from their old garden – one item always drew her hand first. It was a small wooden giraffe, its elongated neck and gentle eyes carved with exquisite detail. This wasn't merely a decorative item; it was a cherished symbol, a tangible piece of her roots, intricately linked to stories of resilience passed down through generations, and a constant reminder of the unyielding strength that flowed through her veins. As her fingers closed around its polished form, she felt an immediate sense of grounding, the smooth wood connecting her to the red earth of Nairobi, bridging the vast geographical gap between her past and her present in Langside, Winnipeg.

The soft chime of a video call connecting pulled her from her reverie. Amani's heart swelled, quite literally, as the screen flickered to life, revealing her parents' faces. Their smiles were wide, their eyes beaming with a profound mix of hope and gratitude that seemed to reach across the continents. Her father's infectious joy radiated from the screen as he enthusiastically gestured, offering a virtual tour of their newly renovated kitchen. He pointed out the gleaming new countertops, the strategically placed spice racks, and the vibrant, freshly painted walls, his voice brimming with pride. Her mother's eyes, usually deep wells of quiet wisdom, sparkled with a newfound optimism, a glint of excitement reflecting in her gaze as she nodded along with her husband's commentary, occasionally interjecting with a soft, pleased sigh.

"Fancy dinner tonight?" Amani couldn't help but tease, her voice laced with a bittersweet longing that caught in her throat, yet underpinned by a fierce determination. In that shared moment, the thousands of kilometers separating them seemed to shrink, replaced by the palpable presence of their shared spirit of resilience and an unbreakable love that transcended not only borders but also the very fabric of time. The familiar warmth of their bond wrapped around her, a comforting blanket against the chill of distance.

Later that evening, after the call had ended but the warmth lingered, Amani found herself on the small balcony of her flat, perched high above the quiet hum of Langside. The crisp late summer breeze, carrying the faint scent of damp earth and distant woodsmoke, wrapped around her like a comforting embrace. As she gazed eastward, the sky transformed before her very eyes, a majestic canvas painted with astonishing vibrancy. Fiery oranges bled into the deep, mysterious purples of the vanishing night, swirled with delicate ribbons of rosy pink. This was a view she had cherished countless times before, finding solace in its quiet grandeur, yet today felt particularly poignant, each brushstroke of color a whisper from another sunrise, another land.

The riot of bright colors instantly transported her, igniting vivid memories of her true home, of Nairobi's bustling energy and the boundless warmth that came from her family's love—an unyielding foundation that had anchored her through every challenge and propelled her relentlessly towards her dreams. It was the faint, phantom sound of laughter, rich and resonant, drifting up from what felt like a busy ground floor below, that momentarily blurred the line of distance for her. It conjured memories so vivid they left her heart aching with a familiar longing. She closed her eyes, letting the imagined sounds wash over her, and envisioned her parents, bustling with tireless energy, in the heart of their newly opened restaurant, the "Phoenix Kitchen." It was more than just a restaurant; it was a beacon, nestled within their new community center, a place of gathering and healing. She pictured the gleam of stainless steel, the controlled chaos of a busy kitchen, the rhythmic chop of knives, and the sizzling of pans.

"Amani! You're going to love it here when you visit!" Her sister Malaika's exuberant voice, brimming with uncontainable excitement, bubbled over in her memory. But now, it was so real, she could almost hear her sister calling her name from across the airwaves. Even though her family was continents away, the sheer force of her love and imagination made her feel as if they were right there with her, their hands moving deftly, crafting the fragrant, soulful dishes that had filled her childhood with so much joy and nourishment. She could almost taste the rich spices, the tender meats, the comforting rice.

The image of her mother, her face serene, humming a soft, familiar tune as she meticulously sliced vibrant vegetables - red peppers, green zucchini, firm onions - made a tender smile bloom on Amani's lips. She could almost hear her father's deeper voice just behind her, his movements precise and deliberate as he added carefully measured spices, a pinch here, a dash there, the air thick with their earthy aromas. It was all part of their shared ritual, a dance of flavors and affection, an enduring effort to preserve their rich heritage and share it, not just as food, but as a story, with a new community. It was their profound way to rise from the ashes of their old life's challenges and build something even more beautiful, more resilient.

The imagined laughter, so vibrant moments ago, gently faded into a comforting silence, replaced by the insistent, yet welcome, ping of her phone. With a yearning heart that still vibrated with the echoes of her memories, Amani opened WhatsApp. With a few taps, she was connected to her family back home, the distance momentarily erased by the power of technology. As the call connected, her younger brother Amir's face, brighteyed and eager, lit up the screen like sunshine breaking through a lingering cloud.

"Amani! You won't believe it!" His voice, high-pitched with youthful excitement, practically burst through the speaker. "The kitchen smells amazing! Mom's making her famous curry!" His eyes twinkled with unadulterated joy, the innocence of youth shining brilliantly through every syllable.

"Oh, Amir, I can practically smell it from here!" She chuckled, a genuine, full-bodied sound that belied the physical distance. In her mind's eye, she envisioned the familiar, delightful chaos in the kitchen—her mischievous brother, perhaps already sneaking a taste from a simmering pot, their parents exchanging playful banter amidst the clatter of pots and pans and the comforting hiss of steam. The scene brought a powerful wave of nostalgia, so potent it felt like a physical warmth spreading through her, a comforting, unwavering reminder of home and belonging.

"Are you coming home soon?" he asked, a fleeting hint of worry, a genuine longing, creeping into his voice. "I miss you."

Amani felt a familiar tightening in her chest, a bittersweet pang. "I miss you, too, little one, more than you know," she replied, her voice softening. "But remember, I'm always with you. I'm in your hearts, just like you're in mine. You all inspire me every single day to work harder, to chase my dreams. Just make sure to take plenty of pictures of everyone's smiling faces while you eat, okay? Show me how much fun you're all having."

"I will! And I'll save you some food next time!" Amir beamed, his cheeks puffing out in mischief, a wide, genuine grin stretching across his face.

"Deal," Amani replied, a profound warmth spreading through her and settling deep in her core, as if they had just shared not only a conversation but a comforting meal together, side-by-side. As the call ended, her heart felt noticeably lighter, invigorated by the tangible, emotional connection that defied geography.

Settling back into her coursework, her textbooks and notes spread across her small desk, thoughts of her family danced in her mind, intertwining beautifully with her studies. The vibrant image of the Phoenix Kitchen, a place of nourishment and rebirth, became a powerful metaphor for her own rapidly growing ambition. She felt drawn, with an even greater sense of purpose, to her chosen path of becoming a psychiatric nurse, wishing, with every fiber of her being, to offer healing, understanding, and profound empathy to those who needed it most. Just as her parents were doing for their community with the comforting, restorative power of food and culture, she wished to foster a true sanctuary for the minds in need—

a "Phoenix Kitchen" not for the body, but for souls seeking solace, a place where broken spirits could find warmth, connection, and the strength to rise again.

As she stood there, the sun resumed its ascent, brightening the breathtaking landscape before her. Solitude enveloped Amani, but she knew she wasn't truly alone. Her heart ached for those across the street—there she spotted homeless persons who seemed worlds apart from her own life, yet bore stories resembling threads in her own tapestry. She knew some of those people. She always stopped to say hi, and whenever she had food or coffee to share, she did.

It was time to go to work at Third Cup; she needed a few minutes to talk to the homeless individuals before her shift began. Amani ambled down the well-trodden path toward the sidewalk, her sneakers tapping lightly on the concrete. Having moved to the city nearly two years ago with dreams weaving through her mind—dreams of becoming a mental wellness writer whose words could illuminate the shadows of others' experiences—she found herself challenged by an underlying loneliness, despite the throngs of people around her.

As she passed, she noticed a man sitting on a weathered blanket, a scruffy beard framing his face, with crinkles etched by time and hardship. His name was Elias, or at least that's what the kind-hearted barista at the nearby café had called him when he once acknowledged him with a smile and an offered pastry. Amani often watched, heart heavy, as he gazed past the people rushing by, his eyes holding vast, unspoken stories of loss and resilience.

"Good morning, Amani!" Elias called, his voice warm and weathered like the afternoon sun.

"Morning, Elias," she replied with a soft smile, pausing to share a moment. "How did you sleep?"

He shrugged, a twinkle of humor lighting his eyes. "As well as you can on a bed of concrete. It's all about perspective, isn't it?"

Amani nodded, intrigued by his profound demeanor. "The dawn is beautiful today, isn't it?"

He followed her gaze toward the horizon. "Yes, but the beauty lies in the light that'll catch the waves. Ever think about how the ocean holds secrets?"

"It holds stories, for sure. Like those of you and me," she said, more to herself than to him.

"Then it's a wise sea, indeed. Each wave could tell tales of heartache, adventure, and belonging," he mused, his face softened by the morning glow. "Sometimes we just need to listen."

"Would you tell me a story?" Amani ventured, intrigued.

His eyes narrowed thoughtfully, as if searching through a trove of memories. "There was a time I had a home, a small house with a garden where my daughter would chase the butterflies, giggling as she ran barefoot. That house—though small—held the laughter of friends and family, the warmth of the sun, and the aroma of baked bread wafting from the kitchen."

Amani felt a pang in her heart, imagining the joy intertwined in his words. She longed to write his story, to give voice to the silent echoes of his past. "What happened?"

"Life is a fickle friend, dear Amani. One day you're crafting dream castles, and the next, they're scattered by the winds," he reflected, his eyes cast downward, sadness clinging to his voice. "But that doesn't mean those energies are lost. They live on in our hearts, don't they?"

She contemplated the weight of his words, feeling something shift within her—a dawning realization that home transcended mere possession. "You're right. And what if home isn't about the place, but the connections and memories we carry?"

Elias smiled, his face brightening with newfound understanding. "Exactly. We're all searching for our own versions of home, even if we're drifting far from it. It may not be here, but it's still within us, like a comforting embrace."

Amani's curiosity piqued as she pondered how Elias ended up living on the streets, but she could sense that the story was not ready to be told today. The time felt too fragile, the connection too tender to press further. As she glanced at her watch, a flutter of anxiety took hold—her shift was starting in fifteen minutes, and she couldn't afford to be late.

"I have to go now, Elias. But I'll be back after my shift, okay?"

"Take the light with you, Amani. Share it," he said with a gentle nod, encouraging her.

"I will," she promised, her heart swelling with gratitude.

As she turned to leave, she couldn't shake the feeling that their conversation had changed her. It was as if Elias had woven a new thread into her tapestry—a strand of resilience amidst despair, a flicker of the hope that lay in connection.

The sun continued to rise, illuminating her path as she walked away, mind racing with both the weight and beauty of the stories resting around her. She felt a resolve settle in her—a desire not only to craft words that could change perceptions but to cultivate a deeper understanding of the lives intertwined with hers.

The customers at Third Cup would soon begin trickling in, eager for their morning caffeine and comfort. But she would carry Elias's story with her, reflecting on the slices of longing and hope that spanned across their lives. Today might find her behind the cash register, but she would leave space in her heart to listen, to share, and perhaps, later that evening, to write.

Chapter 08

The sun hung low in the September sky, its warm golden rays filtering through the trees surrounding Long Plain First Nation. As the long weekend arrived, Christina was buzzing with excitement. She had invited her best friends—Maya, Samantha, and Amani—to join her for the Pow Wow, a vibrant celebration of Indigenous culture and tradition. For Amani, a newcomer to Canada, this would be her first true immersion into the heart of First Nations community life.

As they approached the Pow Wow grounds, Amani's eyes widened at the vastness of the gathering. Colorful tents dotted the landscape, and the deep, rhythmic beats of drums resonated through the air, inviting her into the heart of a living tradition. Christina, noticing Amani's wonder, took her hand and led her toward the entrance.

"Get ready for the Grand Entry," she smiled, her excitement contagious.

The four friends found a spot among the crowd, and in a moment that felt both solemn and electrifying, the Grand Entry began. Honourees and dancers adorned in intricate regalia entered the space. A sense of reverence enveloped them as eagle staff-bearers and flag-bearers gracefully dipped their staffs toward each cardinal direction before planting them securely. Aami gazed in awe, feeling the weight of history behind each movement, the echoes of countless generations fueling this sacred celebration.

When the veterans were honored, a wave of energy swept through the crowd as everyone was invited onto the field to express gratitude. Amani watched as her friends exchanged handshakes and warm embraces, their faces lighting up in earnest appreciation. It was a moment that connected not just the present with the past, but also each individual with a shared sense of community and respect.

After the Grand Entry, the atmosphere shifted into spirited joy and celebration. Intertribal dances commenced, welcoming everyone to join—First Nations or not. The vibrant costumes twirled and swayed, reflecting the colors of the earth and sky, while the pulse of the large drum reverberated through each participant, pulling them into a rhythm that felt effortless and exhilarating. Some dances honored missing and murdered Indigenous women, and Amani felt a poignant mix of sadness for the lives lost and admiration for those who carried their memory forward through such powerful expression.

Amid this tapestry of movement, Amani spotted children clad in bright regalia laughing as they learned to dance. Their innocent joy was infectious, beckoning her to join in. Maya and Samantha were soon dancing alongside, their laughter harmonizing with the rhythm of the drum as Amani stepped into the circle, her heart swelling at the sensation of becoming part of something bigger than herself.

They took a break to wander around the Pow Wow, exploring the edges where artisans showcased their crafts. Amani watched potters shape clay, their hands skillfully molding traditional designs, while stone carvers chipped away at rocks, creating arrowheads and tools. She was fascinated, imagining nights around a fire long ago, where stories were passed down through generations, skills lovingly honed.

As they strolled past the vendors, a familiar scent wafted toward them. A food vendor caught their eye and recommended Indian tacos, a treat Christina insisted they should not miss. The spicy meat, fresh vegetables, and smooth sour cream piled on warm frybread were an explosion of flavors that made them all laugh in delight as they shared bites, each savoring the handmade treat.

Amani stood at the perimeter of the Pow Wow grounds, her heart swaying to the beat of the drums that resonated through the air, echoing the very pulse of the earth beneath her. The vibrant tents and stalls danced lightly in the wind, their colorful fabrics fluttering like the banners of a jubilant community. It was a day filled with celebration, family, and storytelling—an elaborate tapestry woven with laughter and movement, much like the fabric of her own existence.

As she piled her plate high with a delicious selection of traditional dishes—smoked salmon, bannock, and moose stew—Amani felt a warm sense of belonging wrap around her. Each mouthful was a connection, linking her not only to the land but also to the generations who had thrived here long before she arrived in Canada.

Families gathered around her, their faces glowing with happiness. Elders shared tales with the younger ones, who listened with wide eyes, their imaginations ignited by stories of courage, resilience, and adventure. Laughter rang out like a joyful chorus, blending with the lively melodies sung by performers showcasing traditional dances passed down through the ages. Amani admired the intricate beadwork on the regalia, appreciating the uniqueness of each piece and the stories they must carry.

"You look like you've just arrived in our land," a voice beside her said, pulling her from her thoughts. She turned to see a young woman with a radiant smile, her dress sparkling with every hue of the sunset.

"I suppose I do," Amani replied with a laugh. "Everything is so beautiful and vibrant. It feels like I'm part of something sacred."

"It is indeed sacred. This isn't just a celebration; it's a gathering of our histories. I'm Kira, by the way," the woman said with a warm nod.

"Amani." She extended her hand, feeling an immediate sense of welcome.

"So, what brings you to the Pow Wow?" Kira asked, her curiosity sincere. Maya, Samantha, and Christina joined the conversation.

"I moved to Winnipeg two years ago," Amani shared, her gaze drifting.

Kira nodded with a thoughtful expression, her eyes sparkling with insight. "I understand. Pow Wow is woven into our identity. It brings our ancestors' stories to life and invites everyone to connect with that heritage."

A gentle breeze danced around them, carrying laughter and melodies through the air. As their conversation flowed, a group of children dashed by, their cheerful voices blending with the rhythmic beats in the background. Amani turned her gaze, enchanted by the vibrant colors of their movements—fabric swirling like the energy of the day.

"Would you like to join us for the next dance?" Kira asked Amani, Christina, Samantha, and Maya, excitement lighting up Amani's eyes.

"Oh, I... I wouldn't want to interrupt," Amani replied, feeling a mix of shyness and thrill at the invitation. Kira's offer felt like a warm embrace. Sensing Amani's hesitation, Kira's radiant smile invited her deeper into the celebration. The sounds of the townsfolk and the laughter of children ignited Amani's enthusiasm. "Dance is a universal language," Kira had said, and in that moment, Amani felt the truth of those words resonate within her.

As they stepped into the next dance circle, Amani took in the joyful faces around her. Each dancer infused energy into the rhythms pulsing from the drummers. The outside world faded away, leaving only the vibrant present alive with spirit. Taking a deep breath, she joined Kira, Maya, Christina, and Samantha in the dance. That breath felt electric, filled with potential.

Kira spun gracefully to her left, the fabric of her dress swirling with the motion. "That's it, Amani! Feel the music!" she encouraged, her eyes sparkling like the sunlight filtering through the canopy of trees above them. Amani couldn't help but mirror Kira's enthusiasm, her laughter bursting forth like butterflies taking flight.

Samantha and Maya danced nearby, their movements fluid and effortless, embodying joy as they interwove their limbs in a playful display of friendship. Christina, with her infectious smile, joined hands with Amani and twirled them both, laughing as they spun. Amani felt an exhilarating mix of freedom and connection, her shyness slipping away like grains of sand through an hourglass.

As the song reached its crescendo, Amani's heart pounded in tandem with the drums, each beat invigorating her spirit. Soon she was no longer mirroring the others but forging her unique rhythm, a blend of her essence combined with the jubilant energy of the dance.

The world around her melted away into a kaleidoscope of shades and sounds—vivid colors of fabric, joyful laughter of children, and the pulse of community forming an invisible thread that connected them all. Amani's soul ignited with the realization that the festival was not merely an event, but a living, breathing tapestry of their heritage, weaving together the stories of their ancestors and the hopes of future generations.

Suddenly, the music slowed, and the drumbeats softened, allowing a moment of stillness. Kira turned to Amani, her eyes shining. "How do you feel?"

"Like I've awakened a part of me that was hiding," Amani admitted, breathless but alive with excitement. "I've never felt so connected... It's as if I belong here."

Kira reached out, taking Amani's hands in her own. "You do belong. This is our space, our history, our celebration. You are part of it, whether you've known it or not."

Just then, a mother called out to her children, and the kids began to form a circle once again, clapping their hands in rhythm, ready for another round of dancing. Kira turned to Amani, her voice filled with anticipation, "What do you say? Another dance?"

Amani nodded fervently, her heart racing with joy. As they joined the children in the circle, the vibrancy of the festival enveloped them all like an embrace. This time, Amani led the way, her laughter swirling with the music, an unbreakable bond forged between her and her new friends, woven into the very fabric of their shared celebration.

In that moment, amidst the laughter, rhythm, and connection, Amani understood: she was no longer an outsider, but an integral part of this beautiful tapestry—rooted in the stories of her ancestors, alive in the present, and hopeful for the future. And as she danced under the open sky, Amani felt the light of her heritage shine brightly within her, illuminating the path forward.

The day was very beautiful, the sun casting a warm golden glow over the vibrant colors of the Pow Wow. Amani and her friends felt the love of everyone around them, a palpable energy that surged through the air like a gentle breeze. The rhythmic beats of drums echoed in the background, blending seamlessly with the laughter and chatter of families celebrating their heritage.

As the last participants began to filter out of the gathering area, Christina turned to her friends Amani, Maya, and Samantha. Her eyes sparkled with excitement, and Amani could see the joy radiating from her.

"Can you believe how amazing this day has been?" Christina exclaimed, her voice bubbling with enthusiasm. "We've seen dancers from all over, and the stories—oh, the stories!"

Amani nodded, her heart swelling with pride. She had been longing for a sense of belonging, and today had filled her with a deep connection to her culture. The colorful beaded regalia, the intricate patterns of the blankets, and the sounds of laughter reminded her of her grandmother's stories about their ancestors—the ones who had danced like this, proudly showcasing their traditions.

Maya, always the dreamer, piped in: "I loved watching the Round Dance! It felt like we were all part of something bigger, something timeless."

Samantha, who had been quiet since the beginning of the celebration, finally spoke up. "I wish we could keep this feeling forever," she said softly, her eyes reflecting the flickering lights of the bonfire nearby. "It's like we really belong here, surrounded by everyone we love."

"Hey," Christina said, a bright smile on her face. "Would you like to come to my apartment? I've got some snacks and drinks, and we can chat more about the pow wow and your stories!"

"Oh, absolutely! We'd love to," Maya replied, her excitement evident. The other girls nodded.

They walked together through the neighborhood, the streets abuzz with post-Pow Wow energy. Christina's apartment was a cozy little space on the third floor, with large windows that offered a view of the tree-lined street below. As they stepped inside, the inviting scent of baked goods—chocolate chip cookies and banana bread—welcomed them.

Wow, it smells amazing in here!" Amani exclaimed, her eyes lighting up as she spotted the treats laid out on the kitchen counter.

"Thanks! I whipped up a few things this morning," Christina said modestly, her cheeks flushing at the compliment. "Nothing like a little sugar to keep the good vibes going, right?"

Samantha picked up a cookie, breaking it in half to let the steam escape. "These look incredible, Christina! You always outdo yourself. Can you give me your secret recipe later?"

"Sure thing!" Christina chuckled, grabbing her own cookie and sinking into the comfy couch. The others followed suit, sinking into the cushions that were adorned with bright, traditional patterns reminiscent of the tribal garments they had seen at the Pow Wow.

As they took their first bites, a delicious silence filled the room. The warm, gooey chocolate melded perfectly with the sweet banana flavor in the air, encouraging the girls to reminisce about the day they had just experienced.

"I can't believe that drum circle!" Maya said, her eyes still sparkling with excitement. "The way everyone moved together like one big heartbeat was magical."

"I loved how people just opened up," Amani added. "I heard so many stories I'd never known before. It felt like we were really connecting on a deeper level."

Christina nodded, her heart swelling with agreement. "And the dancing! Everyone was just so free, so alive. It reminded me of my grandmother, how she used to share the stories of our ancestors through her dances."

The conversation flowed naturally, each girl taking turns to share her thoughts and experiences. They talked about the beauty of their heritage, the pride they felt in their cultures, and how important it was to pass these traditions on to younger generations.

As the sun began to set, casting an orange hue over the apartment, Samantha pulled her guitar onto her lap. "You know, with all this talk of stories and connections, I think I want to write a song about it. Can you guys help me out?"

"Absolutely!" Christina exclaimed. "We can create it together!"

Amani and Maya leaned in, brimming with ideas. The energy shifted as they brainstormed lyrics and melodies, laughter punctuating their discussions. They took turns singing their versions of the stories shared at the Pow Wow, their voices blending harmoniously in the small living room.

After what felt like hours of creativity, they finally settled on a simple but heartfelt chorus that encapsulated the spirit of the day. As Samantha strummed softly, Christina felt a warmth fill her heart—not just from the melodious sound of their voices, but also from the camaraderie and love that surrounded them.

With a deep breath, Christina allowed herself to bask in the moment. She thought back to the Pow Wow, the way she saw the lines on her friends' faces illuminate as they danced and shared. This gathering, now transformed into an evening of music and memories, was far more than just a series of events strung together. It was the essence of community—the power of relating not just through words, but through heart, mind, and spirit.

"Here's to us," Christina raised her glass, filled with sparkling lemonade. "To our stories and our connections. May we always carry this energy with us, wherever life takes us."

"To us!" the girls echoed, their glasses clinking together, the sound ringing like a bell of promise in the warm, cozy room.

With that, they dove back into creation, their voices rising and falling, weaving a tapestry of their experiences into a beautiful song that they would carry with them forever, a testament to the bonds formed and the stories shared at the Pow Wow.

Chapter 09

The air wasn't just crisp; it hummed with an electric charge, sharp and clean, cutting through the last vestiges of summer's languor. It was invigorating, a breath of pure life pulled deep into her lungs, carrying the heady, sweet-earthy scent of damp, decaying leaves – a rich, fertile perfume that spoke of life and decay in equal measure. And beneath that, a distant, tantalizing hint of woodsmoke, perhaps from an early morning fireplace or a neighbor's first autumnal bonfire, adding a nostalgic warmth to the cool embrace. This wasn't a chill that bit at her skin, but a comforting, almost maternal hug, a caress that settled deep into her bones. It was a promise, whispered on the gentle, shifting breeze, that summer's oppressive, lingering heat was finally, irrevocably giving way to something lighter, clearer, more defined. A delightful, almost anticipatory shiver, not of cold but of pure, unadulterated exhilaration, traced its path down Amani's spine, a profound and eager welcoming of this much-needed change.

Around her, the venerable, ancient oaks and towering maples that proudly lined the winding campus pathways were not merely changing; they were ablaze in a breathtaking, riotous spectacle of color. Ruby reds, deep and sumptuous like spilled wine, blazed alongside fiery oranges, vibrant as molten sunsets, and brilliant golds, shimmering with an almost ethereal light. These hues danced and swirled in the gentle morning breeze, a silent, majestic ballet, before detaching themselves and fluttering earthward like vibrant, delicate confetti. Each falling leaf was a tiny, perfect jewel, unique in its intricate veining and flawless hue, joining the ever-expanding mosaic on the ground. Together, they formed a plush, impossibly soft carpet that muffled the sounds of the waking campus, softening the world around her, and crunching with a satisfying, almost musical whisper with every deliberate stride Amani took.

This wasn't just any ordinary Tuesday; it was, for Amani, the official, eagerly anticipated inauguration of her absolute favorite season – the first undeniable day of autumn. And with its arrival, a profound, almost spiritual sense of new beginnings cascaded over her, a wave of clarity washing away the stagnant, heavy sluggishness of a summer that had, at times, felt interminably long and emotionally draining. In its place, a keen, invigorating sense of purpose surged through her veins, a clear direction emerging from the haze. It felt, profoundly and refreshingly, like turning a crisp, clean page in the meticulously kept, yet sometimes messy, book of her life, ready to inscribe new narratives.

Amani paused at a bend in the path, deliberately, almost reverently, taking a deep, expansive breath, allowing the cool, clean air to fill her lungs to their very capacity. It was saturated with that distinct, signature aroma of autumn – the rich, intoxicatingly musky perfume of decaying leaves, a scent both earthy and ethereal, mingling exquisitely with the sharp crispness of the morning dew that still clung to the grass blades. This was a scent infused not just with autumn, but with the very essence of the earth's timeless cycles: life, death, decomposition, and rebirth. It was more than merely a pleasant smell; it was a potent, visceral reminder of renewal, of the necessary process of growth that often required letting go, of shedding the old, tired skin to make way for the vibrant, limitless potential of the new.

And intricately, inextricably woven into that earthy, grounding fragrance, into the very promise of the season, was the exhilarating, almost tangible potential of the semester stretching out before her. New classes loomed – courses promising intellectual stimulation and fresh perspectives, new challenges meant opportunities for growth, and countless new discoveries patiently waited to be made, not just within the hallowed walls of lecture halls but also in the quiet, contemplative corners of the library, where insights often bloomed in solitude. Yet, deeper, far deeper than any academic anticipation, there was another, profoundly more personal reason for her heightened emotions, for this deep resonance she felt today. This afternoon marked her scheduled appointment with Dr. Alex. The mere thought of stepping into Dr. Alex's calm, understanding office brought with it a complex, almost overwhelming mix of profound relief, unwavering trust, and a familiar, yet quiet sense of apprehension. Their sessions, over the past months, had solidified into the unshakeable bedrock of her healing journey – a meticulously constructed safe harbor where she could, without judgment, slowly and carefully unpack the tangled, painful threads of her past, threads inextricably linked to the trauma of rape. It was the sacred space where she confronted the raw, undealt emotions of that agonizing experience, facing her deepest vulnerabilities not with fear, but with a growing, hard-won courage. It was where, painstakingly, piece by painstaking piece, she was learning to stitch herself back together, mending the profound rips in her psyche. This particular visit, occurring on this symbolic first day of fall, felt exquisitely poignant, almost fated. There was so much to discuss: the small, hard-won victories – a night without nightmares, a moment of unburdened laughter, the ability to assert a boundary; the lingering shadows – a sudden flashback, a wave of undeserved guilt; the undeniable, measurable progress she was making; and the difficult, often uncomfortable truths she was still bravely learning to acknowledge and embrace. It wasn't merely therapy; it was a journey of profound, soul-deep transformation, a courageous rebuilding from the ground up. And as she continued her walk, the vibrant leaves crunching underfoot, Amani felt a potent surge of quiet, unwavering determination. She was ready. Ready for the vibrant, challenging embrace of fall, ready for the intellectual demands of the semester, and most importantly, ready – truly, fundamentally ready – for the next, crucial step in her profound and courageous healing.

Entering the third year of her Bachelor of Science in Psychiatric Nursing program felt monumental. The past two years had laid the foundation for her knowledge and skills, but she knew this year would challenge her in ways she had yet to imagine. Twenty-four course credits awaited her, each demanding its own space in her already busy life. But Amani had never shied away from a challenge. She was tough, with a heart that beat fiercely for both her education and the people around her.

The familiar melody of laughter drew her attention as she made her way into the bustling student union. Spotting Christina, Samantha, and Maya at their usual table, Amani's heart swelled with joy. They were her anchors, her sisters in a world sometimes too chaotic and unpredictable. As she approached, they looked up, grinning ear to ear.

"Is it cliché to say you look like a ray of sunshine?" Christina teased, her eyes sparkling.

"Only if you admit we're all just jealous of your perfect hair," Amani shot back, ruffling her friend's glossy waves as she pulled up a chair. They spent the next hour chatting about their summer adventures, the latest campus gossip, and their hopes for the new semester. The laughter spilled around them like bubbles, distracting Amani from the weight of her commitments. But as the conversation shifted to upcoming classes, a flicker of anxiety sparked in her chest.

"Are you really thinking about continuing to work at Third Cup? On top of everything else?" Maya asked, her brow raised in concern.

"I have to," Amani replied, determined to strengthen her voice. "It's not just a job to me. It gives me perspective, you know? Plus, Mr. Jenkins and his friends—they've become my family, too. I can't just abandon them."

The vibrant hues of orange, red, and gold that danced in the fall air affirmed her resolve. Amani's heart ached for the moments spent at Third Cup, the small café nestled in the corner of their college town. Each interaction, each cup of coffee handed over with a warm smile, peeled back another layer of her understanding of the human experience. She needed that connection.

"I get it, but you're talking about a full course load and a job that requires your heart and soul. You have to take care of yourself, too," Christina advised, her gaze searching Amani's.

"I appreciate that, but taking care of myself means staying involved with the people I care about," Amani explained, the determination unmistakable in her voice. "If I can manage it, I will. Besides, it's not just work; it's part of who I am."

"Okay, okay, Miss Independence," Maya chuckled, rolling her eyes affectionately. "Just promise us you'll be careful. We love you too much to lose you under a pile of textbooks."

Amani laughed, but deep down, she understood Maya's concern. It was a delicate balance she walked, like a tightrope suspended over her aspirations and responsibilities. But as she looked into her friends' supportive faces, she felt fortified. Their bond provided her with strength, a promise that they would help each other navigate the challenges ahead.

As they wrapped up their session in the student union, Amani felt a familiar surge of excitement pulsing through her veins. The air buzzed with potential, and as they ventured out, the sun dipped lower in the sky, painting the horizon in shades of lavender and gold.

"Come on! Let's take a quick walk around the campus before class," Samantha chirped, her energy infectious.

The four friends strolled down the pathways, laughter echoing off the brick buildings adorned with ivy. They marveled at the decorations welcoming fall: pumpkin patches, scarecrows, and the tantalizing scent of cinnamon wafting from the nearby bake sale. The world felt alive, wrapped in warmth despite the cooling temperatures.

Later, as Amani settled into her first class of the semester, the room began to fill with familiar faces and a few new ones. The instructor, Dr. Patel, stepped forward, her presence commanding attention.

"Welcome to Advanced Psychiatric Nursing. This course," she said, her voice steady, an authoritative yet calm demeanor settling over the rows of expectant faces, "is designed to push your boundaries. You'll be confronted with complex cases and ethical dilemmas that will challenge your understanding of caregiving, forcing you to look beyond textbooks and into the nuanced depths of the human mind." Her gaze swept across the room, piercing yet reassuring, lingering for a moment on Amani.

Amani's heart raced—a tumultuous mixture of thrilling anticipation and a shiver of trepidation. Challenging? Yes, profoundly so. Necessary? Absolutely. This was her calling, the gritty, demanding path she had chosen. As Dr. Patel, a figure of quiet strength, launched into the syllabus, outlining the rigorous modules and demanding practicals, a potent spark of motivation ignited within Amani. Each word from the instructor, delivered with a measured cadence, heralded a new adventure, a call to deepen her comprehension and empathy for those she aspired to help, a chance to truly become the compassionate, insightful nurse she envisioned.

When the lecture concluded, the fluorescent hum of the classroom filling the sudden quiet, Amani lingered, absorbed in the last whispers of discussion around her. Her mind buzzed with theories and questions, and she diligently jotted down notes and formulated queries for the upcoming weeks, already anticipating the challenges ahead.

"Amani?" A voice, gentle but clear, interrupted her concentration. It was Dr. Patel, who had approached her desk with a warm, knowing smile. The classroom was almost deserted now, only the faint hum of the building remaining. "I sense your determination," Dr. Patel continued, her eyes crinkling at the corners. "That's an excellent quality in this field. But remember, this course delves into challenging territory. Don't hesitate to seek help when things get tough. We're here to support you."

A wave of relief and gratitude washed over Amani. She hadn't realized how much she yearned for that validation, for someone to see her earnestness and her nascent vulnerability. "Thank you, Dr.

Patel," Amani said sincerely, her voice imbued with genuine appreciation. With a grateful nod, she gathered her things and practically ran, propelled by a renewed sense of purpose, to her last lecture of the day: Indigenous Studies.

At 3:30 pm, the sharp, percussive ding of the bell shattered the heavy silence of the lecture hall, its sound piercing and precise. It ripped violently through the oppressive quiet that had settled in, a thick, suffocating blanket of shared sorrow, after nearly an hour of Amani listening, mesmerized and horrified, to her Indigenous Studies professor. The reverberation of the bell echoed against the soaring, high ceilings, seeming to linger in her ears, a metallic tang mingling with the cold, leaden knot of dread and utter exhaustion that had solidified deep within her chest. That visceral knot had formed insidiously during the class—a tangible manifestation of the anguish she felt as she listened intently. The guest lecturer, an elderly woman whose face bore the lines of sorrow and resilience, her voice a raw, unvarnished lament, painted a vivid, agonizing tableau of the systemic struggles and unspeakable tragedies faced by Missing and Murdered Indigenous Women and Girls. She spoke of stolen sisters, unsolved cases, and the chilling silence of state apathy. Amani's stomach recoiled, a gnawing pit of anxiety, profound sadness, and bone-deep fatigue, as if all her accumulated worries had pooled into a small, painful ball, twisting and tightening into a perpetual cramp with every passing, harrowing minute.

Moving her hand slowly, almost supernaturally, to gather her bag seemed an insurmountable feat of strength, a monumental effort that tested the very limits of her will. Each movement felt deliberate, heavy, her limbs weighted, as if her body itself was resisting the effort, refusing to carry the burden further. Her mind, a relentless loop, replayed the faces she'd never seen, the unjust silences, the stories she had just heard, sticking like agonizing splinters in her thoughts, each one a fresh prick of pain. The speaker's voice, a haunting, sorrowful song echoing in the vast space, resonated deep within her—filled with an unbearable sorrow, an urgent, desperate plea that pulled relentlessly at her conscience, a plea for justice, for remembrance. It was thick with emotion, a palpable entity wrapping itself around her, a suffocating shroud that refused to let go.

As she finally pushed open the heavy, resistant doors of the hall, which groaned in protest like ancient, weary guardians, her heart hammered in her chest, a frantic, desperate drumbeat. It wasn't just the everyday nerves she was accustomed to—it was the crushing, invisible weight of the stories she now carried, the heartbreaking narratives of women who had vanished into thin air or been brutally taken too soon. Stepping outside, the sprawling campus loomed before her, a vibrant, lively tapestry of motion and sound, yet everything around her felt distant, alien, almost surreal. Her head felt leaden, a dense fog clouding her thoughts, brimming with phantom memories she couldn't shake, chilling images that played on repeat. The blissful, carefree cacophony of the campus seemed to clash violently, dissonantly, with the storm of tumultuous feelings raging inside her.

She could hear the distant, exuberant shouts of students in the gym, the sharp squeak of sneakers against the polished floors, the rhythmic, booming pounding of basketballs echoing like a percussive rhythm, and the triumphant cheers that moved through the air like a vibrant celebration. It all sounded so loud, so full of unburdened life—so agonizingly far removed from her own heavy, broken heart. This normal, indifferent joy seemed to mock the aching hollowness within her. She quickened her pace, each step deliberate, propelled forward by a desperate need for sanctuary, making her way toward the quieter, dust-laden theatre hall where she hoped to find some small, forgotten peace away from the world's harsh noise, a place to simply be with the immense weight she now carried.

The journey to Dr. Alex's office was more than just a walk across campus; it became a quiet, relentless battle inside her mind, a psychological odyssey through her own fraying mental landscape. The harsh, fluorescent lights in the hallways flickered softly overhead, casting an unforgiving, sterile glow over everything, exposing the raw vulnerability she felt. The amorphous hum of students rushing by, their chatter a jumbled, indecipherable layer over her own quiet turmoil, grew muffled in her ears as her thoughts took over, consuming her. She felt the thick, almost suffocating tension rising within her, like an unspoken storm ready to break, threatening to dismantle her fragile composure. When she passed through the gym's open, echoing doors, she was met with a different kind of noise—a cacophonous, unruly maelstrom of sound and motion, filled with an uncontained energy that contrasted sharply, almost cruelly, with the profound heaviness she carried. The insistent squeak of sneakers intersected with the resonant echo of bouncing basketballs. Raucous cheers and shouts, fueled by friendly rivalry and youthful exuberance, filled the vast space, but they all blurred into a distant, meaningless hum in her mind. Each sound seemed like a fading echo of a world that was lively, carefree, whole—so utterly different from her own inner chaos, her personal abyss. She sought refuge in the quieter, dust-laden theatre hall, a forgotten pocket of peace, where the nostalgic scent of old costumes and faded velvet curtains seemed to hold memories of past performances, moments of profound silence that now longed for her presence, offering a promise of solace.

With each arduous step toward Dr. Alex's door, she made a desperate assertion of will, tightening her grip on her body and mind. It was as if she was trying to carve out a fragile mental space, a tiny, fortified sanctuary, creating a barrier against the storm raging inside her. The crushing weight of the statistics about Missing and Murdered Indigenous Women and Girls (MMIWG)—of countless women going missing or being murdered—hit her with the force of an avalanche. They weren't just cold, impersonal numbers anymore; they were stark, chilling reflections of someone's stolen reality, a life extinguished, a family shattered. They echoed her own deeply ingrained feelings of helplessness and profound pain, resonating with a chilling familiarity. These stories, once distant, had become deeply personal, intertwining with her own history, even though they were about strangers. She thought of women she knew, women who shared her ancestry or her experiences, a vulnerable tapestry of shared vulnerability. The memories came flooding back—a torrent, a cascade of unwelcome images—the ones where men, from her childhood in Kenya to her life now in Canada, had crossed boundaries they shouldn't have, violating her space, her autonomy. Her firm "no," once clear and strong, a desperate claim to her own body, had been ignored—met with cunning manipulation, relentless pressure, or dismissive, infuriating smiles. Those moments had left indelible scars, hollow echoes in her mind, forcing her to perpetually question her own sense of safety and autonomy in a world that felt increasingly hostile.

Finally, she reached the modest door of Dr. Alex's office, a simple wooden panel that felt like a portal, a space she knew had once promised, and truly delivered, understanding and deep comfort. She paused for a long moment, inhaling deeply, a ragged gasp for air. The cool air in the corridor felt like a fragile balm, a fleeting whisper of calm, trembling as she took a shaky, desperate breath. Her chest rose and fell with each exhale—long, trembling, a silent, desperate plea. The air was thick with unspoken hopes, silent prayers for clarity, for strength, for healing. Her mind clung to those hopes as she prepared to step into the room, longing for the wisdom that could help her untangle the Gordian knot of years of trauma. She thought about the persistent, spectral shadows that haunted her—those lingering ghosts from her past, stubborn and unyielding, refusing to dissipate. She longed for someone to shed light on those shadows, to illuminate a path, to guide her through the suffocating darkness that refused to fade. Standing on the threshold now, Amani felt the immense weight of her journey—one arduous step closer to healing, yet still teetering on the very edge of confronting the deepest, most terrifying ghosts that loomed within her. She knew, with a profound clarity, that this moment marked a pivotal turning point, a chance at profound understanding and ultimate release, and despite the fear, she was finally ready to face what lay ahead.

Amani arrived precisely at 3:45 **PM**, the very moment the clinic's waiting room, usually a quiet hum of hushed conversations and the soft rustle of magazines, seemed to collectively hold its breath for her arrival. The subtle shift in the air was palpable, as if the usual gentle current of muted chatter and the distant ring of phones had momentarily paused, focusing its energy on the expectant hush that now filled the space. Before she even had a chance to fully take in the familiar, calming muted tones of the decor or settle into one of the soft, inviting armchairs, Dr. Alex's secretary, Eleanor, a woman whose impeccably tailored demeanor matched her perpetually serene expression and neatly coiled silver bun, offered a soft, knowing smile. It was more than mere politeness; it was a silent understanding, a reassuring beacon in Amani's anxious moment. "Right this way, Amani," she murmured, her voice a soothing balm, gesturing with a gentle, inclusive sweep of her hand towards the subtly lit doorway of the therapy room, a portal to the sanctuary Amani sought.

Amani's heart, a frantic hummingbird beating a rapid staccato against her ribs, fluttered with a complex mix of old nerves and a profound, almost desperate anticipation. The nerves were echoes of past anxieties, ghosts of conversations yet to be had, whispers of vulnerable truths she would soon lay bare, a residue of the raw vulnerability required for deep healing. But the anticipation was a potent counter-force – a burning ember of hope, the promise of a safe space, a haven where she could finally untangle the stubborn knots of her mind, piece by painstaking piece, and find a fragile, much-needed sense of peace. This therapeutic space, a sanctuary she had slowly, painstakingly come to rely on, built brick by painstaking brick through trust and consistency, truly represented more than just hope; it was a lifeline. She inhaled deeply, consciously drawing in the air, allowing the familiar, grounding scent of lavender, subtly diffused and almost imperceptibly sweet, to fill her lungs. It mingled perfectly with the rich, aged leather of Dr. Alex's well-worn armchair, a scent that spoke of countless hours of shared stories and quiet comfort. It was a sensory anchor, a soft landing pad for her spiraling thoughts, instantly settling a fraction of the agitation that had coiled tightly in her stomach, a gentle hand smoothing the crumpled edges of her unease.

As she stepped across the polished wooden threshold, crossing a quiet boundary from the cacophony of her inner world into a dedicated space for reflection, the soft, diffused light of the therapy room enveloped her, a warm, golden embrace that was a stark contrast to the sharper, harsher edges of the world outside. The room itself was a haven of muted tones – soft greens and blues, artfully placed to soothe – and plush comfort, from the deep pile rug underfoot to the inviting cushions on the sofa. And there, rising from his own worn but comfortable chair, grooved by countless hours of quiet presence, was Dr. Alex. His tall, reassuring frame and calm demeanor were a quiet, steadying force. His eyes, deep pools of understanding framed by the crinkling lines of genuine warmth that spoke of countless hours of patient, non-judgmental listening, met hers with that gentle, perpetually inviting smile. It wasn't just a polite gesture; it was a visible manifestation of his unwavering empathy, a silent, profound invitation to disarm, to lay down the heavy, tangled skeins of her burdens and allow them, for an hour, to be shared, received, and processed. Amani felt a powerful wave of profound relief wash over her, a physical loosening in her chest, a letting go she hadn't realized was so tightly wound, as if her shoulders had finally dropped the imperceptible weight they had been carrying all day. She took her first breath of true ease.

Taking her usual seat in the plush, worn armchair that seemed to mold perfectly to her form, a tangible surge of profound relief washed over her, a physical loosening of the knots in her stomach. Here, in this quiet, sun-drenched room, she felt an unburdening, a readiness to articulate the tangled threads of her thoughts and emotions. The therapist, a steadying presence, welcomed her with his characteristic warmth, his voice a low, calm timbre that seemed to resonate with the very air in the room.

"How was your summer?" Dr. Alex inquired, leaning back slightly in his own chair, his posture open and attentive, a silent cue for her to take her time.

Amani responded with a soft, almost nostalgic smile, her gaze drifting momentarily to the sun-drenched window, reflecting on the previous months. A contented sigh escaped her lips. "It was truly wonderful," she replied, her voice infused with a deep, genuine contentment that resonated with the ease of summer days. "I worked throughout the summer, keeping myself relentlessly busy with shifts at the cafe and the library. Honestly, the sheer volume of tasks, the constant need to focus on something external, helped to keep my mind occupied, preventing it from spiraling into those dark places it sometimes goes. But amidst the busyness, I also made sure to carve out precious time with friends whenever possible, clinging to those moments of pure joy and effortless connection like a lifeline. We went to the lake," she continued, a brighter spark, almost a shimmering light, in her eyes, "splashing in the cool water, devoured picnics under the vast, endless sky, and just cherished simple moments of laughter and easy, unburdened company. It was a period of intense activity, yet profoundly enjoyable, and it helped me feel more rooted, more connected to the vibrant pulse of the present. I suppose I truly needed that respite, that breathing room, from everything that usually weighs me down, from the ceaseless hum of anxiety." Her face brightened further with a sincere, almost radiant smile, as if the very memory brought sunlight into the room, indicating the profound significance of those experiences, a lifeline in a turbulent inner world.

Dr. Alex nodded slowly, a thoughtful and deeply empathetic expression settling on his face, acknowledging her sentiments with quiet, unwavering empathy. "That's truly wonderful to hear, Amani," he remarked, his voice gentle and warm, a soothing balm in the quiet space. "Sometimes staying busy, actively engaging with the world around us, aids our coping in various, often underestimated, ways – it can be a healthy distraction, a profound sense of accomplishment, a vital connection to life beyond our internal struggles, a way to re-anchor ourselves." He adjusted his position slightly in his chair, a subtle movement that subtly widened the already inviting space between them, a non-verbal cue that eloquently conveyed his readiness for her to delve deeper when she felt ready. "What would you like to concentrate on today?" he gently asked, his tone inviting her to unburden the true, heavier weights pressing upon her mind and spirit.

Amani paused for a long, heavy moment, gathering not just her thoughts, but also her breath, and most significantly, her courage, which felt like a fragile, fluttering bird within her chest. The easy warmth, the comforting glow of summer memories, began to recede like a tide, replaced by the familiar, unsettling thrum of anxiety that had long been a constant companion. A tremor ran through her, almost imperceptible. When she finally spoke, her voice was soft, almost tentative, a fragile whisper that seemed to battle against the air itself, yet undeniably filled with a deep, aching emotion that resonated in the quiet room. "I want to comprehend why I feel such deep apprehension around men," she began, the words a raw, honest confession that felt like tearing open an old wound. "It's like my body instantly tenses up, my entire being goes on high alert, every nerve-ending screaming a silent warning, whenever I encounter a man I don't implicitly trust. It's a purely physical reaction—my shoulders hunch, as if bracing for a blow, my jaw tightens, aches with the effort, my stomach clenches into a hard, cold knot, as if bracing for a physical impact."

She continued, her voice gaining a quiet, almost fierce intensity, the words flowing with a newfound urgency. "I am acutely aware that some men seem to enjoy teasing or mocking me, especially when my reactions don't align with their expectations—when I don't laugh at their crude jokes, or shrink away as they expect, they just amplify their intimidation tactics, their voices growing louder, their stares more piercing. Occasionally, they intrude on my personal space uninvited, stepping too close, their bodies a looming threat, touching my arm with a touch that feels like a violation, or cornering me in a room, the walls seeming to close in around me, leaving me feeling utterly trapped or profoundly unsafe, like an animal caught in a cruel snare, cornered and helpless."

A deep, shuddering sigh escaped her, carrying the immeasurable weight of years, of countless memories, of endured pain. "Moreover, I carry the crushing weight of past trauma from when I was raped by Usiku. And even when I think I am healing, when I believe I've made progress, taken steps forward, that memory—the searing fear, the profound violation, the consuming shame—it continues to haunt me in ways I can't always articulate, like a ghost that never quite leaves the room. It's a phantom limb of pain, an ache that isn't physically there but is felt just as acutely, always present, just beneath the surface, a constant throb." Her hands, previously relaxed and open, now clasped tightly in her lap, her knuckles white with the effort of control, a visible manifestation of her internal struggle. "I desperately want to overcome this feeling, to shed this constant dread, this heavy cloak of fear, but I can't seem to rid myself of it. It's as if my mind intellectually understands I should be wary, should protect myself, yet my heart is utterly overwhelmed by the sheer magnitude of it all, by the relentless emotional onslaught. I constantly question why, after all this time, am I still so afraid? Why do these feelings persist so strongly, so viscerally, gripping me with such unwavering intensity? It's bewildering and utterly exhausting because, deep down, I yearn to trust again, to connect without this pervasive shield, this impenetrable barrier, but something within me clings obstinately to the pain, to the terrifying memory of what happened, as if letting it go would erase a part of myself."

Her voice, which had begun strong and resolute, wavered precipitously on the final words, thinning to a fragile whisper that barely filled the quiet, empathic space between them. A raw vulnerability exposed. She immediately lowered her gaze, her focus fixed not on Dr. Alex's kind, intent face but on the tightly clasped hands in her lap, as if they held the answers she desperately sought, her knuckles still white with the effort of control, of holding herself together. Her eyes burned, a fierce, internal heat as she battled back the hot, insistent prickle of tears that threatened to spill, a betrayal of the carefully constructed composure she had fought so hard to maintain for so long. Releasing them felt akin to unraveling completely, to dissolving into the very pain she sought to contain, and she wasn't ready for that public collapse, not yet, not in front of him. She sought more than just advice, more than clinical recommendations; she craved a deep, resonant understanding, a profound acknowledgment of the complex, often contradictory, labyrinth of emotions and experiences she navigated daily. It was a silent plea for someone to witness the unspeakable weight she carried, to truly see it, without judgment, without diminishing its profound impact.

Her past experiences had irrevocably shaped her view of men, creating a distorting lens of suspicion and fear that colored every interaction, every perceived glance, turning even innocuous gestures into potential threats. She was desperate to discern whether these pervasive feelings, this suffocating fear, were typical, a natural and understandable response to the profound trauma she had endured, or if they were aspects she could actively alter, could somehow heal from and transcend, finally breaking free from their oppressive grip. She longed, with an aching, desperate intensity that felt like a physical pang in her chest, to feel secure around men again, to not instinctively brace herself for an invisible impact, to not prepare for flight or fight whenever she encountered one, however innocuous the situation. The simple act of existing in the same room as a man, of merely sharing space, had become an exercise in constant vigilance, an exhausting internal battle that consumed her energy and peace.

The moment was thick with unspoken questions, a palpable tension in the air, a silent testament to the raw vulnerability Amani had just laid bare, a sacred trust placed in Dr. Alex's hands. She hoped that, with time and the unwavering, empathetic support of Dr. Alex, she could finally begin to unravel the tightly wound fear that had taken root within her very being, constricting her life and her spirit, suffocating her potential for connection.

She now waited, her posture still, her gaze still fixed on her clasped hands as if they held the answers she sought, for Dr. Alex to speak, to offer some thread, some path, no matter how tenuous, to help her with a move forward through the daunting, seemingly endless landscape of her fear. The silence stretched, filled only by the soft hum of the building's ventilation system and the rapid, almost frantic beat of Amani's own heart against her ribs, a drum against the quiet.

"Amani," Dr. Alex began, her voice a calm and steady murmur, a low, soothing balm against the tumultuous storm in Amani's soul. The words seemed to settle gently, like snowflakes on parched earth. "I am glad you are allowing those feelings to take root, to surface here in this space." Her gaze, warm and unwavering, met Amani's without a hint of reproach. There was no judgment in her tone, only a deep, bottomless well of acceptance that seemed to envelop Amani, offering a rare sense of safety. "There is no quick fix to those emotions and fears you're experiencing," Dr. Alex continued, her voice empathetic yet firm in its realism. "What you have gone through, what you've endured, is a lot. It is natural that it has left its mark, deep and intricate, upon your spirit." Amani instinctively felt a small, almost imperceptible knot of tension in her chest begin to loosen.

There was a comfortable, therapeutic silence then, not empty, but rich with unspoken understanding, allowing Amani to absorb the quiet validation. It was a space to breathe, to simply be with the enormity of her own suffering without the immediate pressure to perform or explain. Dr. Alex leaned forward slightly, her posture mirroring Amani's vulnerability, her expression gentle yet purposeful, like a skilled artisan approaching a delicate task. "Sometimes, the first step towards untangling these complex emotions is simply to name them," she suggested softly, her words a quiet invitation, a gentle hand extended in the darkness. She was inviting Amani to explore further, to excavate and articulate, to put words to the nuanced layers of pain, confusion, and raw frustration Amani held deep in her heart, a jumbled mess she rarely dared to inspect. "Can you tell me more about what that 'profound pain' feels like, for instance? Is it a dull ache, a sharp stab, a crushing weight? Or what specifically makes you feel 'bewildered'? Is it a sense of disorientation, a lack of clarity, or a feeling of being completely lost?"

Amani paused, the sudden quiet of the room amplifying the frantic beat of her own heart. It was a long, drawn-out moment, where the air seemed to thicken, becoming a tangible weight pressing down with her unvoiced struggle, a battle fought entirely behind her eyes. Her fingers worried the frayed seam of her jeans, picking at the denim with a focused, almost compulsive energy – a nervous habit she'd long since developed as an anchor in moments of overwhelming emotion. She could feel the words building, a pressure behind her teeth, as if pushing through a thick, resistant barrier of fear, shame, and the long-held conditioning to keep silent. Then, with a subtle clench of her jaw, she started to speak, her voice a little softer than she'd intended, a slight tremor underlying the words, but undeniably clear and carrying a new, fragile strength. "I feel annoyed and violated when men try to tease me or violate my space."

The confession hung in the air between them, stark and raw, a single, flickering flame in the vast darkness of her unspoken pain. She had, with immense and painful effort, named the feeling, pulled it from the murky, tangled depths of her subconscious where it had festered for so long, and laid it bare, exposed for both of them to see. A profound, almost disorienting sense of vulnerability washed over her now, chilling her to the bone. It was as if she had peeled back a layer of her own skin. She waited, her eyes fixed on Dr. Alex's face, searching for a sign, a flicker of comprehension, an answer. She expected the professional, wise man across from her to deliver the instruction, the magical phrase, the definitive answer: what to do with this feeling, how to make it disappear, how to heal it instantly.

Dr. Alex met her gaze for a long moment, his own expression an impenetrable mask, absorbing the raw vulnerability she had just laid bare. Then, as if the intensity became too much to sustain, his eyes dropped, not in avoidance, but in deep contemplation, staring intently at the intricate, almost hypnotic, pattern on the carpet between his feet. He knew, with a certainty that settled like a lead weight in his chest, the immense weight of the truth she had just shared – a fractured piece of her soul, courageously offered. The session's remaining time, a mere handful of minutes, felt brutally short, a cruel, almost mocking irony given the seismic shift that had just occurred in the room. He recognized the profound, staggering depth of her revelation, understanding intrinsically that it deserved far more space, more careful, unhurried, gentle exploration than the loud, insistent ticking of the clock would possibly allow. This was undeniably a core issue, a foundational stone of her being, a conversation that needed not just to continue, but to unfold slowly and meticulously in the next session, perhaps even several more, layer by painstaking layer.

Yet, he also knew, with a clear professional and ethical certainty that was ingrained in his very being, that he couldn't simply end this session without providing some form of gentle closure, a carefully constructed bridge rather than an abrupt, perilous cliff edge into the following week. That would be irresponsible, potentially re-traumatizing. Taking a slow, deep, deliberate breath, he mentally recentered himself, gathering his thoughts, his composure. He looked up, his expression softening, transforming from unreadable to one of profound understanding, gentle yet undeniably firm in its resolve. His gaze met hers with a steady warmth, a silent promise of continued support.

"Amani," he began, his voice calm, even, and imbued with quiet strength, "Can you name just one small, manageable thing you would like to work on this week? Something that feels like a foundational step, however tiny, to help you begin the process of healing and integrating what we've touched upon today?"

A fragile, hopeful smile bloomed on Amani's face, a stark contrast to the heavy atmosphere that had pervaded the space moments before. "I would like to draw my feelings," she said, the simplicity of her request profound in its implication of self-expression and internal processing.

A genuine, unbidden smile broke across Dr. Alex's face, and a slight, almost boyish jump in his step betrayed his professional composure, revealing his genuine enthusiasm. "I like the idea, Amani, truly. And I cannot wait to see your art," he affirmed, the warmth in his voice palpable. With that, he swiftly but smoothly ended the session, rising to open the door, a silent invitation for her to step back into the world, carrying this new task with her, a flicker of empowerment in her eyes.

"See you next month," he said, extending his hand, his grip firm and reassuring as he shook Amani's hand, watching her walk out, already contemplating the path ahead for their next meeting.

A leaden weariness, profound and insidious, had settled deep within Amani's very bones. It wasn't merely fatigue; it was a dense, invisible anchor, each limb feeling weighted, each thought moving through treacle. The sensation was akin to a heavy, sodden cloak she grudgingly trailed behind her, a monumental effort just to keep it from completely engulfing her. The morning's emotional excavation in her therapy session had left her raw, as though her most guarded internal landscapes had been exposed to a harsh, unfeeling light. Every nerve ending felt frayed. This intense vulnerability, coupled with the relentless information deluge of her university classes – a torrent of facts, theories, and critical analyses that blurred into an oppressive cacophony – had left her utterly hollowed out. It was a sensation akin to her brain being physically wrung out like a damp, depleted cloth, leaving behind only an empty echo chamber, while her spirit felt utterly raw, an exposed and tenderwound.

Yet, the immutable reality of her schedule loomed over her like an approaching storm front. There was no reprieve, no pause button. She still had to report for her shift at Third Cup, a non-negotiable demand of her fragile independence. The very thought of the relentless chime of the cash register, the clatter of ceramic, the insistent hiss of the espresso machine, and the constant, purposeful movement of the café floor already sent a fresh wave of exhaustion through her. It was the steady, unwavering stream of income vital for her very upkeep; for the rent that kept a roof over her head, for the groceries that filled her sparse fridge, and, most profoundly, for the lifeline of sending much-needed money to her family struggling back in Kenya. Their faces, their needs, were a constant, quiet burden that outweighed even her deepest fatigue.

Her mind, still buzzing with the insistent echoes of the session's raw revelations, threatened to replay every vulnerable moment, every painstakingly unearthed memory, every aching realization. It was a relentless reel, threatening to pull her back into the very depths she had just struggled to escape. To ward off this introspective descent, this spiraling fall into the abyss of her own thoughts, Amani instinctively hunched her shoulders, pulling her worn denim jacket tighter against the crisp, biting autumn air. It was a physical act of self-preservation, an attempt to create a small, insulating cocoon. Then, she began to hum. It was a wordless melody, a low, resonant thrum that vibrated through her chest, a gentle, mental shield she constructed note by repetitive note. The simple, almost hypnotic tune filled the space where unwanted thoughts, sharp and insistent, might otherwise gather, creating a small, private world around her. She focused intently on the insistent, rhythmic fall of her footsteps on the cold pavement, letting the humming create a steady, comforting rhythm that quieted the internal clamor as she walked, one foot in front of the other.

Third Cup, she knew, would be her immediate sanctuary, a beacon of luminous warmth and familiar, contained chaos after the quiet, almost suffocating intensity of her day. She pictured its inviting glow, the warm light spilling onto the darkening street, already anticipating the precise moment she'd step through its heavy glass doors. There, among the comforting symphony of the café – the soft, undulating murmur of countless conversations blending into a background hum, the rhythmic hiss and gurgle of the espresso machine, almost a living breath, the sharp clatter of ceramic on saucers, and the occasional, uninhibited burst of laughter – she could finally decompress. The distinct, rich, almost seductive perfume of freshly roasted beans mingling with the sweet warmth of baking pastries would envelop her, a familiar, encompassing embrace she craved. Here, amid the familiar, non-judgmental faces of colleagues and the fleeting glances of regulars, she could simply exist within the comforting, predictable structure of her shift. She could let the external world's insistent, comforting rhythm quiet the tumultuous currents within her, allowing her mind to be occupied by the simple, repetitive tasks of her job. It was a silent pact, a temporary truce: her physical energy traded for their comfort, her inner turmoil momentarily subsumed by their outer peace, a desperate, necessary exchange.

The bell tinkled as she entered, and the familiar scene brought an instant smile to her face. "Just in time for the evening rush!" Mr. Jenkins called from behind the counter, a jovial sparkle in his eyes. "Can't wait to serve up some warmth and smiles!" Amani replied, rolling up her sleeves.

Within the walls of Third Cup, she became a part of a community, discovering stories behind every face that entered. She understood the weight of their joys and sorrows; they, like her, were navigating life's complexities.

As Amani steamed milk and poured coffee, she thought about the long road ahead. The challenges, the classes, the friendships, the laughter—all were woven together in the tapestry of her experience. With each sip she served, she gathered strength for the days to come, grounded in the awareness that she was exactly where she needed to be.

As the first day of fall came to a close, Amani smiled to herself, fully embracing the promise of new beginnings. She looked forward to the challenges ahead but, more importantly, to every connection, every moment she'd share within her journey. Today was just the beginning, and she was ready.

Chapter 10

Amani inhaled deeply, the crisp October air biting at her exposed skin but refreshing her lungs, a sharp, invigorating contrast to the turmoil within. She attempted to find her balance, not just on the uneven sidewalk but within herself, as she walked through the bustling, vibrant thoroughfares of Langside and Portage Avenue. Sunlight, filtered through the thinning canopy of autumn leaves, dappled the pavement, painting the scene in hues of gold and rust. The constant, cheerful crunch of fallen leaves beneath her worn boots provided a rhythmic backdrop, a simple pleasure that somehow amplified the complex chaos she felt churning beneath her ribs.

The streets hummed with life: the cheerful clang of the streetcar bell nearing its stop, the distant blare of a car horn quickly forgotten, and the low murmur of countless conversations. Laughter, unrestrained and carefree, drifted from groups of students spilling out of a nearby coffee shop, their voices mingling with the soft, inviting tunes of jazz drifting from a café with steaming windows. Yet, despite being surrounded by this lively cacophony of human connection, Amani remained profoundly isolated, enveloped in a silent, suffocating bubble of her own making.

The world around her was a vibrant, intricate tapestry, each thread bright and distinct. But Amani felt utterly adrift, a single, frayed strand unraveling from the fabric, lost and unnoticed in its grand design. Lately, Usiku's presence had loomed larger than ever in her mind, a persistent, chilling shadow that managed to eclipse even the brightest, liveliest atmosphere. The name itself felt like a physical weight in her chest, a constant, aching reminder of a past she both desperately longed to escape and, paradoxically, yearned to finally comprehend. A faint tremor ran through her as she remembered the sole purpose of her journey: she was fortunate enough to finally talk about it today with Dr. Alex; it was her long-anticipated October therapy appointment.

Each step toward Dr. Alex's office felt increasingly heavy, a monumental mental struggle between the visceral, overwhelming desire to avoid confronting the past trauma and the deep, persistent ache for healing. Her breath grew shallow, her heart a frantic drumbeat against her ribs, echoing the internal debate. Turn back, escape this, bury it deeper. The thought was a siren song, tempting her with the immediate relief of avoidance.

As she neared the university's Student Center, its large, welcoming windows already beginning to glow warmly against the fading light, reflecting the brilliant, fiery hues of the sunset that bled across the western sky. Oranges melted into deep purples, painting the clouds in a dramatic farewell to the day. Amani paused at the main entrance, her hand hovering just inches from the cool metal of the doorknob. What words could she possibly find? How could she articulate the tangled, suffocating knot of fear, shame, and simmering anger swirling within her? A chilling whisper, Usiku's cruel words, echoed in her mind, insidious and persistent: Wasn't it simpler to remain hidden? To pretend it never happened, to let the past stay buried?

Yet, deep within her, a stubborn, tenacious spark of determination began to flicker, growing warmer, brighter. She recalled the quiet, resolute purpose behind her decision to seek help, a promise she'd made to herself on a particularly dark night. Despite her trembling hesitations, she yearned for healing—not just for the Amani she was now, burdened and scarred, but for the vibrant, curious, unburdened girl she had been before Usiku's shadow had darkened her world. With a renewed surge of conviction, she took a deep, fortifying breath, pushed the heavy door open, and stepped into the warm, bustling lobby. The immediate chatter of students, the clatter of cafeteria trays, and the distant thrum of music gradually faded into a gentler hum as she navigated the familiar hallway, each step bringing her closer to the quiet, private space of the therapist's office.

Dr. Alex's door stood invitingly ajar, a sliver of light spilling into the hallway. The secretary's desk beside it was empty, her chair neatly tucked in; she was likely gone for lunch, leaving a quiet, temporary void. Amani took a moment, consciously slowing her breathing, to smooth her wind-ruffled hair and discreetly wipe the nervous sheen from her forehead. Then, with a soft, almost hesitant rap of her knuckles on the frame, she knocked gently.

"Come in, Amani, you don't have to wait. My secretary just stepped away for a moment, that's why I'm keeping the door open!" Dr. Alex's voice was a warm, steady presence, immediately recognizable and comforting, like a soothing balm applied directly to Amani's troubled spirit.

Amani pushed the door fully open and stepped inside, a complex mix of immediate comfort and lingering anxiety washing over her. The office was a sanctuary of calm: decorated in soft, muted blues and gentle greens, with soft, indirect lighting that cast a warm glow. Uplifting quotes, beautifully rendered in elegant calligraphy script, were framed and strategically placed on the walls, each offering a quiet message of hope and resilience. A large, plush armchair and a cozy, inviting couch, covered in a soft, textured fabric, seemed to beckon her to relax, promising a safe space for vulnerability. Dr. Alex looked up from the notes scattered neatly across his desk, his warm, genuine smile providing an anchor of stability amidst Amani's racing thoughts and internal turmoil.

"Hi, Amani. It's truly great to see you," he said, his voice gentle as he motioned for her to take a seat on the armchair opposite him.

Amani settled into the plush cushion, the luxurious fabric molding around her with a soft sigh of displaced air. Her pulse throbbed a frantic rhythm at her temples, mirroring the frantic hummingbird still caged in her chest. Each breath felt like a conscious effort, weighed down by the immense, leaden burden she carried – a complex tapestry of grief, regret, and unspoken fears that she struggled desperately to unravel, let alone articulate. She opened her mouth, but the words felt trapped, caught beneath the immense pressure. Finally, with a monumental effort that left her feeling weakened, a single syllable escaped: "Hi," she managed to say, her voice barely a whisper, a frail, trembling bridge between her chaotic inner world and the quiet, expectant hum of the tastefully understated room.

The air in the office, usually so calming, felt charged with her unspoken dread. Dr. Alex, seated opposite her in a matching, yet less imposing, armchair, leaned forward slightly, his posture open and inviting. "How have you been?" he asked, his tone a steady, warm anchor in her choppy emotional waters, both gentle and profoundly reassuring, devoid of any hint of judgment or haste.

The immediate, almost reflexive urge was to plaster on the familiar, polite smile and utter the well-worn lie: "I'm fine, thank you." She had perfected that practiced response over years, a shield against probing questions and the discomfort of revealing too much. But as her gaze met Dr. Alex's, she saw not judgment, but a deep, unwavering understanding – a quiet invitation to honesty that disarmed her completely. Her breath hitched. The lie died unspoken on her tongue. "I don't know..." she admitted, the confession a shaky, raw sound, like a first step onto uncertain ground. "I thought I was getting better, or that I should be, but I really don't want to talk about Usiku. Not today. Not ever, possibly." The name hung in the air, a phantom limb of pain.

A small, empathetic smile touched Dr. Alex's lips. He nodded slowly, a deliberate gesture that conveyed profound acceptance rather than mere acknowledgment. "That's perfectly fine, Amani," he said, his voice softer still, like velvet. "We can discuss whatever you feel comfortable with today. There's no pressure to pick up exactly where we left off last session. This space is yours. We can talk about anything you would like us to talk about, or even simply sit for a while if that's what you need."

Taking a deep breath, Amani allowed herself to be open for the first time in a while. "I hate that he still has control over me," she confessed, her voice breaking. "Every time I think I'm okay, something brings him back... everything."

Dr. Alex listened carefully, not rushing to fill the silence, letting Amani's words hang in the air. "What kind of reminders have you been facing recently?" he asked softly.

Amani looked out the window, her gaze following the raindrops as they raced each other down the glass, signaling the onset of summer rain in Winnipeg. The overcast sky reflected her mood—heavy and subdued—as memories of her past flickered through her mind. After a prolonged silence, she finally managed to speak, her voice barely audible.

"The other night, while I was heading home, I heard laughter." She hesitated, nervously twisting the hem of her sweater. "Initially, it felt warm and inviting, like a brief spark of joy amidst the gloom. But then it turned icy, sending chills through me. It turned out to be just a group of students, yet it felt as if they were mocking me, as if they were biding their time to pounce."

Dr. Alex leaned in, listening with keen interest, his expression both empathetic and concerned.

Amani took a sharp breath, memories of Usiku crashing over her like an unrelenting wave. "Back then, Usiku and his friends were exceptionally cruel; they would laugh at me whenever I passed by them at school or on the streets of South B. Even on days when I felt optimistic, their taunts would cast a shadow over my spirit. They whispered hurtful comments behind my back, and each laugh felt like a stone hitting my heart. I felt powerless... just a girl adrift in a sea of mockery."

Her voice trembled as the gravity of her words filled the room. "It was profoundly painful," she continued, her throat constricting with emotion. "I thought I had buried those feelings, but they resurface at the most unexpected times—like when I hear laughter."

Seeing tears stream down Amani's face, Dr. Alex offered her water and tissues. "It's perfectly okay to cry," he reassured her, allowing Amani the space to process her emotions. He waited patiently, his presence a comforting anchor amidst the swirling tide of her distress.

Amani took a deep breath, the cool water soothing as it flowed down her throat. "I keep wondering," she said, brushing a tear away with the back of her hand, "why their laughter still impacts me so profoundly. I'm no longer that girl, but their voices seem to echo in my head, haunting me."

"Maybe it's about more than just their laughter," Dr. Alex suggested gently. "Perhaps it symbolizes a deeper wound—one that goes beyond their mocking laughter. It's about vulnerability, about feeling rejected when you just wanted to fit in."

His words struck a chord within Amani, resonating with the multitude of emotions she had suppressed. "Do you think I'll ever truly get past it?" she asked, her voice wavering, as if the mere thought of healing felt precarious.

Dr. Alex nodded thoughtfully. "Healing isn't linear. It's a journey—one filled with setbacks and breakthroughs. But with each step, you'll find strength you didn't know you had. Acknowledge those feelings when they arise; let them wash over you, but don't let them define you."

Amani took another deep breath, allowing Dr. Alex's words to sink in. "I want to feel free, to not be chained to the past. But some days, it feels impossible." Shifting in her chair, she gazed back out the window as the rain began to soften, the droplets forming networks on the glass. "Why can't I just let it go?"

Dr. Alex smiled softly. "Because it was a part of your life. Your experiences shape who you are, but they don't have to control your narrative. Each drop of rain is followed by a moment of clarity, a reminder that storms eventually pass."

Amani considered his words, the weight of her memories still heavy but somehow less suffocating. "Maybe I need to start reclaiming those moments. Flip them on their heads."

"That's a powerful insight," Dr. Alex encouraged. "Every time you hear laughter, pause. Remind yourself that laughter can also be a source of joy, a connection. Find the laughter that warms you rather than the echoes of your past."

As the rain began to lighten, Amani's heart felt a little less burdened. "I'll try," she said, tentative yet hopeful. "I'll try to find warmth in laughter, to break this pattern."

"Good," Dr. Alex replied, his tone encouraging. "Remember, it's okay to seek help as you navigate these emotions. It takes courage to share your story, and even more so to begin rewriting it."

Amani took another glance at the rain-slicked streets outside, where the resolute echoes of laughter now felt less like traps waiting to ensnare her and more like distant reminders. She would choose to laugh—to reclaim her joy, to step out from the shadows. Perhaps it was time to let the summer rain wash away the remnants of pain, leaving room for new beginnings.

As Amani leaned back in her chair, she felt a shift inside her, a subtle tug nudging her toward the possibility of change. The storm clouds outside matched the tempest of emotions she had carried for so long, but now, as the rain began to taper off, she sensed the first glimmers of sunlight breaking through.

"Do you remember what made you laugh as a child?" Dr. Alex prompted, his eyes sparkling with curiosity. "What brought you joy before the laughter became a painful echo?"

Amani closed her eyes, allowing memories to tumble through her mind like a kaleidoscope. "I loved storytelling," she confessed, her voice warming. "I would tell my friends wild tales of magic kingdoms and brave heroes, my imagination taking flight with every word. Those were the moments that felt... free."

Dr. Alex's expression transformed into one of encouragement. "There it is—the essence of you, the girl who found solace in her creativity. What if you revisited that part of yourself? Writing, storytelling, perhaps even creating a narrative where your voice emerges triumphant?"

His words sparked a small flame deep within her; perhaps reclaiming her joy could start with the very stories that had once liberated her. "That... that could be something. Writing has always been a refuge for me, an escape. Maybe it's time to let that girl back into my life."

"Absolutely," Dr. Alex replied, his enthusiasm palpable. "Through her stories, you can release the weight of the past. Allow yourself to create new memories, tangled up in laughter, joy, and imagination."

With every passing moment, Amani felt lighter. "I think I want to write a story," she said, her heart racing with the thrill of a new endeavor. "I want to write about my experiences but transform them—give them new life. I want to show that the girl they teased is now a woman who deserves to tell her truth."

"That's powerful," Dr. Alex said, nodding in approval. "Writing can be incredibly therapeutic. Don't be afraid to be raw and honest. What's going to matter is that you're reclaiming your narrative."

Taking a quiet moment to breathe, Amani felt inspiration budding, a delicate blossom unfurling after a long winter. "I want my story to inspire others," she mused, feeling a newfound sense of purpose growing within her. "I want to show them that they can turn their pain into strength, just like I'm trying to do."

Tears brimmed in Amani's eyes again, but this time they were not borne from sorrow; they were tears of hope and acceptance. "It feels like I'm finally starting to see the patterns in the rain," she whispered, her voice stronger now. "I want to be that person who can help others find their sunshine, too."

Dr. Alex smiled broadly, his pride evident. "You're on the right track, Amani. Healing isn't just for yourself; it can ripple outward, touching others who may carry similar burdens."

Just then, the sun broke through the clouds, casting a warm golden glow throughout the room. Amani squinted against the brightness, her heart fluttering with a mix of fear and excitement. "What if I'm not good enough?" she breathed, the shadow of doubt creeping back in.

"Remember, it's not about perfection," Dr. Alex reassured her gently. "It's about expressing yourself and allowing your voice to resonate. Every drop of rain you've weathered has built the foundation for your creativity. Embrace the imperfections; they are part of your story."

Amani's face lit up, and she clasped her hands together in her lap. "Then I'll embrace every drop. I'll write through the echoes and the shadows. I'll channel my hurt into something beautiful."

After her ninety-minute therapy session concluded, Amani rose to leave, turning to Dr. Alex with a newfound lightness she hadn't felt in months. "Thank you for listening. I really needed this today."

Dr. Alex offered a warm smile. "Remember, Amani, it's perfectly fine to take your time. You're making more progress than you realize. Shall we plan for six weeks from now?" Amani's insurance only covered therapy sessions every four weeks, leaving students to cover any extra costs themselves.

"Absolutely," Amani responded, filled with determination. As she stepped back into the world, the sounds of laughter from her fellow students filled her mind, but this time it felt less intimidating. It became a reminder of life moving forward, a life she was determined to reclaim piece by piece.

With each step, Amani sensed a growing sense of freedom and control. Although she had a long journey ahead, for the first time, she could glimpse a spark of possibility on the horizon. Her journey was just beginning.

As Amani strolled across the university campus, she allowed the lively atmosphere around her to envelop her senses. The trees were dropping their golden foliage, and the cheerful laughter of her classmates resonated in the crisp autumn air. While this sound had often felt like a jarring reminder of her insecurities, today it represented something new—hope and a sense of belonging.

As she approached the library, Amani took out her phone to check for messages. A few notifications appeared: her friends Maya and Christina had organized a study session for Saturday, followed by a get-together at Saint Frank Café in Osborne village. For a brief moment, she hesitated, but the thought of disappointing Christina and Maya, who had been her guiding lights in Winnipeg, pushed her to respond. They always managed to highlight the positives in her life.

Taking a deep breath, she quickly typed a message: "Hey! I'd love to join the study session this Saturday. Just let me know the time and place." A flicker of excitement ignited in her heart, soon accompanied by a familiar wave of anxiety, but she hit 'send' regardless. With each passing moment, that anxiety began to fade away.

As she stepped into the library, the aroma of aged books blended with the rich scent of fresh coffee from the nearby café, evoking memories of peaceful moments spent immersed in tales. The library, with its towering shelves and cozy corners, felt like a sanctuary, a place where time stood still and the outside world faded away. She headed to her favorite nook, a small alcove nestled between two tall bookshelves, where sunlight poured through the windows, casting a warm glow on her textbook. The golden rays illuminated the pages, making the text seem almost alive, and Amani felt a sense of comfort wash over her. Thoughts of healing and creativity danced in her mind, merging seamlessly with her studies as she opened her book and delved into the lesson ahead.

Time flew by in a joyful haze, the hours slipping away unnoticed as she lost herself in the intricate world of her studies. The library was a symphony of soft whispers and the occasional rustle of pages turning, a backdrop that encouraged her to explore the depths of her imagination. Just as the sunlight began to wane, casting long shadows across the floor, Amani's phone buzzed, pulling her attention away from the comforting embrace of her textbook.

It was a message from Maya: "Awesome! Can't wait to see you! We'll meet at the library at 3 PM on Saturday. Bring snacks!"

Amani felt a warm smile spread across her face at the thought of the laughter and friendship that awaited her. It was a straightforward plan, yet it promised a sense of warmth and belonging. For a long time, she had felt like an outsider, peering into a world that seemed just out of reach; now, she sensed that she could finally join that circle of friends that had once felt so distant.

The idea of Saturday filled her with excitement, but as her enthusiasm grew, so did a nagging sense of doubt. "What if they notice my flaws? What if I'm not interesting or fun enough?" Although she had spent countless moments with Christina and Maya, something inside her was unsettled, and she couldn't quite put her finger on it—it just wasn't her best day.

Yet she remembered Dr. Alex's advice about the beauty of embracing imperfection. "They're just as flawed and wonderful as I am," she murmured to herself.

That night, Amani sat in her small apartment, her notebook open on her lap. The blank pages beckoned like empty canvases, waiting for her emotions to spill onto them. She traced her pen across the paper, scribbling fragments of thoughts, snippets of dialogue, and raw emotions. With every stroke, she poured her heart onto the pages, reflecting on her struggles and her resilience.

The blank pages called to her like unpainted canvases, eager for her feelings to flow onto them. Amani inhaled deeply, sensing the day's burdens lifting as she settled further into her chair. She glided her pen across the paper, jotting down snippets of thoughts, bits of conversation, and unrefined emotions.

"Every drop of rain," she whispered softly, coaxing the idea to take shape in her mind. It was a metaphor that had emerged during a moment of stillness, perfectly encapsulating her journey. Rain reminded her of the tears she had cried, the storms she had navigated within herself.

As she continued to write, she reflected on the fears that had weighed down her spirit—each painful memory like a stone lodged in her chest—heavy and suffocating. Amani recalled the heartaches that had left her feeling empty and shattered—the friendships that had fallen apart, the relationships that had fractured under the pressure of her anxiety. Each line carried the burden of those memories, yet also sparkled with a hint of resilience.

She thought back to the countless hours spent journaling, where she had learned to unravel the threads of her thoughts, reweaving her identity like a fragile tapestry. Each writing session had served as a small fortress against her inner demons, a battleground for the shadows that haunted her mind.

But tonight felt unique. Amani gazed out the window, noticing the trees swaying gently in the breeze. The laughter from the street below now felt welcoming instead of isolating. A smile crept onto her face as she wrote about the friends who had gradually entered her life, healing companions who had revealed the beauty of sharing burdens.

With each stroke of her pen, she infused life into the pages that had once felt desolate. It was like a ritual—each word a brushstroke crafting a new story. The shadows of doubt faded as her words morphed into something real. This was her healing; this was her voice—raw and unfiltered.

As Saturday approached, Amani's excitement bubbled up into a palpable energy. She prepared herself, not just physically, by picking out an outfit that felt like her, but also mentally, reminding herself that she was worthy of connection. Standing in front of the mirror, she took a deep breath, recognizing the reflection of someone who had decided to embrace life despite its uncertainties. When Amani stepped into the library, the cheerful hellos from Maya and Christina enveloped her like a warm hug. The trio nestled into a comfy nook, their laughter blending with the soft sounds of pages turning and conversations buzzing around them.

They swapped study strategies, nibbled on snacks, and reveled in the lively friendship that Amani had been longing for.

"Alright, Amani," Christina said, her grin contagious. "What's been inspiring you these days?"

Amani paused for a moment, then recalled her newfound bravery. "I've been writing... about my journey and how healing can extend beyond ourselves," she started, sharing bits of her therapy experiences and the influence of her creativity. Her friends listened closely, the warmth in their gazes urging her to keep going.

Maya leaned in, her excitement shining through. "That's incredible! You should think about sharing that with a wider audience, maybe even at the campus open mic night!" Amani beamed at the suggestion.

As they walked to Saint Frank Café in Osborne Village, their laughter echoed louder. Once they arrived, they opted for burgers and fries, savoring a wonderful time together.

As they settled into a cozy corner of Saint Frank Café, Amani felt a fresh wave of enthusiasm wash over her. The café buzzed with energy, the comforting aroma of roasted coffee mingling with the mouthwatering scent of burgers sizzling on the grill. The trio claimed their spot by the window, the sun casting warm golden rays over their table.

"I can just see you up there, sharing your story," Christina exclaimed between bites of her classic burger. She leaned forward, her eyes wide with excitement. "You've gone through so much, and your journey is so inspiring. Others need to hear it!"

Amani's heart fluttered at the thought. The idea of speaking in front of an audience had always sent her spiraling into anxiety, but the way Maya and Christina believed in her ignited a flicker of courage she hadn't felt before. "You really think I could do that?" she asked, her voice laced with both disbelief and hope.

"Absolutely!" Maya chimed in, waving her hands animatedly. "And you can even incorporate some of that creativity you've been exploring. Maybe throw in a poem or even a spoken-word piece. You already have the story; just let it come alive!"

As their conversation danced between topics, Amani felt the weight of her uncertainties lift like a morning fog chasing away the night. The notion of sharing her story started to take root in her mind, intertwining with the laughter and dreams that filled the air.

"You know," Maya said suddenly, her eyes gleaming with mischief, "if we're talking about a weekend gathering, I propose a theme."

Amani raised an eyebrow, intrigued. "A theme? Like what?"

"Oh, I don't know," Maya mused, tapping her chin thoughtfully. "How about a 'Glow-Up' party? Everyone comes dressed as their most confident self, sharing what makes them shine! You could even practice your open mic piece!"

Christina nodded enthusiastically. "That sounds amazing! It's like a mini celebration of ourselves. Plus, it gives you a chance to test the waters with your story!"

The idea electrified Amani's spirit. "I love that! It's like we're giving each other permission to be ourselves, to be who we're becoming."

"And," Maya added, her voice conspiratorial, "we can have a 'bravery jar' where everyone puts in something they want to share or something they're scared to do. Then we can draw from it and support each other."

The thought made Amani's heart swell. It was a beautiful concept—a tangible way for all of them to express their hopes, fears, and dreams.

As they indulged in dessert—decadent chocolate cake and caramel-drizzled ice cream—their laughter echoed through the café, warming the space even more. Amani felt as if she were tumbling down a hill, the rush of her friends' support propelling her forward.

"Hey, do you guys remember the first time we met?" Amani asked as they strolled through the soft glow of streetlights.

"Oh, absolutely!" Christina laughed. "I thought you were so mysterious, hiding in the corner with your headphones. It made me want to know you more!"

"Right!" Maya chimed in. "And then once we got to know you, you were like this treasure chest of creativity. I couldn't believe how much you had to offer!"

Amani beamed, warmth rising in her chest again. "It's funny how everything has changed since then—how we've all grown together."

"Growth is our superpower," Christina declared, playfully puffing out her chest.

They started sharing stories about the metaphorical transformations that had shaped their paths: Maya stepping into a leadership position in a campus group, Christina conquering her self-doubt to try out for a play, and Amani reflecting on her challenges and victories as she adapted to life in Winnipeg. And in that moment, Amani understood that this journey wasn't just about her healing. It wasn't just about standing up to share her words. It was about the bonds that encouraged her to rise. With every laugh and supportive word shared among the trio, they all lifted each other higher.

That night, as Amani drifted off to sleep, she clutched the soft fabric of her blanket, warmth wrapping around her like a promise. The world was ripe with possibilities, and in the shared light of her friendship, she felt as if she could truly shine.

Chapter 11

The sun was just beginning to rise over the city, casting a soft golden light across the balcony where Amani sat, cradling her steaming cup of black coffee. The familiar sounds of early traffic and distant chatter surrounded her, but her gaze was fixed on the street below. There, nestled against the brick walls of the shop across from her apartment, was a group of homeless individuals wrapped in layers of worn blankets. Among them was Elias, a figure she had often seen and recognized as the unofficial leader of the small community that formed in their makeshift home on the sidewalk. His silver hair caught the dawn's light, glistening like a beacon amidst the muted colors of the blankets. Amani had watched Elias for weeks now—how he would share whatever food people offered him with the others, how he maintained a sort of ragged dignity despite their circumstances. There was something in his demeanor that commanded respect, an unassailable strength that resonated with her. Today, however, there was a palpable sense of need hanging in the air, as the bite of the morning chill seeped in with the light. She could see the shivering figures huddled together, and something stirred within her.

At that moment, Amani made a decision. She would break her routine and do something to bring them a small splash of warmth in the form of hot coffee—the one luxury that could spark joy in the early morning hour. "It's just a simple gesture," she murmured to herself, but it felt monumental in her heart.

After finishing the last drop of her own coffee, she dashed inside to take a quick shower. The water cascaded over her, washing away the remnants of sleep and leaving her feeling invigorated. She dressed in comfortable jeans and a cozy sweater, letting her long hair dry in loose waves, and mentally plotted her route. The extra time spent on this act of kindness felt like a worthy sacrifice.

With her backpack slung over one shoulder and a sense of purpose in her stride, Amani left her apartment and headed toward Tim Hortons on Broadway. The familiar scent of coffee and freshly-baked goods enveloped her as she stepped inside. After a brief wait, she ordered several large cups of the dark brew, the barista's eyebrows raising slightly as she requested extra cream and sugar packets on the side.

"Coffee run?" the barista asked, curiosity gleaming in her eyes.

Amani smiled. "Yeah, for some friends across the street." She gestured towards the windows, where Elias and his friends still rested beneath their tattered blankets.

With her hands warmed by the cups, she made her way outside and crossed the street. Her heart raced a bit; she had never spoken much to Elias and his group, always hesitant but drawn in by their shared humanity.

As she approached, Elias stirred, his eyes blinking open to the brightening morning. He rubbed the sleep from his eyes and sat up with a polite yawn that turned into a smile when he saw Amani's offering. "Good morning! You're a sight for sore eyes," he greeted, his voice gravelly but warm.

"Good morning, Elias! I thought you all could use some hot coffee to start your day," Amani replied, handing him a cup.

His eyes lit up with gratitude as he accepted the coffee, and soon the others began to wake, drawn by the enticing aroma. "You're too kind," he said, pouring cream and sugar into his cup. "You really didn't have to do this, but it sure is appreciated!"

Amani watched as more cups were passed around, laughter breaking the morning silence. The group shared stories of their dreams and their struggles, simple joys emerging from what could be seen as a bleak situation. Elias spoke about how he once wanted to be an artist, and someone else chimed in about a long-lost job he enjoyed. Amani felt a warmth spreading through her chest, not only from the coffee, but from the connection she had made in the brief moments spent together.

"I have class soon, but I wanted to chat for a little while," Amani explained, her fingers wrapped around her cup for warmth. "I'm really glad I stopped by."

As she listened to their stories and shared a few of her own, Amani realized that this encounter was not just about giving coffee; it was about acknowledging that Elias and his friends were humans with dreams and history, deserving kindness and community.

Soon enough, the time slipped away, and Amani knew she had to go. "I'll be back!" she promised as she stood up, ready to head to her lecture. "Maybe next time, I'll bring some baked goods, too!"

As she walked away, she felt lighter, as if she had gained more than she had given. Leaving the aroma of coffee behind, she glanced back one last time, and there was Elias, lifting his cup in a warm salute, ready to face the day.

Amani knew she wouldn't just see them as a small group outside anymore; she would see them as her neighbors, her new friends, and perhaps her life would intertwine with theirs in ways she had yet to discover. That morning, she realized that sometimes, the simplest gestures create ripples more significant than one might ever anticipate.

As the sun streamed through the large windows of the lecture hall, students settled into their seats, anticipation brewing in the atmosphere. Dr. Patel, with her calm demeanor and insightful presence, examined her class — a mix of budding psychologists, educators, and those interested in mental health. Today's class focused on anxiety and the various factors that could contribute to it.

"Let's take a look at Liz," Dr. Patel began, projecting a slide onto the screen featuring a photo of a young woman with a warm yet tired smile. "Liz is a young assistant professor navigating the complex landscape of academia along with the challenges of family life."

Amani, a diligent student known for her analytical mind, leaned forward, her brow furrowing with concern as she listened to Liz's story unfold. Dr. Patel gave a succinct summary of Liz's journey thus far — the delays in her startup package, the struggles with graduate student recruitment, the battle to gain funding, and the mounting pressure that came with new course preparations.

As Dr. Patel spoke, Amani felt an ache of recognition in her heart. Juggling responsibilities felt all too familiar; it mirrored her own experience of balancing her studies with a part-time job and personal commitments. "She's doing too much," Amani thought, her mind flashing back to her own recent moments of overwhelm.

Dr. Patel continued, detailing Liz's apprehensions—her concerns about student debt, the desire to contribute more to her department through committee work, and the pressures of learning a new language to support her child's education. At the mention of Liz's partner struggling to find stable employment, Amani's gut twisted with empathy. She could sense the weight Liz was carrying, and it only grew heavier when Dr. Patel brought up the impending reappointment application.

"Can you imagine receiving such an email?" Dr. Patel asked, pausing to look around the room. "Liz wonders about her future at the university and whether her chair has concerns about her performance."

Amani's mind raced with thoughts. "How can we create a healthy environment for Liz?" Dr. Patel prompted, facilitating a discussion around solutions. But deep down, Amani found herself wondering why Dr. Patel had chosen this case study. Was it a lesson for her to heed the importance of balance?

The ensuing discussion was lively. Some students suggested creating a mentorship program for new faculty members, while others highlighted the essential need for mental health resources on campus. They proposed regular check-ins with department chairs or colleagues, encouraging a culture of support rather than competition.

Still, Amani felt a sense of frustration bubbling inside her. "What about Liz's happiness? What about her feeling fulfilled, not just as an academic, but as a wife and mother?" she blurted out, her voice resonating with urgency. "She needs time for herself—to recharge, to breathe!"

Dr. Patel nodded thoughtfully, recognizing the depth of Amani's insight. "You're absolutely right, Amani," she replied, her voice steady. "Creating an environment that supports mental wellness isn't just about alleviating stressors; it's also about valuing and nurturing each individual's holistic well-being."

The lecture hall emptied slowly, students drifting out like leaves blown away by a gentle breeze. Amani remained seated for a moment longer, her fingers tracing the lines of her notes, but her mind was already adrift. "Perhaps I need to create my own strategy," she mused, her heart racing with the possibilities she could envision. Limit commitments, manage expectations, and find joy in small victories—it was a roadmap that shimmered with promise.

But even as she pondered her newfound strategy, a familiar knot formed in her stomach. Work at Third Cup consumed her evenings, lectures took over her days, and the weight of being an international student played heavy against her shoulders. The pressure of deadlines, assignments, and the constant need to prove herself gnawed at her spirit. With each step, the comfortable rhythm of her day-to-day life seemed more like an uphill battle.

As she gathered her books and notebooks, Amani weighed her options, nearly convinced that she could juggle it all. The thought of meeting Maya or Dr. Patel made her stomach twist. Their well-meaning concern felt like an uninvited shadow that threatened to engulf her. "Slow down," they would say, their voices laced with genuine care but utterly unhelpful. Amani didn't want to hear it. She was more than capable of managing her coursework and pushing through her shifts at the café. She had no choice; she needed the money.

Stepping outside, she breathed in the crisp afternoon air, the wind wrapping around her like an embrace. The world beyond the lecture hall felt invigorating, filled with promise and possibility. Each stride took her farther from the confines of her thoughts and closer to her self-imposed deadlines. She would show them; she didn't need to be coddled or cautioned. She would redefine her boundaries in the way only she could.

But the reality of the world waiting for her at the café loomed large. Customers were fickle, often impatient, many too absorbed in their screens to offer her a passing glance. Every time the bell over the door jingled, it reminded her that she needed to perform, to smile, to serve, while internally battling the exhaustion that settled slowly in her bones.

The late afternoon sun cast long shadows as she entered Third Cup, the familiar scent of coffee beans grounding her momentarily. Her manager, Alex, greeted her with a wide smile, and for a second, she felt the warmth of camaraderie. She worked with a small team of almost-friends, and laughter frequently rang through the shop. Amani reminded herself—small victories.

As she poured coffee for a regular meal, her thoughts danced back to her earlier contemplation. What did managing expectations mean for her, anyway? She could start small. Maybe she would limit herself to two extra shifts a week instead of three. Or perhaps she would carve out fifteen minutes a day to journal her thoughts. Every little victory might pave the way for something larger.

The evening rush faded, and as she swept the floor, Amani caught a glimpse of herself in the reflection of the café's glass—the girl who dreamed of travel and independence, navigating a path of study and work. She paused, realizing that resilience wasn't only about relentless forward motion; it was also about recognizing one's own limits and adjusting course when necessary.

When her shift ended, Amani walked home under a canopy of stars, the world quieter now, and her resolve strengthening. She would not drown, and she would not ask anyone to pull her back. Instead, she would build her own strategy—layer by layer, day by day.

In the coming days, she shifted her focus. Emphasizing the joy of connecting with her customers, sharing small stories, and finding meaning in the day-to-day banter made the hours at Third Cup feel less like a grind and more like an adventure. And as her studies continued, rather than racing against time, she began to embrace each lecture, savoring the moments in which knowledge unfolded. Amani chose that evening while gazing at the stars to make a commitment to herself—one that echoed her new mantra: balance. She could be a student, a worker, a dreamer, and still find joy, but it required a delicate dance of self-acceptance and the courage to say no when necessary. In the end, it wasn't just about getting through; it was also about enjoying the journey. It was the act of navigating the chaos that painted her path vibrant, giving her every reason to smile at the life she was building, one small victory at a time.

<h1 style="text-align:center">Chapter 12</h1>

Amani sat cross-legged on her bedroom floor, textbooks strewn around her like fallen leaves. The soft golden light of the evening streamed through her window, casting a warm glow that contrasted with her fatigue. She had been looking forward to her shift at Third Cup, the comforting hum of the café a welcome distraction from the relentless grind of studies. But tonight, all she craved was solitude—just her notes, her thoughts, and the memories that seemed to bubble up from the depths of her mind unbidden.

The exam loomed large, its presence felt in the pit of her stomach, but as she cracked open her textbook, her thoughts drifted beyond the page. Images of the Masai Mara sprawled out before her mind's eye like a vivid painting, vibrant and alive. It was a trip she had yearned for throughout months of COVID lockdown, and now that the world had reopened, her family had seized the moment to escape the concrete jungles of Nairobi.

She could almost hear the engine roar of the small aircraft as it took off, cutting through the clear Kenyan skies. The giddiness of the adventure rushed back, recalling the sense of wonder that flooded her as they soared over the patchwork quilt of land dotted with acacia trees and meandering rivers. Amani could still feel the wind whipping through her hair, the thrill dancing in her veins. Below, the vast landscapes of the Masai Mara unfolded, magnificent and unblemished, a stark contrast to the busyness of daily city life.

With each passing minute in the air, Amani's smile grew wider, her heart lighter. She glanced around at her family, her father's eyes sparkling with excitement, her mother bursting with happiness, and her younger brother gazing out the window in awe. It was a moment stitched together with laughter and anticipation, a reprieve from the fears and uncertainties that had overshadowed their lives just weeks before.

As the plane began its descent, Amani pressed her forehead against the cool glass, watching the earth rise up to meet them. She could feel the joy bubbling within her, the thrill of open spaces beckoning her to forget the confined walls of their home that had become too familiar. She knew, now, with every heartbeat, that the Masai Mara would become a sacred sanctuary of freedom—their family's first step back into adventure.

Touching down on the airstrip felt like a rebirth. The scent of earth and wild grass filled her lungs as they stepped out, the warm breeze wrapping around her like a comforting embrace. Amidst the rich hues of warm browns and lush greens, she felt alive, as if the landscape itself was welcoming them home. The backdrop was nothing short of extraordinary—a vast wilderness teeming with wildlife, the symphony of nature surrounding them unleashing a spirit of adventure that no pandemic could suppress.

The golden hues of the late afternoon sun cast a warm glow over the plains as Amani and her family drove through the expansive wilderness. The chatter from the Jeep filled the air, mingling with the rustling grasses and distant calls of wildlife. Amani clutched her camera tightly, determined to capture every breathtaking moment. As they ventured deeper into the reserve, the seasoned guide shared stories of the land's rich biodiversity and the delicate balance of life within it. Amani listened intently, her heart racing with each revelation. When the Jeep finally came to a halt, they found themselves face-to-face with a majestic pride of lions lounging lazily under the shade of a fig tree. She watched in awe as the lioness groomed her cubs, the playful kittens tumbling over one another, their tiny roars breaking the serene ambiance.

"This is amazing," she whispered, glancing at her family who shared her excitement. Her father snapped pictures, while her mother pointed out the subtle nuances of the animals' behavior. Even her brother, typically restless, was mesmerized by the scene before them.

As the sun dipped lower in the sky, painting the horizon with streaks of orange and purple, the guide motioned for them to be quiet. Amani held her breath, the world around her fading into a hushed reverence. When a distant male lion let out a thunderous roar, resonating through the stillness, she felt a thrill of fear and wonder ripple through her body. It was a raw, unfiltered moment, a reminder of the power and beauty of nature.

Their game drive continued, the evening cooling as they witnessed the sky transform into a canvas of colors. Amani felt an overwhelming sense of gratitude for this experience—the opportunity to be part of something so grand, so removed from the chaos of her life. This trip was a balm for her soul, a reminder of the world's vastness and the sheer joy of connection—both with her family and the stunning wilderness around her.

As they returned to the campsite under the blanket of stars, laughter echoed around the fire. They shared stories of their favorite animals of the day and planned their next adventure in the Mara. Amani knew this trip would leave an indelible mark on her heart, a cherished memory of freedom, discovery, and the unbreakable bond of family. Little did she know that this was just the beginning of her deep-rooted love for nature and wildlife that would shape her future in ways she could never imagine. For now, the exam could wait.

The following day the driver drove them to the heart of the Masai Mara, where the golden grass rolled like waves beneath a bright and watchful sky. Amani found solace and magic. The driver slowed the vehicle as they approached a small watering hole, the perfect spot to witness the daily rhythms of the animal kingdom. Eagerly, they grabbed their cameras, eyes glued to the scene unfolding before them. A herd of elephants punctuated the landscape, their majestic forms silhouetted against the sun, while a few graceful impalas pranced nearby, ever vigilant for predators.

"Look over there!" one of the travelers exclaimed, pointing toward the horizon. The others turned to see a pride of lions lounging lazily under the shade of a solitary acacia tree, their golden coats blending seamlessly with the grass. The sound of a distant roar sent shivers of thrill down their spines, a reminder that they were truly in the wild.

As the afternoon wore on, they watched in awe as a majestic cheetah, poised and powerful, vanished into the tall grass, seemingly oblivious to the onlookers. Time seemed to stand still as they absorbed the beauty and raw power of nature surrounding them.

Later, as the sun began to dip beyond the horizon, painting the sky in hues of orange and pink, the group gathered around a small campfire. They shared stories and laughter, the warmth of the fire contrasting with the cool evening air. The sounds of crickets chirping and the occasional rustle of bushes reminded them that they were not alone out there; the wilderness was alive.

Some of her favorite moments unfolded under the sprawling branches of an acacia tree. They would gather as a family, their laughter intertwining with the soft rustle of leaves as they shared meals crafted from the bountiful earth around them. Stories would flow, each recounted tale infused with the warmth of kinship. Amani would listen, sketching vivid pictures of their lives back in Nairobi—dreams of career aspirations, memories of bustling marketplaces, and late-night conversations that stretched until dawn. In these stories, they found a tether to their past, a thread that connected them to the vibrant city, even as the wildness of nature enveloped them.

But each moment, no matter how beautiful, carried a bittersweet reminder of the lockdowns that had confined them to their homes for what had felt like eternity. The walls of isolation had smothered them, and though they had shared laughter and love through screens, nothing could replace the depth of experiences shared in the wild. They had traversed the landscape of fear and uncertainty, emerging resilient and united, ready to celebrate the splendor around them.

As they explored the vastness of the Mara together, Amani understood that each sighting of a lion pride lounging in the tall grass or a cheetah sprinting across the plain renewed their bond as a family. The thrill of the hunt, the beauty of survival, all played out in front of their eyes, a reminder that life was precious and transient—a lesson they had all learned too well during their months of separation.

In the hush that followed a day filled with adventure, Amani felt a shift within her; the Masai Mara was not merely a destination. It stood as a sacred signpost, indicative of her family's journey—one of exploration, discovery, and triumph. Each day out in the wild ignited within her a profound appreciation for life in its purest form. The sunsets, the shared meals, and the laughter echoed in her heart, reverberating like a drumbeat of affirmation: life was meant to be lived, to be explored, and to be celebrated.

Amani adjusted her glasses and let out a soft sigh as she closed her eyes for a moment. The faint rustle of leaves outside her window whispered of the evening breeze, and she could almost hear the soft murmur of the African wilderness, a distant echo of her recent trip to the Masai Mara. Just days ago, she had been surrounded by vast grasslands, vibrant colors, and the raw beauty of nature that only seemed to exist there. It was a stark contrast to the dimly-lit confines of her study, but it was a comfort she clung to.

The trip had been a whirlwind of experiences. From the moment Amani's feet touched the soil of the reserve, her spirit ignited with energy. She had witnessed a pride of lions lounging lazily under the acacia trees, their golden fur illuminated by the sun. She had watched herds of elephants meandering gracefully, their presence commanding and gentle. Each moment had etched itself into her heart, planting seeds of inspiration that would grow with her determination to excel in her studies.

As she packed her bags, Amani felt a sense of nostalgia wash over her. The vibrant sunsets, the thrill of spotting wildlife, and the warmth of the local community had woven unforgettable memories into her heart. Each day had brought new adventures, whether it was watching a lioness and her cubs or being surrounded by the sounds of nature as she sipped chai with Maasai villagers.

She recalled the laughter shared with her guide, who had become a family friend, and the stories of the land that painted a picture of rich culture and history. Amani knew that she had left a piece of herself in the Masai Mara, and this trip was just the beginning of a lifelong connection.

As she boarded the plane, her heart soared with excitement and anticipation for her next journey back to the wilds of Kenya. Until then, she would carry the spirit of the Mara with her, eager to share her stories and inspire others to experience the beauty she had encountered. The Masai Mara was not just a destination; it had become a cherished part of her soul.

Now, as she flipped open her textbook, the words began to blur together. Amani shook her head, fighting against the inertia of fatigue. She remembered the vibrant colors of the sunset over the Mara River, how the sky transformed into hues of orange and purple, a breathtaking tableau that wrapped around her like a comforting shawl. The beauty of it lingered in her pensive heart, pushing her to find a way to channel that inspiration into her work. "Focus," she whispered to herself, fingers dancing over her notes. She started to scribble down the main concepts she needed to master for her upcoming exams, but the numbers danced on the page. In a moment of frustration, she closed the book and leaned back in her chair, allowing the memories to wash over her once more.

That night, under the starlit sky of the Mara, Amani had sat with her fellow travelers, sharing stories and laughter. The air was charged with hope and possibility as they talked about their dreams, ambitions, and challenges they faced back home. Amani had felt a sense of camaraderie, a tether to others that gave her strength. Remembering their encouragement fueled her resolve to push through this moment of doubt.

With renewed determination, she opened her book again, this time with the intention to conquer it, page by page. The math equations that had once seemed daunting began to feel like the puzzles she had encountered on her journey.

With every smile that crept across her face—from the memory of laughing with her friends as they traveled to the look of awe shared with strangers at the sight of an elusive leopard—Amani felt the chaos of stress begin to ease. This was more than studying; this was a celebration of her growth and resilience.

Amani drifted again, her mind a gentle tide pulling her back to sunlit afternoons spent at Alliance Girls School. The green grounds and brightly-painted dormitories faded in and out of focus, but one figure remained clear amidst the marsh-mallowed edges of her memories: Grace Nyamboki.

Amani could almost hear Grace's laughter, a melody that danced in the air like birds teasing the sky. Grace was the kind of girl who could turn even the most mundane moment into an occasion. With wild curls framing her face, she had a way of making every story seem like a grand adventure. Whether it was a school project or a simple game of double-dutch, Grace's vibrant energy made everything more enjoyable.

After school, the two friends would often escape the rush of homework and bustling dorm life. They would traverse the flower-laden paths, their laughter echoing against the school's red bricks. One afternoon, as they laid on the grass, watching clouds morph into fantastical shapes, Grace suddenly sat up, her eyes sparkling with mischief.

"Amani, let's start a club!" she declared, her voice bubbling with enthusiasm.

"What kind of club?" Amani asked, propping herself up on her elbows.

"A smile club! We'll make people smile every day." Grace's eyes gleamed mischievously as she sketched an imaginary logo in the air.

"We could do it secretly. Leave little notes in their lockers, or do silly dances in the cafeteria!"

Before Amani could respond, Grace was off on a streak, crafting plans that twinkled with spontaneity. For weeks, they became the architects of joy, slipping cheerful notes and drawings to classmates who needed brightening up. The smiles they collected acted like currency, and Amani found herself more enchanted by the joy they created rather than the attention it garnered.

But there was one memory that always stood out—a cool evening when the school hosted a fundraising event. The hall buzzed with nervous energy. Grace stood on stage, fidgeting with her microphone, trying to calm her jitters. Amani could see the flicker of uncertainty in her friend's eyes.

"Amani, what if I forget my lines? What if they laugh at me?" Grace whispered frantically, pacing like a caged bird.

"Just be yourself, Grace. No one is here to judge you. They love you for who you are," Amani reassured, feeling a surge of support for her friend.

Grace nodded, but it was clear that her nerves hadn't dissipated. As the spotlight beamed down, she stepped forward. The audience fell silent, and a deep breath later, Grace let her heart lead the way. She started speaking about kindness and the power of connection, weaving in anecdotes from their smile club escapades. Laughter erupted as she mimicked their failed attempts at dance moves, and soon everyone was caught in a whirlwind of happiness.

When she finished, the hall erupted in applause, and Amani felt tears prick her eyes as she saw Grace shine, her earlier fears evaporating like morning fog. In that moment, Amani realized that Grace could light up the darkest room simply by being true to herself.

Now, tucked away in the folds of her memories, Amani remembered that night with a warmth that felt like a cozy blanket on a winter's day. Amani missed those exuberant days with Grace, but she also found comfort in knowing that the world had been a little brighter for their laughter and their dreams.

Returning to her studies, Amani experienced an unexpected rush of optimism, reminiscent of the exhilarating surge just before a wave of motivation washed over her. The relentless grip of exhaustion finally loosened, and she felt prepared to confront the pharmacology exam that had loomed above her like a gloomy shadow for weeks. Sunlight poured into her small, cluttered room, illuminating the various textbooks and scattered notes sprawled across her desk.

The previous night had been a struggle through fatigue as she desperately crammed details about enzyme interactions and drug mechanisms into her mind. Each passing minute felt stretched, and every concept appeared as insurmountable as a towering mountain. At one point, tears almost escaped her as she found herself engulfed by a sea of flashcards and highlighters. However, with the break of dawn, her weariness seemed to dissolve, receding like a bad dream chased away by morning light.

Sipping her chamomile tea, she let the warmth envelop her as she immersed herself in the realm of pharmacology. The weathered pages felt like old friends, sharing wisdom without judgment and encouraging her to explore deeper. It was as though the textbooks recognized the effort she had invested to get here and were finally ready to reveal their secrets.

Her imagination wandered as she visualized molecules swirling and dancing like performers in a grand ballroom—gliding through the bloodstream and weaving gracefully between cells, each with a purpose, each sharing a unique story. She could envision adrenaline racing through the body in preparation for a sprint while neurotransmitters conveyed messages of joy or pain, depending on the circumstance.

A recollection of last week's study session with Maya and Christina drifted into her mind, their laughter brightening the otherwise dim corners of the library. Maya had been pouring over her notes, a frustrated expression on her face. "How do you even remember all this?" she had grumbled, brushing her hair back. "It feels like a whole new language!"

"But it is a language," Amani had responded, feeling a spark ignite within her. "These medications are characters in a story we're learning to narrate. Each mechanism of action, each side effect—it all fits together like pieces of a complex puzzle."

Maya had rolled her eyes but smiled, recognizing the enthusiasm in Amani's voice. It was contagious, especially when Christina eagerly stepped in to quiz them both, testing their recall of vital facts. "What's the antidote for acetaminophen overdose?" she had asked, excitement written all over her face.

"N-acetylcysteine!" they both chimed in, the words bursting from them like a triumphant shout. It felt empowering to reclaim knowledge that once felt distant.

Fueled by the rekindled spirit of camaraderie, Amani dove back into her textbooks, purposefully navigating the lessons. Each pharmacokinetic principle sprang to life, akin to a theatrical performance unfolding in her mind. The liver transformed into a bustling factory metabolizing drugs, while the kidneys acted as diligent workers filtering out toxins to preserve balance.

Late in the afternoon, her phone buzzed, disrupting her serene study session. "Hey, want to study together tomorrow before the exam? Bring the tea!" Maya texted. Amani smiled, reflecting on how her world had shifted in such a brief time. The prospect of studying together filled her with warmth; it was a reassuring reminder that she wasn't alone in this endeavor.

"Of course!" she replied, her heart grateful for her friends. She glanced at her textbook, still energized by the thought of collaboration. The narratives of each drug and their interactions, the delicate balance maintained in the human body—these were no longer just theoretical concepts. They had transformed into lessons in empathy, teaching her about resilience and the human experience while deepening her understanding of medicine.

Time flew by, and the hours were both productive and satisfying. The sun dipped lower in the sky, bathing her room in warm shades of amber and gold. Amani took breaks to clear her mind, gazing out the window at the magnolia tree that stood firmly in her yard, its branches swaying gently in the wind. She thought of her classmates, some likely lounging while others buried themselves in their own textbooks, sharing the same dreams and challenges.

In the back of her mind, she felt lingering anxiety, but it no longer felt suffocating. It resembled the weight of fatigue—something she could shed with determination and clarity. Her worries about performance faded away, replaced by an exhilarating sense of anticipation. Tomorrow wasn't just about an exam; it represented a culmination of her hard work and passion.

As evening settled in, she lit a lavender-scented candle, filling the room with a comforting aroma. Amani reviewed her notes one last time, pride swelling within her as pharmacological terms effortlessly twirled across her mental stage. With every term recalled, her confidence blossomed further.

As sleep began to creep in, she crafted a final plan for the morning, setting her alarm and organizing her exam materials. Tucking herself under the covers, a calming sense of peace enveloped her. Drifting off into slumber, she felt assured that she had prepared thoroughly and, no matter the outcome, she had confronted her fears directly.

Softly, the clock ticked in the background, its rhythm synchronized with her heartbeat. Tomorrow would come, and she would rise, ready to meet the challenges ahead, equipped with knowledge and a revitalized spirit. Embracing that thought, she surrendered to sleep, blossoming into the possibilities awaiting her at dawn.

Before she knew it, dawn beckoned her into a new day. Amani looked around her room, now bathed in the gentle light of morning, mirroring her resolve. She felt lighter, as though the burdens she had carried had been replaced by an exhilarating sense of purpose.

Chapter 13

Amani always looked forward to Saturdays, as they were the perfect balance of work and play. She had an early morning shift at Third Cup, where she enjoyed the lively atmosphere and the interesting customers. After work, she had the rest of the day to herself or to spend with her friends. On this particular late fall Saturday, Amani had plans with her friends Christina, Maya, and Samantha. They were going to visit the Birdhill Provincial Park, which was just twenty minutes north of Winnipeg.

As they walked, the sun dipped lower in the sky, casting a warm golden hue over everything. Amani, feeling a wellspring of joy, suggested they play a game of "I Spy" to keep the energy up. Christina eagerly jumped in, pointing out everything from the vibrant red and orange leaves to the squirrels scampering about. Samantha, always the jokester, made up silly clues that had everyone bursting into laughter.

The group reached a small clearing where they could catch their breath and take in the breathtaking view. The landscape stretched out before them, a patchwork of colors ranging from deep crimson to sunny yellow. Maya, inspired by the scenery, rummaged through her backpack and pulled out her sketchpad, inviting everyone to sit still for a moment while she captured the essence of the scene.

As Maya focused on her drawing, Amani and Christina engaged in a gentle debate about their favorite seasons. Amani loved autumn for its crisp air and cozy sweaters, while Christina championed spring's blooms and fresh starts. Samantha, always the peacemaker, declared that they were lucky to experience the beauty of every season.

After a while, they began their descent back to where they had set up their picnic. On the way, they spotted an old wooden swing hanging from a sturdy branch of an oak tree. Without hesitation, they ran over, Amani feeling a rush of nostalgia as she took her place on the swing. The others soon joined, pushing each other higher and laughing freely.

As the last rays of sunlight painted the sky in hues of pink and orange, Amani turned to her friends, her heart swelling with gratitude. The chirping of birds gradually quieted, replaced by the rustle of leaves in the gentle breeze. "I can't believe how lucky we are to have days like this," she said, her voice filled with warmth.

Christina, with a content smile, agreed, "It's moments like these that remind me how important our friendship is. We should do this more often!" Maya chimed in, suggesting they make it a monthly tradition, a notion that excited everyone. Samantha quipped, "Next time, I'll bring my famous cookies! They're even better than these!" Laughter followed as they teased her about her "famous" recipes, which occasionally turned out more adventurous than intended. They shared stories, each recounting their own favorite mishaps and adventures, igniting bursts of sincerity amidst fits of laughter.

As the sun dipped below the horizon, casting the landscape in shadows, the air turned cooler and Amani pulled her sweater tighter around her. They decided to begin their hike back, taking a different trail that meandered along a small creek. The sound of water trickling over the stones added a soothing soundtrack to their walk.

The group continued to share their hopes and dreams, chatting about their aspirations. Amani spoke about her aspirations for the future, touching on her desire to travel and experience different cultures. Maya excitedly shared her plans for starting her own art studio, while Christina elaborated on her passion for environmental activism.

"Can you imagine if we all travelled together?" Samantha said with a gleam in her eye. "Exploring the world and having more adventures!" The idea thrilled them, and they started dreaming about where they would go first—Italy, Japan, or maybe a road trip down the coast.

Eventually, they reached the parking lot, the sky now dark, dotted with stars. Amani felt a sense of fulfillment wash over her. Despite the chill in the air, the warmth of her friends enveloped her like a cozy blanket. They hugged goodbye, promising to coordinate their next adventure soon.

As Amani drove home, the memories of the day replayed in her mind like a favorite song. The laughter, the camaraderie, and the shared aspirations warmed her heart. She parked her car in the driveway and sat for a moment, appreciating the stillness of the night. The stars twinkled like tiny diamonds scattered across the velvet sky, and she couldn't help but feel a tug of wanderlust stirring within her.

Once inside her home, she nestled onto the couch with a cup of chamomile tea, the steam curling around her like a gentle embrace. She grabbed her journal and began to jot down the ideas they had brainstormed about their potential travels. Amani wanted to capture every moment, every dream they had shared. The pages filled with notes on Italy's charming streets, Japan's vibrant culture, and the stunning coastline they could explore together. Writing it all down felt like making a promise to herself and her friends—a promise to chase those dreams, no matter how far-fetched they seemed.

As she closed her journal, Amani's phone buzzed with a message from Christina. It was a picture of the beautiful sunset they had witnessed earlier, along with the caption: "Grateful for today and even more excited for tomorrow's adventures!" Amani responded with a heartfelt emoji-filled message, reinforcing the bond they all cherished.

Amani felt a mix of relief and happiness in her heart. This message from Christina was a small yet important sign of their progress and dedication to each other. She recalled the uncertainty she felt after the incident at Grand Beach, when she had given a ride to a stranger on Highway 59 and Christina seemed upset. Amani had worried their friendship was in trouble, but now, reading Christina's message, she felt hopeful again.

She responded quickly, saying, "Definitely! It's great to make progress together. I feel fortunate to have you in my life!" Amani clicked send, feeling a surge of excitement. Their friendship had withstood challenges and difficulties, evolving into something even more valuable. While waiting for Christina's response, Amani thought about the growth they'd experienced together. The challenges they faced brought their bond to light, encouraging them to face their fears and misunderstandings. Both of them improved their communication skills and became more comfortable expressing their emotions without worrying about criticism.

The sound of her phone ringing interrupted her thoughts, and Christina replied: "You're my partner in crime! You're stuck with me Let's make tomorrow's breakfast amazing!" Amani laughed in response. The phrase "stuck with" held great significance, signifying not only friendship but also a strong and unwavering support that had developed through shared moments of joy and sorrow, and now, a journey of healing bathed in the colors of the setting sun.

She responded, saying, "Being awesome is what I do best! When are we meeting again?"

 Christina responded after a brief pause, suggesting meeting at Grapes Restaurant on Corydon at eight AM. Amani's smile grew even bigger. She was thrilled for the upcoming day. Every new journey they took was a leap into unfamiliar territory, an opportunity to make lasting memories and strengthen the connection they worked hard to preserve. "Okay, okay! I will be prepared! I am excited!"

As the clock struck ten PM in Winnipeg, Amani knew it was six AM in Nairobi, where her mother was beginning her day. The time difference allowed for a brief window before her mother would be fully awake and engaged in her morning routine. Amani hesitated, torn between sending a simple text message or making a call—each option weighed her down with significance, but she was leaning towards a desire for a deeper connection.

Amani picked up her phone, her fingers hovering over the screen as she debated whether to send a text or just call. After a moment of contemplation, she decided a call would be more personal.

She pressed the dial button and waited, listening to the ringing tone, each beep amplifying her anticipation. Finally, she heard her mother's groggy voice on the other end.

"Amani? Is everything okay?" her mum asked, still half-asleep.

"Hey Mum! It's me! I just wanted to hear your voice before I drift off," Amani replied, a smile spreading across her face.

Her mother chuckled softly, the sound comforting despite the early hour. "You know I love waking up to your calls, no matter the time. How was your day?"

Amani settled back against her pillows, feeling the warmth of the conversation wash over her. "It was good! I went to the new café down the street. They have the best pastries! I thought of you when I tasted the chocolate croissant."

"Oh, now I'm craving one! You'll have to bring some home when you visit," her mum said, her voice starting to gain more energy.

They continued to chat, sharing stories about their day. Amani recounted her plans for the weekend, and her mother shared the latest updates from family back home.

As the conversation flowed, Amani felt the drowsiness creeping back, but it was comforting to know that even miles apart, they could connect like this.

"Mum, I should let you get back to sleep," she finally said, stifling a yawn.

"Alright, sweet girl. Just remember, I'm always here for you, no matter the distance. Sleep well and dream sweet," her mother replied, her voice laced with love.

"Goodnight, Mum. Love you!" Amani said, and they exchanged their usual goodbyes before hanging up.

Feeling lighter and more at ease, Amani buried her head into her pillow, letting the sound of her mother's voice linger in her mind.

With a smile, she finally closed her eyes, cocooned in the warmth of their connection.

As the calendar page turned to November, she felt a surge of motivation. Amani made a pact with herself to start planning: researching destinations, budgeting for travel, and learning a few phrases in languages that would come in handy. With every step, she was one step closer to making their collective dream a reality.

Chapter 14

Amani found herself once again working at Third Cup, this time alongside her colleague Leo. Leo seemed unusually quiet compared to his usual chatty self, leaving Amani feeling reluctant to inquire about his mood. Choosing to distract herself, she poured her attention into the intricate process of operating the coffee machines, skillfully grinding beans and frothing milk to perfection. She made a conscious effort to maintain a cheerful ambiance by filling the café with the comforting sounds of her tasks. The delightful scent of freshly-brewed coffee permeated the atmosphere, mingling with the bustling arrival of customers to create a vibrant and dynamic scene. After a brief period of quiet, Amani made the decision to initiate a conversation with Leo. She greeted him with a casual "Hey Leo, how are you doing?" However, despite her best efforts to sound nonchalant, her underlying worry was evident in her voice. Leo lifted his gaze from the counter he was cleaning. "Everything is okay," he answered, yet his eyes revealed a complexity that contrasted with his words. They appeared unfocused, as if immersed in deep contemplation. Amani took a moment to gather her thoughts, pausing with her hands gently resting on the counter. She expressed her concern to the other person by questioning if everything was alright, noting that they appeared to be feeling a bit different or uneasy that day. With a heavy sigh, she watched as his smile slowly disappeared. "I'm not sure, really. Lately, I've been pondering various things, reflecting on life and all its complexities." Amani could sense that Leo was holding in some emotions and that it was weighing on him. She felt a strong urge to provide him with a safe and supportive environment to open up about what was bothering him. She gently offered, "I'm here for you if you need to talk. It can be therapeutic to express your thoughts and feelings to someone who cares." After a moment of contemplation, he gazed at her with a slight glimmer of appreciation reflected in his eyes. "I appreciate it, Amani. I'm just feeling a bit stagnant, I suppose. It's like I'm in a rut and not making any progress with my musical career." Leo had a profound love for music that was apparent in his actions, as he would frequently hum or play tunes while they were working. Amani recognized the significance of music in Leo's life and how much it meant to him. She acknowledged his talent, telling him, "Your music is fantastic. Have you been composing anything new lately?" "No, not really. I have come up against a creative block, and it's really bothering me." He ran his fingers through his hair in frustration. "I feel this immense pressure to come up with something extraordinary, but the more I push myself, the less I seem to achieve." Amani nodded in agreement, acknowledging the overwhelming burden of that particular pressure. She offered some advice, suggesting that perhaps the weight of expectations was becoming too heavy. She emphasized the idea that sometimes the most wonderful outcomes occur when one is not actively striving for them. In essence, she encouraged a more relaxed and natural approach to achieving goals. Leo carefully contemplated her words, remaining quiet for a brief moment as he absorbed her perspective. After a pause, he acknowledged, "Perhaps you have a point. It's just that I long to rediscover that inner fire within me." "Would you be interested in a proposition? What if we synchronized our breaks to enjoy some music together? We could delve into different genres, experiment with your creative concepts, and simply have a good time without feeling any stress or obligations. It's just a casual suggestion to alleviate some of your workload," she proposed, aiming to offer him some relief. "Of course, that sounds like a great idea," he responded with a subtle smile reappearing on his face. Expressing his gratitude, he added, "Thank you, Amani. I am truly grateful for your kindness." As the café buzzed with a steady stream of customers, Amani experienced a sense of satisfaction and purpose as she extended her help. She was committed to assisting Leo in rediscovering his passion for music that once ignited his soul. Through the budding conversations between them, Amani hoped that they could both uncover their inner desires and aspirations in unison.

The day progressed with a renewed sense of energy as Amani and Leo synchronized their breaks. Amani was eager to create an atmosphere where Leo could feel free to express himself, away from the pressures of their work environment. She knew how important it was for him to regain that spark of creativity.

When the time finally came for their break, Amani led Leo to a cozy corner of the café, one that was slightly removed from the hustle and bustle of customers. She had brought along her small portable speaker, eager to set the mood. As she connected it to her phone, she asked, "What genre do you feel like listening to today?"

"Let's start with some jazz," Leo suggested, his eyes lighting up at the thought. Amani couldn't help but smile at the way his demeanor shifted as music filled the air, the mellow sounds providing a soothing backdrop.

They sat together, letting the music weave around them like a comforting blanket. As the soft melodies enveloped the space, Amani gently encouraged him to share more about his current block. "Is there a particular place where you feel the most inspired?"

Leo leaned back, thinking, "Honestly, it used to be when I'd play in front of audiences. The energy of the crowd always fueled my creativity. Now it feels so isolating." His brow furrowed in frustration, the weight of unexpressed thoughts still lingering on his shoulders.

"Have you considered playing somewhere again?" Amani prompted. "It doesn't have to be a big venue—maybe just in front of friends or at an open mic night? Sometimes the pressure of performing can shake off those cobwebs."

Leo considered her suggestion, a spark of hope flickering in his eyes. "I haven't thought about that in a long time. I suppose I've been too caught up in my fears."

With an understanding nod, Amani continued, "It's completely normal to feel that way. Just remember, it's okay to be imperfect. The joy of music is in the expression, not in the perfection. Why not try playing a few notes here, just for fun?"

He hesitated, but ultimately the warmth of her encouragement melted away his apprehensiveness. "Alright, I'll give it a shot," he said, a mixture of nervousness and excitement evident in his voice. Amani handed him the guitar she had brought along, and she could see the tension in his shoulders easing as he held it. Strumming the strings tentatively at first, he slowly fell into a rhythm, the music flowing more effortlessly than he anticipated.

As he played, the café's ambiance shifted; customers paused to soak in the unexpected serenade. Amani clapped along softly, her light-hearted enthusiasm infectious. With each note, Leo began to smile more, the creative block seemingly crumbling under the weight of his own music.

"See? You still have it!" Amani cheered. "What you create doesn't have to be a masterpiece; it just has to be a reflection of you."

After a few minutes, Leo stopped, laughing with a sense of relief. "I really needed this. It feels good to just play without the pressure."

The break was coming to an end, and Amani knew they had to return to work soon. "How about we make this a regular thing?" she suggested, excitement bubbling in her voice. "A little jam session every week to keep the music flowing and let you explore your creativity again."

"I would love that," Leo replied, a genuine smile finally returning to his face. The burden of stagnation began to lift, replaced by the warmth of support and friendship.

As they returned to their tasks, there was a newfound lightness in the air. Amani felt fulfilled not just in her role at Third Cup, but in knowing she had helped her friend find joy again. She couldn't wait for their next session together, eager to witness Leo rediscover the passion that brought music to life for both of them. In this little café, surrounded by the rhythm of customers and the aroma of coffee, Amani and Leo were on the cusp of creating something beautiful together—both in music and in their friendship.

As the days passed, Amani and Leo transformed their café breaks into a cherished ritual. Each week brought fresh melodies and the comforting hum of creativity. Their sessions became a safe haven—an escape from the demands of work where notes danced freely in the air and laughter mingled with chord progressions.

Amani would bring her ukulele, its strings worn but vibrant, while Leo often found himself coaxing sounds out of his old guitar, a relic from his teenage years. They would sit in a cozy corner of the café, away from the hustle and bustle, the light filtering through the windows casting a warm glow on their half-finished songs and whimsical ideas.

One afternoon, as the sun bathed everything in golden hues, Amani strummed an upbeat tune that filled the room with energy. "How about we write a song about our daily adventures here? The coffee spill incidents, the quirky customers, all the little moments that make Third Cup special?" she suggested, her eyes sparkling with inspiration.

Leo nodded enthusiastically, his heart swelling with the affection he had for their shared space. "I love that idea! Let's make it a celebration of this place." His fingers moved nimbly over the strings, weaving in a soft melody to complement her playful rhythm. The news of their sessions gradually spread among the café staff, and before long, a small audience of coworkers began to gather, enjoying the tunes that echoed through the walls.

Their little jam sessions became an event, drawing in not just colleagues but regular customers who found themselves enchanted by the impromptu concerts. Amani felt a rush of pride at how their music fostered connection; it was as if the café had transformed into a sanctuary where creativity thrived and friendships were strengthened.

One rainy afternoon, as droplets painted the windows with streaks of silver, Amani suggested that they invite the regulars to share their stories. "What if we create a song that tells the tales of the people who come here?" she proposed, her voice barely audible over the sound of the storm. Leo, ever the encourager, instantly agreed. "Let's make it a collaborative piece, a tapestry of voices and experiences."

They placed an open call on a chalkboard by the entrance, inviting patrons to jot down their favorite café memories. To their delight, the response was overwhelming. Notes filled the board, and the duo read them aloud during their sessions. Stories of first dates, bittersweet farewells, and serendipitous meetings poured forth, each one infused with the magic of connection that Third Cup represented.

With each story, their song evolved, an organic blend of narrative and melody. As Leo strummed the evolving chords, Amani worked on the lyrics, capturing the essence of every tale. The café transformed into a hive of creativity, with customers chiming in, offering suggestions and harmonies, turning their informal sessions into vibrant community events.

 Leo and Amani had a conversation with Mr. Hargrave, who is the proprietor of Third Cup, regarding turning Friday evenings into a music and storytelling event at the café. Mr. Hargrave enthusiastically embraced the idea, expressing his eagerness to listen to stories from customers and witness transformation and solace in people's lives. Over time, the café experienced a transformation in its ambiance, evolving from a peaceful setting to a vibrant space filled with laughter, music, and reminiscences.

Leo and Amani, inspired by the multitude of stories they heard, collaborated on a distinctive musical composition that fused together the tales of their customers into a harmonious blend of sound. Every Friday night was eagerly awaited as a time when the café was filled with the lively stories of various people. The usual customers came in early to save their preferred spots, excited to share and reminisce about significant moments in their lives. The chalkboard was filled with a mix of fun and meaningful memories, each one weaving together the café's community.

On a Friday, Grace, a kind-hearted woman, bravely stood to recount her story. She reminisced about her deceased spouse, who had a tradition of taking her to Third Cup every Sunday morning for coffee and chats that lasted for hours. As she shared her recollections, a silence enveloped the audience, filled with deep emotions. Leo, without thinking, started playing a gentle tune on his guitar, blending with the unspoken sentiments in the space, while Amani wrote down phrases that beautifully encapsulated Grace's memories. As they collaborated, Leo and Amani's connection strengthened, with Leo appreciating Amani's poetic thoughts and Amani inspiring Leo with her colorful descriptions. Their meetings typically concluded in a comfortable nook of the coffee shop, filled with notes and traces of their work, where they would laugh and come up with ideas for incorporating new stories into their evolving song.

As the locals became more involved, they started bringing in their own musical instruments, adding to the diverse range of voices and sounds. One day, a talented violinist from the area was inspired by the lively music gatherings and decided to participate, blending her tunes seamlessly with the group. An older man brought along a harmonica, sparking impromptu duets and fostering a sense of unity among everyone present.

The word about their Friday night activities quickly circulated among the residents nearby, leading to a surge in new customers eager to see the imaginative spark born from collective moments. Mr. Hargrave, pleased with the excitement, opted to establish a cozy spot in the café where a small stage could be set up, turning intimate meetings into a full-fledged area for performances. Leo and Amani considered documenting their developing project as it picked up speed. They imagined creating a collection that captured the essence of the café—a fusion of experiences from the people who sought comfort there. The music went beyond mere notes; it transformed into a medium for healing, sharing stories, and fostering connections within the community.

Chapter 15

It was well past midnight when the phone started ringing. Amani
was deep in sleep. Groggy, she stumbled over to the landline that
was ringing non-stop.

When she finally answered, it was her dad on the other end. A wave
of worry hit her; it was unusual for anyone in her family to call the
landline, and it was her dad, not her mom.

"Amani, it's Baraka, your dad."

"Is everything alright?" Amani asked, her heart racing.

"Yeah, everything's good. I just wanted to tell you that we got you a
ticket to come home for Christmas," Mr. Baraka replied.

"What's going on?"

"We miss you! It's been over two years since we've seen you, and
your siblings and mom have been really wanting to see you," he
explained.

Amani felt a mix of emotions. She was thrilled about going back to
Kenya for Christmas, escaping the cold of Winnipeg, and reuniting
with her family. But at the same time, she couldn't shake the feeling
that her parents had given up so much for her.

"It's... it's really a surprise! Thank you, Dad," Amani replied, her
voice a little shaky with excitement and guilt. The thought of her
family waiting for her back home stirred a longing she had tried to
suppress over the past few years.

"I know it's last-minute, and I'm sorry about the late call, but we
wanted it to be a surprise. We've been planning this for a while," he
said, a hint of pride in his voice. "You deserve to be home, to be
with us."

Amani swallowed hard, fighting back the tears that threatened to
spill over. "I've missed you all so much. I just... I just feel bad for

being away for so long. You've sacrificed so much for my education and everything else."

"Listen to me, Amani," he said, his tone softening. "We're proud of you. Every late night you spend studying or working hard is worth it to us. You're building a future, and we know it isn't easy being away. But we want you to come back home, even if it's just for a little while. Family is everything."

His words hit Amani like a wave, mingling her gratitude with a bittersweet ache. "I know," she said, her voice barely above a whisper. "I want to be there. I can't wait to see everyone. The kids must have grown up so much!"

"They're unstoppable!" Baraka laughed. "Fatima is taller than you now, and Ibrahim has taken up football. You won't recognize them. And your mom, she's been cooking your favorite dishes, just in case you'd come home."

Amani smiled through her anxiety. "What about you?"

"I'll be just as I always am," he chuckled. "Trying to keep up with your mother and the chaos of the household. Ready to spoil my favorite daughter," he added, teasingly.

"Seriously, Dad. Thank you. I can hardly believe I'm finally coming home," she said, envisioning the vibrant streets of Nairobi, the familiar sounds of her family bickering and laughing, and the comforting aroma of her mother's cooking.

"Get some rest, Amani. We'll pick you up from the airport, and I promise it will be a Christmas to remember. Just like the old times," he said, his voice filled with warmth.

As Amani hung up, she felt a surge of hope and yearning. The prospect of home was intoxicating. It felt like the world outside her window faded into silence, leaving her with the comforting thought of family and connection. She crawled back into bed, a smile creeping on her lips as she imagined the welcoming embrace of her family, the laughter echoing in their little house, and the way everything would feel right again, if only for a fleeting moment.

With that thought in mind, she drifted back to sleep, clutching the phone tightly, her heart filled with the promise of the upcoming reunion.

She lay awake, her mind racing with thoughts. She was excited to see her little brother Amir and her sister Malaika. She pictured cooking with her mom and going shopping at the big Two Rivers Mall. She also thought about visiting her grandparents in Mombasa and spending time with all her cousins. The things she wanted to do during the two weeks of Christmas break seemed never-ending. Amani found herself drifting back to her childhood, recalling those cozy evenings around the kitchen table. Her mom's laughter blended with the sounds of dinner sizzling away. She could almost hear her little brother cracking jokes like their dad and her sister softly singing in the background. Those simple times felt like pure gold now, and just thinking about them made her heart feel full.

For a brief moment, the guilt of being away slipped away. Her family always got the sacrifices she made to chase her dreams; they were her biggest cheerleaders, reminding her that her education was the ticket to a better life. But now, she felt a strong urge to give back, to show them how much their support meant to her.

As she gazed at the ceiling, the stars twinkling outside her window, she started dreaming about the gifts she wanted to bring home. There was something magical about Christmas that turned even the smallest gestures into heartfelt gifts. She envisioned surprising them with thoughtful presents—books for Malaika, a new football for Amir, and maybe a little something special for her parents. Just picturing their reactions filled her with joy.

Each gift she envisioned felt like a hug, a way of wrapping her love around them despite the distance. The thought brought warmth to her chest, illuminating her heart with gratitude for everything they had sacrificed for her.

The excitement of the holiday season began to wrap around her like a cozy blanket, and with each passing moment, Amani's resolve grew stronger. She wouldn't just be coming home to visit; she would bring little pieces of herself as a thank-you—a promise that their support had not gone unnoticed. This Christmas, she would make it magical not just for her family but for herself as well, reconnecting with the love and laughter that had shaped her into who she was today.

With newfound determination, Amani grabbed a notebook and began jotting down her ideas. Maybe she'd bake some of her mom's favorite cookies, surprise her dad with a vintage album from his youth, or even craft a special gift for each of her siblings—something handmade that reflected their unique personalities.

Each idea flowed onto the pages like a gentle stream, filling her with a sense of purpose. Amani smiled as she envisioned the laughter that would soon echo through the halls of her childhood home. Baking cookies with her mom would be more than just a culinary act; it would revive cherished memories of flour-covered counters and warm conversations that felt timeless.

The thought of presenting her dad with a vintage album brought a spark of joy. She could already picture his eyes lighting up with the surprise and nostalgia of reliving old tunes that had once filled their living room with melodies. Music had always been a thread that connected them, and this gesture would weave a new layer into that fabric of shared experiences.

For her siblings, Amani's heart thrummed with creativity. She wanted each handmade gift to encapsulate not just their interests but also the bond they shared. Perhaps a hand-painted mug for her sister, who loved her morning coffee rituals, and a custom skateboard deck for her younger brother, blending his passion for art and skating. Each thoughtful creation would serve as a reminder that no matter the miles between them, her heart was always their home.

As she penned down the plans, Amani felt an electric thrill of anticipation. She yearned to step into the whirlwind of holiday preparations—the bustling markets, the scent of pine, and the warmth of togetherness. This season, she would not only give gifts but also share pieces of her heart, crafting an experience filled with connection and gratitude. Each thoughtful action would be her way of stitching together the fabric of love that distance had momentarily frayed.

With each item on her list, Amani realized that she was creating the kind of magic that was often overlooked in the frenzy of holiday shopping. This year, she would bring not just presents, but also laughter, love, and a renewed sense of belonging. The spirit of Christmas would breathe life into her intentions, transforming simple gestures into lasting memories. And as the warmth of family enveloped her when she finally walked through that front door, she knew that this would be the most special holiday yet.

Yet the thrill of her plans made it difficult to close her eyes. Amani could already envision the taste of her mom's cookies, the way the kitchen would fill with warmth and laughter. Her mind danced with images of her dad's joyful surprise, the nostalgic melodies of his favorite music floating through the air. As for her siblings, she imagined their delighted expressions as they unwrapped the carefully-crafted gifts, each one a testament to the bond they shared. Finally, fatigue washed over her, and Amani set the notebook aside, knowing she'd have more time to refine her ideas later. She nestled under her blankets, her heart still buzzing with excitement. The anticipation of making this holiday one to remember lulled her into a peaceful sleep, dreams filled with twinkling lights, joyous reunions, and the clinking of glasses during family toasts.

When dawn broke, she woke up to the soft golden light filtering through her curtains. Amani jumped out of bed, her mind racing with fresh inspiration. She readied herself for class, her thoughts buzzing with her holiday plans. The world outside was crisp with winter, a fresh blanket of snow shimmering under the sun—a perfect backdrop for the season of giving and gathering.

In her class, staying focused was a challenge. She found herself doodling in her notebook, sketching out ideas for gifts and writing down decoration plans that would fill her childhood home with holiday cheer. The thought of twinkling lights and the scent of pine from their Christmas tree made her smile, especially since it was so different from the busy campus life surrounding her.

With Christmas in Kenya approaching, Amani realized that she needed to buckle down. She had a lot on her plate in the three weeks before her trip; three lengthy papers to write, two exams to study for, and a job at Third Cup that required her to work at least four days a week. On top of that, she had Christmas shopping and crafts to tackle, friends and coworkers to catch up with, and if she could, she wanted to visit Ahmad, Fatima, and their kids, Leila and Ali. It seemed like a lot, but she was determined to make it all happen.

Amani took a deep breath, trying to quell the rising tide of anxiety. She pulled out her planner, the pages bursting with to-do lists and deadlines. Organizing her thoughts always helped, and she began jotting down her priorities. First on the list was the looming academic workload; she couldn't let her grades slip if she wanted to ensure her scholarship for the next semester.

She set specific goals for each day. "Monday: Paper draft. Tuesday: Study for exam. Wednesday: Finish the second paper..." Amani's mind drifted for a moment, envisioning the cozy gatherings at home, laughter echoing in the air, and the warmth of family. She quickly shook off the daydream—she needed to stay grounded.

Next, she turned her attention to her job at Third Cup. Serving coffee was a pleasant escape, but the busy holiday season meant that every shift was a rush of orders and murmured conversations. She decided to fit in her work schedule around her study times, so she could maximize every moment.

Christmas shopping loomed large in her mind, too. Amani had set aside a small budget, and she was determined to find meaningful gifts without breaking the bank. Maybe handmade crafts for her family—thoughtful and personal. Amani was always inspired by the traditions they had growing up, and she'd love to bring some of that creativity to her gifts this year.

Visiting Ahmad and Fatima was a priority; they were like family to her, and it had been too long since she'd seen their kids. She would need to coordinate with her friends at home to finalize plans without overwhelming herself.

As the weeks sped by, Amani tackled her papers diligently, and with every page that she turned into her professor, she felt lighter. Each study session brought her closer to her exams, and her shifts at Third Cup became moments where she could connect with her community.

Amani took a moment to breathe, feeling a sense of accomplishment as she ticked off items on her planner. With the semester nearing its end and the holiday season in full swing, every detail mattered. She picked up her phone, the screen lighting up with a familiar comfort. After a few rings, Fatima answered, her warm voice instantly lifting Amani's spirits.

"Hey, Amani! It's been a while! How have you been?" Fatima's enthusiasm was palpable, making Amani smile.

"I've been good, just trying to juggle school and work. It's a bit hectic, but I'm managing! I was actually hoping to see you and the kids soon," Amani said, her heart swelling at the thought of catching up.

"Oh, we'd love that! The kids have been asking about you. How about this weekend?" Fatima suggested.

"Let me check... Friday should work! I'm free after my shift at Third Cup," Amani replied, mentally planning out her Friday.

"Sounds perfect! We can have a little get-together, make some hot cocoa, maybe do some Christmas crafts with the kids," Fatima replied, excitement bubbling through her words.

"Great! And I also have some exciting news to share with you all— I'm finally planning my trip to Kenya!" Amani couldn't help but let her joy spill over as she mentioned her plans.

"Kenya? That's amazing! We need to celebrate! How about inviting your friends Christina, Maya, and Samantha over, too?" welcomed Fatima.

"Absolutely! I'll text everyone today and organize a little gathering," Amani said, her mind already racing with ideas for decorations and snacks.

After they hung up, Amani felt a renewed sense of motivation. She quickly drafted a group message, her fingers flying over the keyboard as she shared her exciting news and proposed two options for the gathering. The flurry of "yeses" came in almost immediately, solidifying plans for a fun Friday night filled with laughter, catching up, and the warmth of friendship.

Feeling a sense of balance in her social life, she turned her attention back to her planner, a newfound clarity washing over her. She meticulously jotted down notes for the upcoming gathering, listing everyone's preferred snacks and beverages, determined to leave no stone unturned. Confident in her ability to juggle schoolwork and meet deadlines before her trip, she recalled her past experiences of thriving under pressure, ready to rise to the challenge once more.

As Amani immersed herself in the meticulous planning of her gathering, her thoughts drifted excitedly to Kenya—safaris, vibrant cultures, and breathtaking landscapes danced in her mind. She daydreamed about the exotic wildlife she might encounter and the rich history she'd explore. It was a trip she had long anticipated, and now it was finally coming to fruition.

With a determined glance at her planner, she set aside her swirling thoughts and focused on the logistics for Friday's gathering. She made a list of fun themes that could brighten up the evening. Perhaps a "Safari Night" theme, complete with jungle decorations and Kenyan-inspired snacks? Amani chuckled, picturing her friends dressed in animal print or colorful attire.

Next, she considered the menu. With Christina's love for sweets, Maya's vegetarian preferences, and Samantha's knack for bringing unique drinks, she wanted to cater to everyone's tastes. Amani noted down "samosas and chapati" as a nod to Kenyan cuisine, along with a selection of fresh fruits and a special punch that would incorporate flavors from her future trip.

Once she felt satisfied with her ideas, Amani set her planner down and made herself a cup of tea. The warmth of the cup in her hands grounded her amidst the excitement. She knew that balancing her schoolwork with planning would be a challenge, but the gathering would serve as a nice break, a chance to connect and celebrate with her friends before her big adventure.

Amani checked her calendar and set aside time for studying since her school deadlines were coming up quickly. She planned to tackle her assignments in the evenings, leaving her weekends open for trip preparations.

Amani sat cross-legged on her bed, surrounded by scattered notes and textbooks, the remnants of her frantic study sessions. The exam pressure was building, a relentless weight pressing down on her chest, but her mind wandered away from her studies, slipping into a labyrinth of memories and emotions. She could almost feel the warmth of the sun from that hot summer day when she had shared her feelings with Dr. Alex in his cozy office. The room had been a sanctuary, filled with the calming aroma of herbal tea that mingled with the soft, soothing cadence of his voice.

"What would you do if you saw him again?" he had asked, his eyes reflecting a blend of curiosity and kindness that made her feel safe enough to explore her deepest fears. That question had lodged itself in her mind, haunting her during her daily life and study times, echoing like a distant bell that refused to be silenced.

Anxiety washed over her like a cold wave, pulling her under. Usiku was a name she had tried to forget, a shadow from her past that loomed larger with each passing day. He was the boy who had assaulted her when she was only eleven, a moment that had shattered her innocence and turned happy memories into painful reminders of betrayal. The laughter of childhood friends, the carefree days spent in the sun, were all tainted by the dark stain of that experience. Those feelings troubled her as she tried to sleep, twisting and turning in her bed, her heart racing with the weight of unresolved trauma.

"I will confront him and go to the police," she thought, the determination sparking a flicker of hope within her. But then, like a dark cloud rolling in, worry crept back. What complications might arise? A legal fight with Usiku's family loomed large in her mind, a daunting prospect that filled her with dread. She imagined the courtroom, the stares of strangers, the weight of her truth against the denial of his family. What if those issues couldn't be resolved before she returned to Canada? The thought of leaving without closure gnawed at her, a constant reminder of the unfinished business that lay heavy on her heart.

She worried about the long-term impact on her family, the ripple effects of her choices. Would they understand? Would they support her, or would they be burdened by the fallout? The fear of their disappointment, their pain, intertwined with her own, creating a tangled web of emotions that left her feeling trapped.

Amani took a deep breath, trying to ground herself in the present. Dr. Alex's gentle wisdom ran through her mind: "Healing is not linear; it's a winding path filled with both pain and joy." Enough of running from the shadows; it was time to reclaim her story, one step, one conversation at a time. As she sat back down, a renewed sense of purpose ignited within her, replacing the fragmented emotions that had once enveloped her heart.

As she opened her journal, a renewed sense of resolve washed over Amani. The pristine pages seemed to call out, urging her to pour in her thoughts, ambitions, and dreams. Each blank sheet held the promise of clarity, a sanctuary in which her fears and hopes could coexist, guiding her toward healing. She aimed to devise a plan for confronting her trauma upon her arrival in Kenya, a land filled with both joyful memories and painful shadows. The prospect of returning ignited a blend of excitement and anxiety within her. She grappled with the question of whether it was worth unearthing Usiku's skeleton—the lingering specter of her past that had haunted her for so long.

The memories of Usiku—the namesake of the dark night that sheltered her childhood agony—loomed like a formidable shadow. Her heart raced at the thought of facing the monster that had robbed her of so much. It demanded great bravery and openness, aspects of herself she wasn't sure she could summon. For years, she had built walls around her heart, using the protective stones of denial to shield her from the hurt. But she knew that the journey ahead would require peeling back those layers, revealing the wounds she'd kept hidden for so long.

With each stroke of her pen, the ink felt like a lifeline. Amani began to sketch out her approach. She wrote about the discussions she hoped to have with her parents regarding Usiku—a name she had once whispered and now longed to reclaim as part of her narrative. She imagined sitting across from them, her hands trembling slightly as she opened up about the darkness that had intertwined with their family history. Would they finally understand? The longing for clarity and connection spurred her resolve.

Her mind drifted towards Rehema, her childhood friend who had once stood by her side. What would it take to confront her about their fractured relationship? Amani needed to understand why their bond had withered in the aftermath of tragedy. Perhaps the conversation would bring closure, perhaps forgiveness, or perhaps the rekindling of a friendship lost in the wilderness of hurt.

Amani also envisioned revisiting the places that once brought her happiness—the sprawling fields behind her childhood home, the sun-dappled paths by the river, and the laughter that used to echo in the community she had nearly forgotten. With every word she scribbled, the idea of reclaiming those spaces from the clutches of her trauma felt increasingly attainable. It promised a potential shift in her reality, a transformation of loss into something more profound and beautiful.

Yet the images of those beloved landscapes were tempered by a pragmatic awareness of what lay ahead. The thought of revisiting haunted sites sent shivers through her resolve. She paused, pen hovering over the paper, and considered the support she would need. Friends, trusted advisors, perhaps even local healers who understood the cultural intricacies of her journey could provide a safety net for her explorations. It was daunting, but knowing that she wouldn't be alone filled her with a glimmer of hope.

As her thoughts flowed, she took moments to consider alternative routes should facing her past become too daunting. Perhaps crafting new memories would be a strategy worth exploring—establishing a life that wasn't solely shaped by her trauma. The beauty of the present, rich with friends and shared laughter, was enticing enough to contemplate. What if she could focus on cherishing these relationships that had blossomed despite the shadows of her history?

The possibilities began to swirl in her mind, weaving between the old and the new. Amani allowed herself to cherish the excitement of exploring both routes—to confront the demons of her past while simultaneously embracing the present that offered warmth and companionship. She imagined her heart gradually expanding, bridging the gap between her past and her aspirations.

With every entry, she crafted a tapestry of hope and resolution, intertwining the need to confront her memories with the joy of creating new experiences. As she closed her journal, Amani felt an undeniable sense of empowerment. This was only the beginning of her journey—a journey not just of pain, but of tremendous courage, growth, and ultimately, reclamation. The pen had become her sword and shield, ready to confront whatever awaited her upon her return to Kenya.